Books in the D BRANCH Series

I0556157

Books in the TALBOT Series

Books in the AGENCY Series

Books in the PANTHEON Series

Books in the COLONY Series

Books in the EMPIRE Series

by Richard F. Weyand:
EMPIRE: Reformer
EMPIRE: Usurper
EMPIRE: Tyrant
EMPIRE: Commander
EMPIRE: Warlord
EMPIRE: Conqueror

by Stephanie Osborn:
EMPIRE: Imperial Police
EMPIRE: Imperial Detective
EMPIRE: Imperial Inspector
EMPIRE: Section Six

by Richard F. Weyand:
EMPIRE: Intervention
EMPIRE: Investigation
EMPIRE: Succession
EMPIRE: Renewal
EMPIRE: Resistance
EMPIRE: Resurgence

Books in the Childers Universe

by Richard F. Weyand:
Childers
Childers: Absurd Proposals
Galactic Mail: Revolution
A Charter For The Commonwealth
Campbell: The Problem With Bliss

by Stephanie Osborn:
Campbell: The Sigurdsen Incident

TOO SHARP TO HOLD

by

RICHARD F. WEYAND

RICHARD F. WEYAND

ISBN 978-1-954903-23-4
Printed in the United States of America

Cover Credits
Cover Art: Luca Oleastri and Paola Giari,
www.rotwangstudio.com
Back Cover Photo: Oleg Volk

Published by Weyand Associates, Inc.
Bloomington, Indiana, USA
January, 2025

TOO SHARP TO HOLD

CONTENTS

Lethargy

Deke Sharp lay in bed. It was morning, and well after the time he should get up to be at work by any reasonable hour, and he didn't much give a damn.

He threw the covers back and looked down his body. He had left his prosthetic legs off last night – he had to leave them off at least one night a week to prevent necrosis of the skin covered by the prosthetic – and his actual legs ended a few inches below the knees.

Artificial knees at that, though covered with his own skin and operated with his own muscles.

Sharp bent at the waist and held his stumps aloft. Bend the knees and back, bend the knees and back. He sighed and put his legs back down on the bed.

He looked at his genitals. Normal looking, but completely prosthetic. He hit the mental switch – without using the delay timer – and had a raging hard-on in seconds. Flipped the switch back off, and he was just as quickly back to a normal flaccid state.

It all worked – he even had feeling, and would orgasm during sex and all – but it wasn't part of what he was born with.

Sharp's arms, too, were prosthetic, from just above the elbows down to the perfectly manicured prosthetic hands.

Again, he had feeling and full function with those arms and hands, just as he had vision and hearing with his camera eye replacements and his microphone ear replacements. He could even adjust his vision up into the ultraviolet and walk at night without a light, or dial it down into the infrared and see

1

humans and warm-blooded animals, no matter how much they tried to hide.

All in all, the doctors had done a nice job, considering how trashed he had been when he got back to D Branch headquarters on Ariel. 'A freezer full of parts.' And not all the parts, just the ones that had stayed in one piece following the pirates' first hit on *Circe*.

Sharp had made it to the medical life-support unit of his day cabin in the zero gravity, his system pumped full of adrenaline and pain blockers by his breached protective suit. He had hit the Freeze button, then woken up in D Branch headquarters, deaf, dumb, blind, emasculated, and quadriplegic.

At that, he was better off than his crew. *Circe* had been lost with all hands, over a hundred of the best-trained and most competent shipmates and crew a fellow could ever have. Murdered by the pirates.

Only Deke Sharp had survived.

Sort of.

Sharp got out of bed and crawled on hands and knees to the adjacent bathroom. He crawled into the shower stall, adjusted the chair there down to its lowest height, and climbed up onto it. He started the water running through the hand unit.

Sharp washed his stumps, first both legs, then the arms one at a time, removing each one, washing, then replacing it. That done, he performed the rest of his shower and rinsed off.

He dried off, then applied salve to his leg stumps. He put the prosthetic legs on, taking them from the rack in which he had left them last night. Standing, he removed the prosthetic arms one at a time, salved the skin at the interfaces, and put them back on.

Sharp looked at himself in the mirror. He looked more or

less normal, even though his ears, his nose, his mouth, and the area around his eyes were all artificial, bonded to the skin. His eyes looked normal too, though they were merely cosmetic overlays of the cameras that lay behind the artifice.

He shaved then, with an electric razor. His hair and beard would grow in splotchy, in patches, due to all the scarring, so he just kept them shaved.

Makeup – to even out his skin color despite all the scarring – he would apply later.

Sharp walked back into the bedroom and made a double espresso on the little machine there. No need to go to the kitchen yet.

He walked nude out onto the balcony, on the top floor of the condo building. It had a southern view out over the ocean, and was private from adjacent units.

He lay back on the chaise in the subtropical morning sunshine and sighed.

D Branch. Officially, D Branch of the Directorate of the Federation of Human Planets, the largest political entity in human space.

D Branch, the secretive intelligence arm of the Directorate.

D Branch, where he had worked for the past fifteen years.

D Branch, which had moved heaven and earth, and spared no expense, to put Deke Sharp back together again.

It had worked for them. Intent on avenging his crew, Sharp had worked himself, over long months of recuperation, back into some sort of shape and gone after the pirates and the people who had supported them.

He had personally killed over fourteen hundred pirates, the crews of the pirate ships and the space stations that had served as their bases.

He had also killed, up close and personal, over a dozen people who had made the piracy possible and profited handsomely from it. Movers and shakers all, they were admirals and corporate executives and high-ranking politicians.

Not murders, they were executions, under an ancient Federation law that gave captains of Federation Navy ships the power of judge, jury, and executioner over pirates.

And Deke Sharp was captain of the Federation Navy Ship *Medea*, the replacement for FNS *Circe*. Like *Circe*, *Medea* was actually a D Branch asset, but it was registered as FNS *Medea*, to allow resupply and maintenance at Federation Navy facilities. Oh, sure, he was being a rules mechanic, but it didn't matter anyway.

They were dead men, for what they had done to his crew and thousands of others over twenty years. The law had nothing to do with it.

Deke Sharp's vengeance didn't care much about rules.

Ultimately, after destroying seven pirate frigates and a destroyer, and two pirate space stations, after killing over a dozen powerful people – after personally announcing to them that 'Aiding and abetting piracy is a capital crime.' – Deke Sharp's burning need for vengeance had been slaked.

The rest of the people supporting piracy, over two dozen in all, were dispatched by other D Branch operatives under the same Federation law.

That had been almost a year ago.

Now Deke Sharp lay out on his balcony in the sunshine and pondered the future.

Escape

Octavius Pasha – the head of field operations for D Branch and Senior Field Operative Deke Sharp's immediate superior – was at his desk in D Branch headquarters on Ariel.

He had two things going on at the moment. More endless paperwork, and worrying about Deke Sharp.

Sharp had not come in today, and he was on-planet. That was not a good sign, one that had been growing in frequency since the anti-piracy operation had concluded.

The incoming call request signaled, and Pasha keyed acceptance. Admiral Kurt Jurgens' face looked out at him.

"Hello, Otto," the Federation Navy's chief of naval operations said.

"Hi, Kurt. What's up?"

"I was hoping you could tell me, Otto. Have you been being good girls and boys over there?"

Jurgens was on Meredith, so 'over there' was quite a few light-years away.

"I think so, Kurt. You see trouble?"

Jurgens nodded.

"I have a cross-jurisdictional request from the Ariel police forces – both planetary police and New Destin P.D. – to arrest and turn over one of your people."

"Why would they need cross-jurisdictional authority? Who is it?"

"Deke Sharp."

"But he's here on Ariel. He's within their jurisdiction."

"Yes, Otto. But he's also the captain of a Federation Navy ship, FNS *Medea*. I guess they don't want to step on any toes.

They also don't want us to let him get away."

"You know that's something of a misnomer, Kurt. Sharp's a D Branch employee, not a Navy asset."

"Well, I'm not so sure about that, Otto. The FNCJ is vague on this one, at least in my interpretation. And I don't want to set any bad precedents. I've sent it on to JAG for a determination."

The Federation Navy Code of Justice, and the Judge Advocate General of the Federation Navy, Pasha knew.

"Did you expedite it to JAG, Kurt?"

"No, Otto. They're always so busy over there, and I didn't want to step on anything else they had going on."

Jurgens was clearly protecting D Branch. It could take JAG months to come back with an answer, and, in the meantime, Jurgens need do nothing. Then again, D Branch had let the Navy – which meant Jurgens in particular – take credit for putting out of business the piracy operation that had harassed Federation shipping for two decades.

That made them friends. It also meant they were the good guys. And if the good guys couldn't stick together, lots of things stopped working.

Pasha nodded.

"All right, Kurt. Thanks for letting me know. I appreciate it."

"No problem, Otto. Stay in touch."

New Destin P.D. was going to try to arrest Deke Sharp?
Oh, boy.
Pasha wanted the video of that encounter.

Deke Sharp, half asleep out on the patio, got a call request. He would have ignored it, but it was the special tone he had assigned to requests from his friend and superior, Octavius

Pasha.

"Hi, Otto."

"Hi, Deke. Hey, I just got a weird call from Kurt Jurgens, Kent Corcoran's old boss."

Vice Admiral Kent Corcoran, the assistant head of naval operations and one of the pirate supporters, whom Sharp had executed last year.

"Yes?"

"He's got a cross-jurisdictional request from New Destin P.D. and Ariel planetary police to take you into custody. To prevent you from leaving Ariel."

"That's curious."

"Yes. You been a good boy, Deke?"

"Oh, yeah. Nothin' goin' on here, Otto. So what did Jurgens do with it?"

"Sent it to JAG for an opinion. Without expedite. It could be months. But it means you need to be careful."

"Understood, Otto."

"Hang on a second, Deke. Something's going on here."

The second stretched out to be five minutes of dead air on Sharp's end, and he grew increasingly concerned. What was going on at headquarters?

Then Pasha came back on.

"Deke! They're here for me. The police. Get out of there. Off planet. NOW!"

The call cut off.

Deke Sharp logged into the condo building's security system the same way he had taken Pasha's call, with his internal virtual terminal processor. He had hacked the building security years ago, when he first moved in.

It had seemed prudent at the time, and proved so now.

There they were. One of those special police tactical teams. Body armor, fully-automatic weapons, maybe a dozen guys.

They overrode the main door's security lock and entered the building. Beyond, in the camera view, Sharp could see their vehicles. Armored vans, one of which had half a dozen armed drones on the roof.

Shit.

Sharp logged into *Medea* and requested the on-planet shuttle to the roof of the building. Even with the emergency request, it would be several minutes for it to spool up and make it here from the New Destin Navy Shuttleport farther down the coast.

At least it wasn't in orbit. That would be more like an hour, depending on where in its orbit the Navy's orbital Ariel Station was with respect to the planetary capital of New Destin.

Deke hadn't liked his bugout ride being that far away.

With the police already on the way up, Sharp didn't bother to get dressed. He had a trellis on the wall behind him, and he was on the top floor. That trellis had been built extra strong for just such a circumstance.

Sharp climbed up the trellis to the top and went over the parapet to the roof. He hunkered down between the air-conditioning unit and the stair enclosure to stay out of the sight of drones. He checked the front security camera of the building again, and no drones had launched yet, but that could change.

Sharp logged into his condo unit's service processor. He had made modifications to that processor's software over the years, and he sent a couple of commands to the unit.

"Defense system active."

"Weapons free."

Police had found all the requirements of search warrants,

arrest warrants, knocking on doors, and the like inconvenient over the years and had largely dispensed with them. The rules hadn't changed, only the excuses had.

Deke Sharp found such excuses uncompelling.

He watched the police tactical team set up outside his condo unit's door, then force entry with breaching tools.

"Fellas, fellas, fellas. That there is what's known as a mistake."

"Go, go, go, go, go!"

The tactical police unit poured through the breached door into the condo unit, sweeping the living room with their machine guns before the lead unit headed into the bedroom, then into the bath.

They began searching in haste, flipping over furniture and the bed, looking out on the balconies.

One fellow pulled a painting off an interior wall and found something behind it.

"Hey, Sarge. What does 'This side toward enemy' mean?"

"What? Let me see that."

The sergeant came over, took one look, and blanched.

"Get out, get out, get out! Everybody out!"

But it was much too late.

Deke Sharp's condo building was a concrete and steel high-rise. It was difficult to heat and air condition units in such a building without an interior wall. So Sharp's unit had purlins on the bare concrete walls, with insulation and a vapor barrier, and drywall over the top.

The claymores Sharp mounted in his living room and bedroom had two-foot-square, half-inch-thick steel plates mounted to the steel-reinforced concrete wall behind them.

They stuck out a bit past the surface of the drywall, and Sharp had covered them with artwork.

Unarmed, they had simply hung there on the walls for the last decade. Once he had given the modified service processor in his unit the weapons-free command, they had been armed.

When the service processor determined from infrared surveillance cameras that all the intruders were inside the condo, not out in the hallway, and none were shielded in the master bath or closet, it took action.

It detonated both claymore mines.

Seven hundred steel ball bearings, propelled by two pounds of plastic explosive, sleeted across each room.

The results were horrific.

The building shook a bit with the double explosion. Sharp checked his surveillance cameras in the corners of the living room and the bedroom.

The entire police tactical unit was down. No one was moving. Their body armor had proven notably ineffective against a claymore mounted head-high in close quarters.

Sharp changed his view to the security cameras at the front of the building. Police there were trying to re-establish communications with the tactical team that had gone in, but they had no idea yet what had happened.

The patio doors in Sharp's unit, both in the living room and the bedroom, had blown out onto the balconies, but that was on the back side of the building, facing the ocean.

The police were getting ready to launch drones when Sharp saw *Medea*'s shuttle screaming in over the water.

The shuttle came in hot, stopping over the condo building and dropping to the roof. Sharp ran for the shuttle, still nude, ran up the ramp and dove through the door. He grabbed at pull-up handholds in the floor, usually used in zero gravity.

"Emergency departure now."

The shuttle closed the door and pulled in the ramp, spooling up the engines.

Sharp saw, in the shuttle's exterior cameras, drones come over the edge of the roof. They started firing pistol rounds at the shuttle. Likely ineffective, but Sharp hadn't stayed alive all these years by taking chances.

"Drone defense active. Weapons free."

The shuttle opened weapons ports and fired forty-millimeter shrapnel rounds at the drones, and they both went down, falling to the ground far below.

At that point the shuttle was off the roof and climbing hard to orbit, where *Medea* waited.

Sharp signaled *Medea* to request departure clearance.

Once the initial hard acceleration, which Sharp took lying full length on the floor, hanging onto a pair of pull-up handholds set into the floor, was over, Sharp got up. He pulled on a spare shipsuit and sat in the command chair of the shuttle.

The shuttle would dock to *Medea*, still in berth, and then *Medea* would leave Ariel Station.

Assuming *Medea* got departure clearance.

Or even if she didn't.

Patrick Mulcahy, the New Destin police chief, was getting absolutely nowhere with Captain Amit Patel, commanding officer of Ariel Station.

"I'm sorry, sir, but I have no authorization to detain the FNS *Medea* or Captain Sharp."

"You don't understand, Captain. He shot his way out of

New Destin, setting off explosives as he departed. I have a dozen men dead down here. Deke Sharp is wanted on a dozen charges of murder of a law enforcement officer. Those are capital charges."

"Did you submit a cross-jurisdictional request before your men made contact, sir?"

"Of course, I did, Captain. Two days ago. I still haven't had an answer."

"Then you have no jurisdiction here, sir, and I have no authority to detain the captain of a Federation Navy ship under local laws, regardless of the charges."

"You won't act on these charges, Captain?"

"No, sir. I'm sorry."

"You will be, Captain. I intend to file a complaint about your failure to act with naval operations on Meredith."

"As may be, sir, but my orders are clear on this point."

Chief Mulcahy angrily cut off the call without a goodbye.

The shuttle docked with *Medea* and Sharp went on into the cabin. It was a small one-room cabin, for *Medea*'s one-man crew. Command chair, galley, bunk – it was all in one room.

Medea was originally a one-off. There were other *Medea*-class ships now, all in D Branch service. She had proven so effective in service they had built more of them.

Medea was built around the engines and power source of an attack ship carrier, but had perhaps ten percent of the tonnage. That meant she was the fastest thing in space.

Medea mounted eight guns from a heavy cruiser, four in each broadside. That made her as powerful on offense as any ship in space.

Medea mounted two shuttles, for redundancy.

And, as FNS *Medea*, she had resupply and maintenance

rights at any Federation Navy station.

Deke Sharp was listed as her captain.

Deke Sharp sat in *Medea*'s command chair and checked for departure authorization. There it was, along with an incoming call request, from the station commander, a Captain Patel.

Sharp accepted the call.

"Good morning, Captain Patel."

"Good morning, Captain Sharp. I thought I would let you know that I got a request from Chief Mulcahy of the New Destin P.D. to detain you and FNS *Medea*. It seems you got people pretty upset down there."

"Yes. When the police break the law and bust your door down without so much as a knock, the top cop gets really annoyed when you kill them all as the criminals they are."

Patel's eyes got wide and then he nodded.

"I see. Well, yes, they are pretty annoyed with you, Captain Sharp. Annoyed with me as well, for denying their request. Without an approved cross-jurisdictional request, I cannot interfere with the movements of a Navy ship or her captain. Such request approvals became required after some local police departments used specious complaints to interfere with Navy operations in the past."

"Ah, that's how it came about. Well, I'm happy for it, Captain Patel. I have other things to do than argue with local charges that won't stand scrutiny anyway."

"And I will let you get to them, Captain. I just thought to let you know."

"I appreciate it, Captain. Thank you."

"Good spacing, Captain Sharp."

Patel waved one hand and cut the connection.

Sharp undocked *Medea* from Ariel Station at his authorized departure time, and followed the traffic pattern leaving the station. Once clear, he accelerated at frigate speed for the envelope.

He had no idea where he was going.

It was reflex and habit that had Deke Sharp accelerating at normal frigate speed to the envelope. That is what his mass reading was, and he didn't like advertising *Medea*'s capabilities to anyone watching.

So getting to the envelope would take some time.

The envelope was a curious thing, discovered early in space flight, and the reason human colony planets existed at all.

Massless particles like photons traveled at the speed of light. Since they were massless, if they didn't travel at the speed of light, they would have no effect on the universe at all.

Massy particles like protons, neutrons, and even electrons, couldn't travel at the speed of light. They could get very fast, though, especially when driven by particle accelerators.

Large, non-sub-atomic objects like spaceships couldn't get anywhere near the speed of light. But a curious thing happened when they got up to a few percent of the speed of light. Spacetime found them so objectionable it formed an envelope around them. It essentially walled them off from spacetime.

When that happened, continued acceleration resulted in much faster velocities, faster even than light. Many times the speed of light. Hundreds and thousands of times the speed of light.

It was the envelope that made interstellar flight possible.

Waiting to get to the envelope was part and parcel of space flight. A few percent of light-speed was still very fast, and it took a while to get going that fast. To get fast enough that the envelope would form.

While waiting, Deke Sharp got another call request. It was from Daphne Duplay.

Duplay was the kind of woman one could meet in certain milieu. Planetary capitals. Financial centers. Wherever the rich and powerful gathered.

Duplay was a professional companion. The newspapers called her a socialite. Some people called her a prostitute, though that was a misnomer. Duplay never accepted a quid pro quo.

She would, however, accept gifts, particularly large gifts of cash, from her many male friends. This allowed her to live a well-funded lifestyle being a companion to many wealthy, older men.

Deke Sharp was one of her male friends. As a Senior Field Operative for D Branch, he was very well compensated. Spending much of his time 'on the road' – and on expense report – he had few opportunities to spend the money.

He was probably one of the youngest – and least well off – of Duplay's many male friends.

Sharp accepted the call, and Duplay appeared immediately. She looked frazzled, something she never did. She was always cool, calm, and very attractive, though not conventionally beautiful.

"Daphne! What's going on?"

"I was going to ask you that, Deke. I've been arrested."

"For what?"

"Prostitution and espionage."

"Are you in jail now?"

"No. A friend bailed me out. He also gave a certain amount of serious talking-to to the police department."

Sharp could imagine that, given the sort of men Duplay called her friends.

"Do you know anything about this, Deke? I wouldn't have associated it with you except for that espionage charge."

"New Destin P.D. tried to arrest me this morning, Daphne. They were unsuccessful."

"Well, good for you. Where are you now?"

"In space. Headed out."

"Good. Stupid bastards."

"Let me ask you a question, Daphne. You know I work for D Branch?"

"Yes. Of course."

"Do any of your other male friends work for D Branch? I mean, I wouldn't ask except for this turn of events. Otherwise none of my business."

Sharp would never have asked such a question normally. Duplay was famously discreet, and wouldn't answer in any case. In fact, you might never see her again if you asked, because she would no longer return your calls.

"I understand, Deke. No. I think one needs to maintain a certain, um, diversity of income sources to ensure financial security."

"OK, Daphne. Good. But that does mean it's probably tied to me. Don't worry about it. They can't bring you to trial. Your friends won't allow it."

Duplay nodded. She knew much too much about way too many powerful men for them to allow her to be compromised.

"All right, Deke. I understand. But be careful. These people are playing hardball."

"Thanks, Daphne. I will."

Familiars

Sharp thought about the implications of Duplay's arrest.

First, it meant that whoever was behind this was on another planet. They couldn't be based on Ariel. Duplay knew too many powerful men – and knew too much about them – for it to be a local play. A local would have known that.

Second, it meant anyone associated with Deke Sharp was in their sights. Otto Pasha. Daphne Duplay.

Who else?

Lydia!

Lydia Thompsen had been Deke Sharp's high school girlfriend. It was Lydia's father who had arranged Sharp's internship with D Branch the summer between his junior and senior year of college, after his mother had died. Without the internship, he would not have been able to afford to finish college. With the internship, D branch had vetted him for employment in its field operations and financed the rest of his education.

More to the point, it had been the adult Lydia Thompsen, now married and with three kids, who had analyzed the pirates' financial data and found that they were being operated at a loss. That the source of their real income was the military, defense suppliers, and insurance companies.

Yeah, somebody unnamed could be pissed at her, too.

Not wanting to risk a direct call to Thompsen, Sharp called Paul Camden, Thompsen's husband.

"Camden."

"Paul. Deke Sharp. New Destin police just arrested my boss and my girlfriend. They tried to arrest me as well, but I wasn't amenable. You need to grab Lydia and the kids and get under cover. I'm on my way."

Camden took it in stride, nodding.

"What about Suzie?"

Suzie Fuller, Sharp's sometimes girlfriend, at least when he was on Humphreys.

Sharp nodded.

"Yeah. Her, too. Someone's going after me and my familiars. I don't yet know who. We're going to have to find out and deal with them."

"All right, Deke. I got it."

"You OK for aliases and all?"

"Sure. When you get here, place a call request to Philip Bernard Daniels."

"All right, Paul. Now get going. I don't know how far in front of them we are."

Sharp cut the connection.

He thought it somewhat curious that Camden hadn't seemed at a loss for how to go underground. Then again, Sharp didn't know what Camden did for a living. Some kind of corporate IT guy, he thought. Consultant or something.

And he already had an alias?

When he reached the envelope, Sharp set course for Humphreys and accelerated at *Medea*'s boat flank speed.

Medea sped through interstellar space at a pace no other ship could match.

Decelerating toward Humphreys, Sharp set *Medea*'s transponder to identify her as FNS *Hera*, one of the false ship IDs, carried in the Navy register, that Admiral Jurgens had given him for the piracy operation.

No sense broadcasting *Medea*'s location.

On the way in from the envelope, Sharp put in a call request for Philip Bernard Daniels.

"Daniels."

But it was Paul Camden in the display.

"You guys all right?"

"Yeah. Incognito, as they say."

"OK, good. I'm on the way in. Once docked with Humphreys Station, I'll send a shuttle down. We're short of seats, so I'll be remoting it."

"Sounds good."

"Where are you?"

"Recall that resort?"

"Oh, yes."

"Two resorts east on the same beach. Westernmost bungalow."

"Parking lot?"

"Behind the bungalow. Empty at the moment."

"Got it. Figure thirteen hours from now."

"Nine in the morning local time," Camden said, nodding. "We'll be ready."

Sharp called up the satellite imagery. When he had vacationed on Humphreys after the anti-piracy operation, Deke Sharp, Suzie Fuller, Paul Camden, Lydia Thompsen, and the kids had stayed right there.

He marked the location and backed the view out.

Two resorts east, the westernmost bungalow.

There.

And there was the parking lot.

This should be easy.

Sharp docked *Medea* to Humphreys Station and then dispatched one shuttle to the planet. He could take it nice and easy on take-off. The adults should have no problem hanging on to the floor grabs while the kids occupied the command chair and the two jump seats.

With the shuttle away, he called up the current imagery of the site to check its status.

Shit.

There was a marked police car sitting in that parking lot. Just sitting there. Probably the advance patrol for a larger group on the way.

Sharp floated into the other shuttle, shedding his shipsuit on the way. He launched the shuttle with an emergency departure authorization while he pulled on a pair of gym shorts.

He reset the landing location on the first shuttle to the beach, and set the autopilot of the second shuttle for a combat drop next to the first.

During the drop, Sharp removed his legs and got into what he called the dog suit, a quadrupedal robotic lower body. With the stumps of his legs connected into the shoulders of the armored unit, he looked like a centaur, half metal and half man.

He hung onto the floor grabs with all four feet – the 'hooves' were actually the balled-up fists of hands at the end of all four legs – and called Camden's alias.

"Daniels."

"Sharp. There's a cop car in the parking lot. I think a tactical team is on the way. So change of plan. Landing will be on the beach. Wait on the lanai. As soon as the dust settles, run for the shuttles. You and Lydia in the command chair in each shuttle, two kids in the jump seats in one, one kid and Suzie in the jump seats in the other. Strap everybody in."

"Got it. What about you?"

"I'll be rear guard. I'll hold the cops off while everybody boards, then jump aboard myself. I don't need a seat. I'll be in a four-legged armored robot, so don't let that scare anybody. I'll fly both shuttles on remote, so don't try to fly it."

"OK. We're good."

Paul Camden hunkered down behind the overturned picnic table on the lanai with Thompsen, Fuller, and the kids. The picnic table was between them and the bungalow doors behind them, to shield from the incoming police unit.

He understood the plan. He in a command seat because he was biggest. He would be a bad fit for a jump seat. Thompsen for the command seat in the other shuttle because she was the mother of children who needed their mother. The kids in the jump seats because they were light. Fuller in a jump seat because, well, she was left over, as was one jump seat.

Sharp, in whatever kind of armored robot setup he had, would hold off the cops and take their fire, jumping aboard at the last second.

It wasn't much of a plan, but it was what they had.

Thompsen crouched behind the picnic table. Camden had briefed them all. She would take Sarah and Camden would take the boys. She could carry six-year-old Sarah, but Camden, big and strapping as he was, could take both four-year-olds, one under each arm.

Suzie Fuller would have to take care of herself.

She didn't know what kind of robot Sharp had, but she wasn't worried about that. Get her and Sarah on the shuttle to the right. That was her part of the plan.

Everybody else had their part to do.

She just concentrated on her part.

During the drop, Sharp loaded two twelve-round cassettes for the dog suit's forty-millimeter mortar launcher. Four smoke rounds, four flash-bangs, and four shrapnel rounds in the first cassette. The second cassette was if it really fell into the pot, and included shrapnel rounds, incendiary rounds, and gas rounds.

He also checked the magazine in the fifty-caliber gun. Forty armor-piercing explosive rounds. If he had to use the fifty, he wouldn't be fucking around.

Sharp bent his knees and lay down in the body of the dog suit, then closed the top over his human portion. He would be immune to small-arms fire in the suit.

Both shuttles would land nearly simultaneously, the second shuttle's more expedited drop catching up to the first shuttle's location. They came in off the water, and they came in hot.

Checking the current imagery, the tactical team had arrived in their vans. They were all out in the parking lot getting organized. Maybe they could be away before the action started.

Then again, maybe not.

Camden saw the shuttles coming in over the water. Damn, they were moving fast, hot and low, kicking up rooster tails. He turned to Sarah and the boys.

"OK, now. Don't be scared, kids. We're just going to go for a ride in Uncle Deke's space ship. How cool is that, huh? But first we have to get away from bad men pretending to be police. The important thing is to get on the shuttle. No matter what, get on the shuttle. Sarah, you go with Mommy, and you boys are with me. But if we drop you or something happens, keep running and get on the shuttle. OK?"

"OK, Dad," Sarah said.

The boys nodded.

"OK. Good. Soon now, we're gonna run for the shuttles. We'll carry you. Suzie? You OK?"

"I'm good, Paul. Good luck, everybody."

"All right, everybody. And Lydia and Suzie, remember. Don't look back. What Deke is up to, what's going on behind us, is not our concern at the moment. We can watch the video later. Get on the shuttles. That's your complete focus. Get on the shuttles, get on the shuttles, get on the shuttles. Nothing else matters."

Thompsen and Fuller looked at each other and nodded. Thompsen looked back to Camden.

"We understand, Paul."

Sharp saw that the police tactical team was advancing on the bungalow from the parking lot as the shuttles came up to the beach.

The shuttles rotated on their landing thrusters to use their main thrusters to slow down as they came up to the shoreline, then settled to the beach. They turned ninety degrees as they came down to present their loading doors to the bungalow.

The doors opened and the boarding ramps extended, but Sharp was already through the door and running for the bungalow.

Camden watched the shuttles land, kicking up a lot of sand. Out of that cloud of sand came a four-legged metal creature, bristling with weapons.

Holy shit.

"Go, go, go!" the creature called out in Deke Sharp's voice.

The sand was mostly settled now, and Camden stood and grabbed up the twins.

"There's Deke. Let's go!"

He ran for the shuttle on the left. Fuller and Thompsen, carrying Sarah, ran for the shuttle on the right.

Behind him, Camden could hear the police tactical team hammering on the bungalow door with a ram.

Deke Sharp saw everybody jump up and run from the lanai, heading across the beach to the shuttles, then turned his attention to the bungalow.

Sharp selected a shrapnel round to shatter the patio doors, followed by two smoke rounds into the bungalow. At this range, he didn't fire the mortar rounds up into the air, but aimed them directly at the doors as direct fire. The mortar cassette rotated to the selected round, loaded it, then fired, three times in rapid succession.

Whirr, cha-chink, FOONT, whirr, cha-chink, FOONT, whirr, cha-chink, FOONT.

The patio doors disappeared in a shower of glass, then the two smoke rounds penetrated the bungalow and bounced toward the front door. They quickly filled the living room with smoke, just as the tactical team breached the door.

Sharp had dialed the cameras of the dog's vision into the infrared, and watched the tactical team enter the room. They ran in and spread out, but they couldn't see. Some fell over furniture they couldn't see in the dense smoke and called out. That prompted others to randomly fire into the smoke.

One guy was carrying a forty-millimeter mortar launcher. That was the only real threat to Sharp or the shuttles. That guy had to go.

One fifty-cal armor-piercing round to the center of mass took down the mortar man. It passed completely through him and took down the guy behind him as well, only exploding when it hit the masonry front wall of the bungalow.

Never stand behind the guy with the mortar launcher.

And what the fuck kind of police force used mortars anyway?

Fuller was following Thompsen, running to the right shuttle. They heard gunfire behind them, but kept running, not looking back.

Then Thompsen called out and staggered. She had taken a stray round through the left calf.

Fuller grabbed Sarah.

"I've got her. Let's go."

Fuller used her free hand to help Thompsen stagger along and they kept running to the boarding ramp and up the ramp into the shuttle.

"Into the command chair and strap in," Fuller said. "I've got Sarah."

"I'm bleeding pretty hard."

"Use your belt to compress the wound for now. More will have to wait until we're outta here."

Camden didn't see Thompsen stagger. He was in front of the women and was completely focused on getting himself and the boys on the left shuttle. Up the ramp, into the shuttle. One boy in each jump seat, strap them in.

"Mommy got shot in the leg," said one of the twins.

Michael, the one he had carried on his right.

"Did they make the shuttle?" Camden asked.

"Yeah. Suzie took Sarah and they kept going. Mommy was limping, but they got inside."

"OK. Good. We all made the shuttles, then."

Camden sent a quick priority message to Sharp.

"All aboard."

When he got the all aboard, Sharp started to spin up the engines on the shuttles. He retracted the boarding ramps on both, and closed the door on the shuttle with Paul Camden and the twins in it.

He popped two more smoke rounds into the bungalow as the police tactical team was still trying to get organized.

Then Sharp turned and ran for the shuttle on the right, the one with Thompsen, Fuller, and Sarah already on board. He had seen Thompsen stagger in his rear-facing camera, and knew she would need first aid.

As he approached the shuttle, he launched a couple of flash bangs as direct fire onto the lanai, then a couple of shrapnel rounds in high arcs to land back down on the beach.

Whirr, cha-chink, FOONT, whirr, cha-chink, FOONT, whirr, cha-chink, FOONT, whirr, cha-chink, FOONT.

Sharp leapt for the doorway of the shuttle as it lifted off the beach. He grabbed for the pull-up hand grabs in the floor and held on with all four feet as the door closed behind him.

The two shuttles, under Sharp's remote piloting, headed out over the water. The quickest way to put distance between them and the police on shore was horizontal, not fighting against gravity.

Once out of range of light-arms fire, the two shuttles angled up and headed for space.

When things settled down to one gravity, Sharp went over to the storage bay for his dog suit. He disconnected his legs from the suit and sat in the suit as he attached his prosthetics.

He then got down off the dog suit and parked it by remote in its storage bay.

He turned to the cabin and its occupants. Lydia looked a little shocky.

"Lydia took a round in the left calf, D.K.," Fuller said.

"Yeah, I saw that."

Sharp pulled his first-aid kit – the shuttle one; there was a bigger, more capable one on *Medea* – and headed to the command chair.

"What are you gonna do?" Thompsen asked.

"I passed EMT, Lydia, so I'm gonna patch you up."

"You did?"

"Yup. Standard field-ops training. Usually we end up using it on ourselves."

"Oh. Right."

Sharp removed the belt she had applied to stop the bleeding. That was smart. Hmm. Clean through. No bone, no artery. Lucky.

OK, lessee. Analgesic first. Acetaminophen and codeine. For a clean-through round, nothing more heavy-duty was necessary.

He administered those to Thompsen, and she took them.

Next, topical antiseptic on the entry and exit, followed by gauze pads and elastic bandage, pulled tight enough to stop the bleeding. She had already pretty much done that with the belt, so he didn't have to overdo it.

Finally, orally administered antibiotic, to make sure the wound didn't get infected internally. Again, Thompsen complied.

"OK, Lydia. That's pretty much it. I'll have the doc on Humphreys Station look at it when we get to *Medea*."

"Is that smart, D.K? How do we know they won't arrest

me."

That was a good point. They wouldn't touch Sharp, as captain of a Federation Navy ship, but Thompsen was a civilian.

"We'll have the doctor come aboard *Medea*. Then everything is under my command."

"OK. Good."

"Now you should call Paul and let him know your status."

"One more thing, everybody," Sharp said. "We're going to be weightless soon, and some people get sick in zero gravity."

"What kind of sick?" Sarah asked.

"They throw up. A lot. And in zero gravity, it floats around and hits everybody. There's vomit everywhere, flying around."

"Oh, YUCK!"

"Yes, indeed. So everybody takes a weightless pill if you don't know you're OK without it."

Sharp sent a message to Camden, in the other shuttle, on the same topic, and told him where the zero-gravity pills were.

The trip to *Medea* was uneventful. The two shuttles docked with their parent ship, and everyone floated on into *Medea*.

Assets

With all seven of them in the one-man cabin of *Medea*, it was certainly cramped. The good part was that they were weightless in the ship – docked to the non-spinning part of Humphreys Station – and the rope meshes for zero gravity were deployed in the cabin.

Everybody used a tether to clip themselves to a portion of a rope mesh as they took stock of their situation.

"OK, so in zero gravity, it's not too bad," Camden said. "What do we do when we're under way to wherever, Deke? There's only so much floor space. Where do we even all sleep?"

"Well, the kids can sleep in the one bunk here," Sharp said. "The couples can sleep in the shuttles. They each have a single bunk as a pullout behind the jump seats. It's like a separate bedroom, as long as you're very friendly. Those single bunks aren't very big."

"And food, D.K?" Fuller asked. "Can this little galley feed us all? And what about stores?"

"I actually take quite a bit of stores normally," Sharp said. "Enough for over a year. We can go probably two months, maybe three, on full stores."

"OK," Thompsen said. "So this isn't too bad, then. We can camp out in *Medea* through whatever the hell is going on. By the way, what the hell is going on?"

"I don't know, Lydia," Sharp said. "My boss was arrested while I was on a call with him. He told me to get out. I almost didn't manage it. The police were already at my building."

"What did you do?" Fuller asked.

"I was on the top floor. I climbed up on the roof and called one of the shuttles to pick me up from the roof of my condo building."

"And it got there before the cops did?" Camden asked.

"No. A couple of claymores set into the walls of my condo unit delayed further police response."

"The tactical team that entered your condo?" Camden asked.

"All dead. A dozen or so. I heard that the police chief was pretty upset about it."

"I shouldn't wonder."

"Busting in my door without a knock or a warrant? Fuck 'em. They only get away with that shit because it's tolerated. I wasn't in a tolerating mood."

"And the Navy didn't detain you, D.K?" Thompsen asked.

"Nope. Against the rules. They had to file a cross-jurisdictional request to detain the captain of a Federation Navy ship, and they had no such approval. They might now, but they didn't then."

"What if they have it now, Deke?" Camden asked.

"For *Medea* and Deke Sharp?" Sharp asked. "But this ship is FNS *Hera*, and my name is Mark Osborn."

"Aliases for a Navy ship?" Camden asked.

"The chief of naval operations is a friend of mine. Something to do with pirates."

Camden snorted.

"So Humphreys police should get the same answer," Fuller said.

"Yep. But that protects *me*. If one of you civilians leaves the ship and goes out into the station, that may not apply to you."

"But we didn't do anything," Thompsen said. "You did all the shooting."

"Yes, but why were they there in the first place?" Sharp asked.

"Good point," Camden said.

"So what do we do now?" Fuller asked. "I think that's the big question on the table."

Sharp shrugged.

"Figure out who's behind all this and stop them."

"I think the big question is why," Camden said. "We need to figure that out first."

"Agreed," Sharp said. "It's probably to do with the whole piracy thing. I'm not sure we got to all the money men behind that whole operation."

"That makes sense to me," Thompsen said. "It took quite a bankroll to set that all up."

Thompsen looked around at the others.

"I guess it's up to us to figure it out," she said.

"Yup," Sharp said. "So let me start with this. What skills do we have? I'm a D Branch field operative. I have a lot of skills, especially weapons and direct-action stuff. Also a wide range of secondary skills, like analysis, computer skills, medical first aid. And I know Lydia is a financial analyst. What do you two do?"

That last was addressed to Camden and Fuller. Camden answered first.

"I'm a Red Team attacker in computer security."

"Really?" Sharp asked.

"What's that?" Fuller asked.

"When a company wants to know how good its computer security is, they hire me. I break into the company's systems and tell them where their weaknesses are. I use a variety of system penetration and hacking techniques."

"That's fucking great," Sharp said. "I knew you were an IT consultant of some kind, but that's about the best thing I could imagine for my purposes right now."

Sharp turned to Fuller.

"You're a financial analyst, too, aren't you, Suzie?"

Thompsen laughed. Sharp looked back and forth between them.

"Sort of, D.K.," Fuller said. "I'm a senior financial corruption investigator for the Humphreys Department of Justice."

"No shit?" Sharp asked.

Fuller nodded.

"Fuck me," Sharp said. "And you didn't see this coming?"

"Well, it's not strictly my department, but no, I had no clue. I don't think this came through Justice. I think the cops are free-lancing this one."

"Which should interest the hell out of you," Thompsen said.

"Oh, you betcha. Because that *is* my department."

The three kids had napped off as soon as they were tethered to the rope meshes and the adults started talking boring stuff. After all the excitement of the escape and the flight to *Medea*, they had all fallen asleep in zero gravity in the warm cabin.

That also meant they had missed out on Sharp's profanity.

Sarah woke now.

"Mommy? I'm hungry."

Thompsen raised an eyebrow to Sharp.

"Well, it's about lunch time. Let's fire up the galley," Sharp said.

"Let me take a look at your stores, Deke," Camden said. "I know what they'll eat."

Of course, much of the stores were for zero-gravity use. That is, tubes of this or that food, which could be heated in the microwave.

Sarah took one look and wrinkled her nose.

"We're eating *toothpaste*?"

"Taste it, Sarah," Deke said.

Sarah looked at him skeptically and smeared one little dab on her finger, then tasted it.

"Oh, yummy!"

She then tried to squeeze the whole tube in her mouth at once.

"No, no, Sarah," Thompsen said. "One mouthful at a time."

The boys, watching all this, tried theirs a little less gingerly, then were also gulping down lunch.

"OK," Sharp said. "Looks like we won't have to worry about them eating properly from the zero-g stores."

"I should probably take a look at your stores order, Deke, and make sure there's enough stuff they'll eat on there."

"Good idea, Paul."

"There's another thing, too, D.K.," Thompsen said.

Sharp turned to her.

"We need activities for the kids. There wouldn't happen to be a toy store on the station, would there?"

"There are some dependents on the station, I think. So the station exchange would probably have some of that stuff."

"But I can't go there, D.K."

"No, but their catalog is on the station network, and they'll deliver everything. Like stores for the ship and all. You order it, Lydia, and they'll bring it to the ship."

"Excellent. There's nothing worse than bored children, D.K. Trust me. Oh, and speaking of which, you have a lot of weapons on board ship, right?"

"Sure."

"What's their status?"

"Locked up until and unless I deploy. Locked under my virtual terminal ID."

"Oh. OK, good. They're good kids, and they know about

guns, but I don't think I want to trust in the good judgment of a child."

"No, we're good, Lydia. Everything's locked up."

"One last thing, D.K.," Fuller said. "We need more clothes. All of us. We had our bags at the resort, but we didn't take anything when we ran for the shuttles. Everything was left behind. All we have is what we have on."

Sharp nodded. They had packed for the rescue, but they had been smart when it became a rescue under fire.

"The station exchange will definitely have civilian clothes in stock. The assortment may not be the best, but they will have things suitable for planet visits."

"OK," Thompsen said. "That's the plan then."

Two hours later, with the children sitting in one of the shuttles – Sarah, as the oldest, got the command chair – happily coloring away in their new coloring books, the four adults took up the conversation where they had left off.

"Let's say it's some big-money type who funded setting up the pirates in the first place, and he's going after D.K. and his familiars because he lost a lot of money and he's pissed," Thompsen said. "What do we do about it?"

"Can we do anything about it?" Fuller asked. "I mean, do we have access to the resources we need?"

"I still have access to D Branch computation and investigation tools," Sharp said.

"Are you sure, D.K? How do you know those haven't been shut down?" Camden asked.

"Well, I have multiple alternate logins that aren't associated with me."

"Really? In D Branch?"

"Yeah. I should be good."

"I probably shouldn't admit this," Fuller said, "but I have multiple alternate logins within the Humphreys DOJ."

Sharp looked to Camden.

"Yes, I still have available logins as well, no matter what they did to my primary," he admitted.

Everybody turned to Thompsen.

"I wouldn't be surprised if my employer didn't tell whoever is behind this to take a hike, but I have, er, multiple supplemental logins as well."

"Remarkable," Sharp said. "Such a law-abiding group, and we all have our little cutouts."

"Yes, to protect us from the not-law-abiding," Camden said.

"Oh, agreed, Paul. Agreed. But it means we are currently unhobbled in wielding our full skills against our attackers."

"Well, I would be better at wielding my skills if we had gravity," Thompsen said. "The weightless pills work, but do not completely kill the symptoms. I'm a little iffy all the time."

"Once we're completely stocked, we can go out a couple light-years to the middle of nowhere and just accelerate around in circles," Sharp said. "We won't hit the envelope doing that, but we'll have gravity."

"Let's do that then, D.K.," Fuller said. "I prefer gravity as well."

"All right. Let's just get our supplies situation in hand, and have the station doctor look at that bullet wound of yours, Lydia. Then we'll head out."

Medea set out from Humphreys Station several hours later.

Camden and Thompsen had met the doctor in the main cabin while Sharp, Fuller, and the kids hid out in one of the shuttles. The doctor had raised an eyebrow at the fresh bullet wound. Camden merely said 'Accidental discharge,' and the doctor had shrugged.

He stitched up the entry and exit wound to minimize the scarring that would result, and pronounced Sharp's first-aid measures appropriate.

"Make sure to continue the antibiotics for two weeks. That should be long enough."

In addition to topping off all of *Medea*'s supplies before leaving Humphreys Station, they had also downloaded a hundred hours or more of kids' movies and games.

Coloring books only got you so far.

Medea dropped out of the envelope about three light-years from Humphreys, and Sharp set it to space in a big enough circle it took three-quarters of a gravity of acceleration toward the center to maintain the circular motion.

Everybody felt better about that, especially the children. They could now eat regular meals, use the regular toilets – not the zero-gravity ones – and otherwise be more comfortable.

And the crayons were easier to keep track of.

After supper, with the kids in one of the shuttles watching a movie before bedtime, the adults were in the main cabin.

"I want to see what went on behind us as we ran for the shuttles," Fuller said. "How did Lydia get shot?"

"I can set that up on the display, or we can watch it in virtual terminal. Are we all equipped?"

Sharp looked around, and everyone nodded, so he split-screened his camera views from the dog suit, front view above and rear view below, and sent them all the footage. The front view was in infrared.

After they had all viewed it, Fuller had a question.

"What were they shooting at, D.K? They were completely in the smoke screen."

"Blindly shooting. They even shot one of their own, who just happened to be in front of one of the other guys."

"Stupid shits," Camden said.

"Oh, yes," Sharp said.

"What if they had killed one of us?" Thompsen asked. "Or one of my kids?"

"Then I would have killed them all. Every damn one of them," Sharp said.

"As it is, you killed two," Camden said.

"Yes. I couldn't let that mortar launcher go. It had the potential to be a real problem. The other guy was just standing in the wrong place at the wrong time."

"Pretty cold-blooded, D.K.," Thompsen said.

"Absolutely. They made it us or them, Lydia. For survivors, I picked us."

"Yeah. Never send a cop to pick up your prom date," Camden said. "He'll bring her back in cuffs, in the back of the car. They only know what they know."

"And the tactical teams are worse," Sharp said. "They'll shoot her dog and tase her, then bring her back in cuffs."

Thompsen and Fuller tried not to smile. Don't encourage bad boys. Then again, they were both happy they had the bad boys on their side.

"OK, so what now, Deke?" Camden asked.

"I think we should all concentrate on our connections first. Find out what we can. Tomorrow morning after breakfast, we compare notes and see if we can come up with a plan."

"Sounds good."

Thompsen went and put the kids to bed when their movie was over. She put them to bed in the shuttle, the boys in the bunk and Sarah in the command chair.

"That gives us the roomier main cabin for the adults. Whichever couple goes to bed first can take the other shuttle."

That made sense to everyone.

As it was, Sharp and Fuller went to bed first. The shuttle bunk wasn't very big, but they made do.

The width wasn't a problem for two if one was atop the other.

Deep into the evening and again in the morning, Sharp poked around inside D Branch systems looking to see what had happened to Octavius Pasha. There was a hidden chat room of D Branch field operatives, of which one of his multiple aliases was also a member, in addition to Deke Sharp.

After breakfast, with the kids playing in what was becoming known as 'their' shuttle, the adults gathered in the main cabin of *Medea* to compare notes.

"I guess I can start off," Thompsen said. "I started looking to see who was highly leveraged on the insurance companies and military suppliers we know were the big beneficiaries of the piracy activity before the piracy actually started. That is, who acted as if they knew those stocks would climb on their greater revenues and income once the piracy started.

"Now this is all twenty years ago, and it was before the laws were tightened – in an effort to aid the fight against piracy – by requiring greater disclosure. So I didn't have all the data available that one would have now.

"Even so, it's clear there was a group of investors who took pretty big positions in these companies, even selling down shares in other firms to free up the cash to invest in the piracy benefactors.

"Some of them were still seriously invested in those firms, and took some pretty big losses in those stocks, when, all of a sudden, their management had a set of reversals – often called death – and the revenues of those companies fell with the cessation of pirate activity.

"I have that list, and that's a good starting point, I think."

"Excellent," Sharp said. "I agree. How about you, Suzie?"

"I've been poking about within DOJ, trying to find out what the motivation was for the police action at the resort. It looks like it came in through the police, not from within the DOJ.

"Once the police had it, though, it went up to DOJ and got approved by a political flunky there. An assistant state's attorney. So I went after his bank accounts. All of that is easier now with the anti-piracy laws.

"And he's been getting payments. Small ones, often, but they've added up over time. This past week, though, he got a much bigger deposit than normal.

"Funny that, huh?

"So I tracked that down to a middleman. The money itself was laundered, but I'm making progress tracking it back using the new legal tools put in place to fight piracy.

"I should have the source of that money nailed down, or at least the next step up in the money laundering, soon."

"Nice. A money trail is always nice," Sharp said. "Paul?"

"I used some special-purpose tools to enter the systems of the New Denver P.D. I was looking for where the orders to that tactical team came from."

"You broke into the police department's systems?" Sharp asked.

"Oh, sure. Corporations have real money and profits on the line. They do a pretty good job. Governments run on tax money, so government systems always have the worst security. Any money they spend on IT is money in their budget they can't spend on higher salaries or fancier offices for the administrators, or more hires to escalate their importance.

"And security is always the first to get cut. They can't cut services. People would complain. So they cut security."

"Wow."

"Oh, yeah. Happens all the time."

"Who did you pretend to be?"

"The head of internal investigations."

Sharp laughed.

"Nobody's going to go checking on him!" he said.

"Exactly," Camden said. "So I poked around on that arrest order. Where did it come from? Turns out it was entered manually by a clerk in the piracy and terrorism unit.

"OK. Fair enough. What was her motivation for entering it? Where was the mail or message or call that motivated her entry of an arrest order?"

"Short story is that there isn't one."

"No source documents?" Sharp asked.

"Nope. None at all. There may be in her private communications, though. I haven't penetrated that yet. That's from a commercial provider, and so it's significantly more secure.

"Also, I think it's likely that there may be a financial incentive, so we can maybe have our finance whizzes here look into her bank accounts and see what they come up with."

"Also nice. Another money trail is good."

They all turned to look at Sharp. Thompsen raised an eyebrow.

"Well, I've been poking around in D Branch. My boss got arrested at the same time they tried to arrest me. He was in the office, though, so he couldn't make quite so flamboyant an escape.

"But there is a problem with arresting and holding the head

of field operations for D Branch.   All the field operatives work for him. And he's a great boss. They like him. A lot.

"Any ideas how much trouble a bunch of D Branch field operatives currently not out on assignment can cause if they get their backs up?"

"Oh, no," Fuller said.

"Oh, yeah," Sharp said, laughing. "You have got to hear this story."

Octavius Pasha

Octavius Pasha had been talking to Deke Sharp when the D Branch security team came in with two New Destin P.D. cops to arrest him. He told Deke to get out, then surrendered to the arresting officers.

No sense making a stink here. If Deke Sharp was on the outside, Pasha was content to wait in jail, if he had to, until Sharp brought this whole charade crashing down.

Which he would. Pasha had no doubt on that score.

The police took him down to the city jail and processed him in. He was allowed to keep his civilian clothes until he was arraigned.

Pasha expected to make bail and be back at the office within a day or so.

But that's not what happened. At the arraignment, the police department made the argument that, like Deke Sharp – who had made a spectacular flight from justice, leaving a dozen dead police officers in his wake – Octavius Pasha was a unique flight risk.

After all, he could just have one of his operatives take him to orbit and depart on a D Branch ship.

An assistant prosecutor, who had clearly just been handed the file minutes before, presented the charges. Peculation of D Branch funds – which wasn't a local charge, anyway, since D Branch was a Directorate operation – and aiding and abetting the murder of police officers by the notorious Deke Sharp.

His last instructions to Sharp to 'get out of there' were the compelling evidence of that last.

So bail was denied, and Octavius Pasha was returned to his jail cell, despite Federation requirements that bail be denied only under the most extreme circumstances.

That's when weird things began happening to the police department.

A policeman returning to his patrol car from lunch got in and turned the key. He got an electric shock. Some of the gauges exploded. There were electrical sizzling and crackling sounds. Smoke began coming out from under his seat, from under the dash, from under the hood.

The police car quickly started on fire, both under the hood and under the dash. The policeman was lucky to get out of the car with his life.

Investigation showed that an outside power outlet on the restaurant used for seasonal lighting displays had been wired to the ignition lead of the car. When the key was turned, turning the ignition on, AC mains power was applied to circuits designed for low-voltage DC, including all the internal electronics and the engine control circuits.

Even the electric seat-position motors.

The fire spread and engulfed the car.

The police car was a total loss.

There were a number of cases where officers returned to their cars and the police car simply refused to work.

It was determined that the engine control modules had been destroyed by an electromagnetic pulse, though they had no clue how such a strong yet localized effect had been created.

Of course, D Branch did have technology they didn't talk about, and policemen did speculate about it.

In other cases, when police walked away from a police car, it simply exploded. The usual cause was a small charge on the fuel tank or battery compartment, depending on the technology.

Whatever it was, it left the officers stranded and other officers had to go out and pick them up.

In all of these cases, the digital security footage from the cars showed nothing.

Forensic investigators determined that the security image had been 'looped,' with an innocuous portion of the footage copied over a portion that may have contained evidence.

The one that really tore it, though, was a series of incidents at police headquarters. On the morning of the second day after the arraignment of Octavius Pasha, the toilets in police headquarters suffered a sudden spike in sewer back pressure.

The toilets and urinals blew the contents of their bowls out into the bathrooms. The empty bowls then allowed sewer gas into police headquarters, and the whole building smelled like a poorly maintained outhouse.

Assured by maintenance that this was a one-time occurrence, the administrative staff at headquarters went back about their business. Maintenance flushed all the toilets and urinals to refill the water traps and mopped up the mess.

It happened again three hours later. This time, Patrick Mulcahy, the chief of the New Destin P.D., was sitting on the toilet, having finished the serious portion of his business and just begun the paperwork.

He was not amused.

His dry cleaner would not be amused, either, but at least Chief Mulcahy had a spare uniform in his office.

TOO SHARP TO HOLD

When someone brought up the thought that holding the popular boss of all of D Branch's field operatives in jail without bond had perhaps not been a good move, Chief Mulcahy dismissed the whole idea.

Until the toilets and urinals blew up again two hours later while Chief Mulcahy was leaving a leak.

Octavius Pasha was brought up on arraignment again the next day. This time, the New Destin P.D. representative *begged* the judge to set bail so they could get this guy out of jail.

The judge set bail, Claude Allard himself – the director of D Branch – showed up to pay it, and Octavius Pasha was released from jail.

The outré incidents involving the New Destin P.D. ceased abruptly.

They never did find the nitrogen cylinder and radio-controlled intermediate-pressure tank connected to the sewer cleanout behind the supplies cabinet in the third-floor maintenance closet of police headquarters.

When Pasha got back to the office, the field operatives currently awaiting assignment brought a cake to his office and sang, 'For He's A Jolly Good Fellow.'

As a joke, there was a hacksaw blade hidden in the cake.

You know. Just in case.

Pasha held the hacksaw blade aloft.

"I don't think I'll ever need this with you guys around."

They all cheered. They had always known that D Branch, in the form of Octavius Pasha, had their back.

He had proved it once again with the cost-be-damned medical rehabilitation of Deke Sharp.

Yes, he had their back, and they had his.

Money Trails

Thompsen, Camden, and Fuller were all laughing when Sharp finished the story.

"Oh, my God, D.K. You've got to be kidding," Thompsen said.

"Nope. The D Branch field operatives on Ariel took the arrest of Octavius Pasha personally."

"Are any of them going to get into trouble?" Camden asked.

"No, Paul. When New Destin P.D. gets in over their heads with an investigation of a crime or apprehending a suspect, they normally call us for help, because D Branch operatives know all the tricks. New Destin P.D. has no chance of figuring out who did any of that stuff."

"How do you even get into police headquarters to place the device that spiked the sewer pressure?" Fuller asked.

Sharp shrugged.

"If you wear a coverall and carry a toolbox, you can go anywhere, Suzie. You're basically invisible."

"Amazing. So somebody just walked in there and did it, then walked out."

"Oh, sure. It takes some nerve, but it's easy."

Fuller just shook her head.

"So Octavius Pasha has been released? He's back in the office?" Camden asked.

"Oh, yes."

"Can we use D Branch to help us, then?"

Sharp considered. Such a move was not without risk.

"Perhaps," he said. "I can contact Otto with one of my aliases. He'll know it's me, but that won't be apparent to anyone monitoring his communications."

"Would somebody even do that?" Thompsen asked.

Sharp shrugged.

"I wouldn't have thought so, but I didn't think anyone would dare to have him arrested, either."

"Fair point," Camden said. "So maybe we could get some help, but it sounds like we're better off on our own if we can swing it."

"Right," Sharp said. "Otto will back us in anything I decide is necessary – and I can call for help if we need it – but limiting contact that can be traced to us is definitely better. At least until we have this resolved."

"OK. So it's back to money trails," Camden said. "Can we get into New Destin P.D?"

"Don't look at me for that," Fuller said. "All my resources are on Humphreys."

"I have that one," Sharp said. "The D Branch operatives who sprang Otto Pasha penetrated New Destin P.D., and I have the hooks."

"Excellent," Camden said. "Using those hooks, I can get Suzie in and she can use her knowledge of police work to track the paperwork."

"If you get me into the police department, I can track their banking as well," Fuller said.

"OK," Sharp said. "I think that's our next step. I think we should go in through D Branch, though."

"Why?" Fuller asked.

"Because, after the recent incidents, if you slip up and the police track your connection back to D Branch, they'll let it drop there."

Lunch and playtime with the kids intervened. Sharp and

Thompsen spent time with the kids in their shuttle to allow Camden and Fuller to work in the main cabin. Before too long, it was nap time, and Sharp and Thompsen returned to the main cabin, but did not disturb Camden and Fuller, who were deep into their penetration of the New Destin P.D.

After naps, Sharp and Thompsen repeated playtime with the kids until after supper. Camden and Thompsen then took their kids back to their shuttle, where the children settled down with a movie.

Once the kids were settled, Camden and Thompsen came back to the main cabin.

"So how did you guys do? Did you make any progress?" Sharp asked.

"Yeah," Fuller said. "Paul just walked me into the police department systems. Whenever I found a system I needed access to, he opened it up. I went anywhere I needed to go."

"Suzie tracked the paperwork through the department," Camden said. "This person to this person to this person. The tactical team was told you were a dangerous criminal, and had murdered dozens of people. Including security people."

"But I'm not a dangerous criminal," Sharp said.

"No, D.K. You're a dangerous law-abiding citizen," Fuller said. "The tactical team didn't know that, though. They walked into an ambush."

"Of course. Dangerous criminal or not, they don't have the right to beat my door down. Break into my home. They broke the law. I won't let that stand. Go quietly in the custody of a bunch of criminals? Not likely."

Fuller waved that away with a hand.

"Anyway, it was all made up," Fuller said. "By one guy in records. Their document server has pretty good tracking tools for who made what changes. I think they were using him for access to the records, and this time they had him create some instead. Same thing for Octavius Pasha and some woman named Daphne Duplay."

"Friend of mine," Sharp said.

"They charged her with prostitution and espionage," Fuller said.

"Daphne's not a prostitute, Suzie. There is no quid pro quo. She accepts gratuities, but not payment."

Fuller raised an eyebrow, but Camden nodded.

"Yeah, they can't make that illegal, or every rich guy with a mistress is in serious trouble. Laws are only meant to ensnare poor people."

Fuller turned to Camden.

"That's because the laws are made by rich people."

"Well, yes. Of course."

"What about payments?" Sharp asked.

"Yes, he was receiving payments," Fuller said. "My Humphreys credentials – my alias ones – got me into his bank accounts. Pretty small payments actually. I guess they add up over time. He got a much bigger payment for this intervention in the records, though."

"Same mechanism? Through an intermediary?"

"Yes, D.K. Same intermediary, in fact."

"OK. Well, that proves that all four incidents are related. The three on Ariel and the one on Humphreys."

"We knew that already, though, didn't we, Deke?" Camden asked.

"Yes, Paul. At least, we guessed it. Now we can prove it."

"So now what, D.K.?" Thompsen asked.

"We need to find the intermediate nodes in the payment stream, Lydia. Track it back. Where did the money start?"

"We might be able to work that from both ends," Thompsen said. "I know the people who were heavily invested in all this. The piracy stuff."

"It may be easier to track it forward than backward," Fuller said. "People concentrate on obscuring the path working back."

"We'll work it from both ends, then, and see where we get," Sharp said.

Camden worked the intermediary back, while Thompsen worked the investors forward. Fuller flitted back and forth between them, using her Humphreys access to bank records to get them into resources as they worked.

By virtue of their jobs, all four of the adults on *Medea* had virtual terminal processors, so all of this work was going on in their heads, not on the physical displays of the ship. They were going in through one of Deke Sharp's aliases at D Branch, so any slip-ups traced back to D Branch and ended there in D Branch's security.

They certainly could not be traced back to Humphreys, just a few light-years away, or to Ariel's civilian systems.

Sharp, for the most part at loose ends, put the kids to bed after their movie, then retired early in the other shuttle.

When Fuller finally came to bed, Sharp woke up.

"Any progress?" he asked.

"Lots."

"Like what?"

"In the morning, D.K. Right now, little Suzie needs to work off some energy if she's going to sleep."

"I can help with that."

"I was hoping you'd say that. Hit the switch, honey. No time delay necessary."

TOO SHARP TO HOLD

The kids had been paying attention to how the shuttle's entertainment controls worked. They had a movie running by the time the adults got up. Sharp was actually first – having retired earlier, despite the interruption – and he was working on breakfast when everyone else got up.

Thompsen and Camden were first, right there in the main cabin where the galley was. The smell of coffee and bacon in the morning was overpowering in the small space.

Fuller wandered in ten minutes later. Even the kids stopped their movie long enough to eat when the aromas hit them in the other shuttle.

Breakfast was a happy affair, then the kids ran off to go back to their movie.

"I understand you made some progress last night," Sharp said.

"Yes and no," Thompsen said.

"Yes and yes," Fuller said.

Sharp looked to Camden and raised an eyebrow.

"I think it's probably yes and yes, but we don't know for sure yet."

"Well, how about you give me the yes everybody agrees on first," Sharp said.

"I traced payments into the last intermediate account to the next account upstream," Fuller said. "Also an intermediary account, I'm afraid."

"I expected that," Sharp said. "I wouldn't think a single account between would be realistic in terms of covering their trail. So how bad does this one look?"

"It looks like it will be harder to crack. I think the deposits were done in cash."

"Cash?" Sharp asked. "Who uses cash anymore?"

"A lot of people," Thompsen said. "The government's tried to get rid of cash, and they can't do it. The market can't work without cash."

"You're gonna have to spell that one out for me, Lydia."

"It's simple, D.K. You need cash for the black market to work, and you need the black market for the open market to work."

"I'm still at sea here," Sharp said.

"If the government over-taxes people, they switch to doing things off the books. For that, you need cash. It's the safety valve. The government hates it, but it also knows that they can't do away with it."

"Why not?"

"Because the government only needs to step over the line in one place, and, with no black market in place, the whole system comes crashing down. With cash in the system, the government can overstep here and there, and it doesn't crash the markets because there's a safety valve that keeps things moving."

Sharp gave her a questioning look and shook his head.

"D.K., think about this one. Let's say the government overtaxes shipping. Interstellar shipping. It's no longer profitable. If interstellar shipping stops, if those companies go out of business, everything else comes crashing down. All the businesses that depend on imports. All the businesses that depend on their export market. Everything.

"But if at least some shippers start running extra cargoes off the books for cash, they can still make a profit. Nothing collapses. The freight rates are still high, but the companies stay in business because of the higher profits on the hidden, cash part of the business. Eventually the government probably corrects the tax rates, but the system has survived."

"OK, now I get it. You don't have to have all of interstellar shipping go to cash, as long as the companies in that business can make a profit somewhere, on part of the cargo."

"Exactly. So the government has never been able to get rid of cash, and never will. They would have to be infallible on everything to keep from crashing the whole economy. They know better, at least that far."

Sharp nodded and turned to Fuller.

"So it looks like the deposits into the second-last intermediary account are in cash?"

"That's right, D.K."

"OK, so what's the maybe-yes/maybe-no part?"

"On the investor side, I can't nail down the funders of the piracy setup, D.K.," Thompsen said. "It could be any of them."

Sharp turned to Fuller.

"So what's the yes part of that, Suzie?"

"I think it's all of them, D.K. An investment club, of sorts."

"Is that a common thing?"

"Sure. You get eight guys investing in potentially high-payoff stuff, that's all gonna be high risk, too. But if each guy has an eighth share in all eight of them, risk is reduced, while the big payoff on a couple makes it really worthwhile. That's how venture capital firms work."

"So we're not just after one guy?"

"Probably not, Deke," Camden said. "I lean toward Suzie on this one."

"Shit. So to shut this operation down, we gotta take out six, eight, a dozen guys, all of whom are super-rich and all of whom probably have excellent security?"

"I think so, Deke."

"Looks like I may have to call Otto after all."

Camden raised one eyebrow, and Sharp continued.

"I'm gonna need backup on this one."

"Maybe not, D.K.," Fuller said. "An investment circle or investment club – even a venture capital firm – usually has something like a managing partner. Some one guy working on each investment. There may only be one guy who's calling all the shots on this one. Take him out and the others are likely to leave it alone."

"How do we figure out which guy it is?" Thompsen asked.

"I don't know yet," Fuller said. "Let me think about it."

Sarah, Michael, and Matthew were good kids, and mostly stayed out from under foot. Movies and coloring were getting old, though.

One day, Deke Sharp realized something he should have thought of right off: *Medea* had a 3D printing facility. There were times when you needed a part, and you couldn't afford the weight and size penalty of carrying spares for everything. With 3D printing, you could just print up the part you needed and repair the ship.

Sharp checked to see if there was a library of toys that could be 3D printed. Of course, there was. Multiples, actually.

He set filters for the amount of feedstock, whether metal or plastic, and the capabilities of his printer, which was mostly a size limitation, and got a whole list of toys that could be made on *Medea*.

The next time Sarah said, "I'm bored. There's no toys or *anything*," Sharp had an answer.

"Well, Sarah, why don't you print some toys?"

A bare fifteen minutes of instruction and the kids were happily going through the library, looking for the best toys to print. Sharp had emphasized there was a limit to how many they could print, so they should print only the best ones.

Soon the printer was turning out a few select toys, and the

boredom issue settled down.

Meanwhile, the adults were trying to track down not just the money trails, but the path the orders took to get from the decision maker to the person who entered the arrest orders.

"They probably follow the same trail as the money, Deke," Camden said.

"Would they do that, Paul?" Thompsen asked. "Wouldn't that make it easier to break?"

"No, dear. Think of it this way. You need one trail for the money, right?"

"Yes. Of course."

"OK, so does having a second trail add to your risk or reduce your risk?"

"I see. A second trail increases your risk. Two chances to lose."

"Exactly. So I think the orders went down the same trail as the money."

Camden turned to Sharp.

"What do you think, Deke?"

"I think you're probably right, Paul. What does that buy us?"

Camden looked to Fuller.

"Maybe we can nail down which of the investors it is. Because the orders are in English – in words, anyway – and we can analyze the language and see if we can compare to public statements by the person. Word choices, syntax, sentence structure, can all tell us a lot."

"It can?" Sharp asked.

"Sure. We do it all the time in corruption investigations."

Camden nodded.

"In which case, I have a question for you, Deke. D Branch

has penetration tools, right?"

"Oh, sure. Really good ones. But I'm not much of an expert in that stuff. I'm not sure I can make much headway, even with D Branch tools."

"Yes, but I *am* an expert in that stuff. Deke, can you get me access to the D Branch tools?"

Oh, now there was a combination. Put Paul Camden on the D Branch toolset? Ouch. That's some horsepower right there.

Could he do it, though? Not really was it possible – sure it was – but was it allowed or advisable? It wasn't something he wanted to break their radio silence for, to ask Pasha for permission. Anything Sharp did would be on his own authority. Probably in excess of his authority, actually.

But would Pasha think it was OK after the fact?

"Let me think about it, Paul. That's sure to step on toes once it comes out at the end of all this. I just have to think my way through it."

"I understand, Deke. But I'm not making much progress with what I have. These guys' security is pretty good."

In the end, Sharp decided to give Camden access to the D Branch tools. It was a pretty easy decision, actually. They had arrested Pasha on bogus charges, then denied him bail. They had sent a tactical team against Sharp, breaking into his home.

And they had sent a tactical team – with fucking mortar launchers! – against Paul and Lydia and their children.

No, this was war. And in times of war, one did what one had to do to win. The rules didn't really play into it much.

Sharp gave Camden one of his fake D Branch IDs. Login, avatar, everything. It was a huge security breach, and Sharp didn't really much care.

He could always delete or modify that fake ID later.

In point of fact, though, from what Sharp had seen, D Branch should probably hire Paul Camden. His level and kind of skills were always in short supply.

He wouldn't even have to move to Ariel. He could do his sort of work from Humphreys. That might even be better from Pasha's point of view. Having someone remote from the center of the action could prove very valuable.

As now, for example.

Being remote from the scene of this kind of war allowed more freedom of action. More security. More chance of success.

And success was what Deke Sharp was after.

Ariel

After his second arraignment, payment of bail, and release from jail, Octavius Pasha went to Deke Sharp's condo building. He met with the building supervisor, telling him he was Deke Sharp's employer, and their insurance would be paying for any damage to the building.

With that, the supervisor took him up to Sharp's unit to survey the damage.

The bodies of the police tactical team had been removed days before, of course, and the unit sealed up, but no other cleanup or work had been done yet. The patio door openings were covered in plastic, but the new doors had not arrived yet. They were a priority of the building management, in order to keep the building weather-tight.

Pasha looked around the unit. The damage was horrific. Seven hundred high-velocity ball bearings had shredded the walls and furnishings in addition to the police tactical team. There were massive holes in the drywall, with clots of insulation hanging out of the openings. Ball bearings were embedded in the drywall remaining. Furniture was overturned and mangled. Blood stains soaked the torn carpeting.

Pasha had never seen the results of something like a claymore detonated in close quarters before. It was a remarkable amount of destruction for such a small device.

"Wow. This is really something."

"I've never seen anything like it," the building supervisor said. "We don't even know where to start."

"All right. Well, let's just gut the whole unit down to the concrete walls. Take out everything right down to the walls and we'll start over. Maybe some of the purlins you can save. Otherwise clear it out.

"Get the new patio doors installed and get it all watertight."

"We also have a lot of debris on the ground."

"We'll pay ten credits for every ball bearing found on the ground, and fifty credits for every pound of glass. Publish that and let people get after it. You can't maintain a high-end building like this with glass and debris on the ground. So let's get that under way."

"Yes, sir. Thank you, sir."

"No problem at all. Let's get all this cleaned up. In the meantime, I'll have an interior designer draw up some sketches and we'll get the unit back into shape in no time. We won't dally on something this important to the property.

"Just bill all the cleanup to me."

"Yes, sir."

"And give every resident a month free on their condo fees and bill that to me as well. We need to make it up to the other owners that there was this annoyance in their building. I know my employee feels bad about being such a problem for his neighbors."

"Very well, sir."

Pasha took one last look around and nodded.

"Get going on all that. I'll be in touch when we're ready to start the reconstruction."

Back in his office, after the party the unassigned field operatives threw for him, Pasha logged into the D Branch servers under one of his alias IDs. He started with the news feeds.

Who else had gotten arrested that day? Deke Sharp, of course, and Pasha himself, but who else?

Daphne Duplay? Oh, my. Somebody didn't know what they were dealing with there. No less a personage than Senator Jeffries, the chairman of the Judiciary Committee of the Ariel Senate, had shown up to bail her out. He had called Police Chief Mulcahy down to the bail counter to personally oversee the process.

Pasha smiled. That had to have been uncomfortable for the police chief. He would have given good money for a recording of that conversation.

Pasha had looked into Duplay when her interactions with Deke Sharp had come to his attention. He had found that she was no more than she appeared to be. Someone who enjoyed the good life – someone after his own heart, in other words – and who found the best way to pursue it was to be the personal companion of wealthy, powerful men.

In particular, she was not an agent of any other interest than her own. A mercenary, in effect.

It had occurred to Pasha that, under the right circumstances, Duplay could be an asset to D Branch, but that was a bullet that could only be fired once. Duplay was famously discreet, and that was what made her powerful.

So Pasha had understood her. Clearly, the police had not. While Pasha had not known that Senator Jeffries was a friend of Duplay's, clearly neither had Chief Mulcahy.

And Senator Jeffries was not a man to be toyed with.

Setting aside his enjoyment of that particular confluence of circumstances, Pasha considered.

Deke Sharp, Otto Pasha, Daphne Duplay. Deke Sharp was clearly the center of things here. If they were going after him and his familiars, who else would be on their list?

What was the name of that financial analyst they had used

for the piracy operation? Pasha looked back through his notes. Here it was. Lydia Thompsen. That was it.

He checked the Humphreys news feeds.

Well, look at that. Lydia Thompsen was a fugitive from justice, fleeing with her husband, Paul Camden, their kids, and another woman, Suzie Fuller. They were apparently in hiding.

Pasha checked on Fuller. Same hometown as Thompsen and Sharp, same school, but five years younger. Had an older brother who was Thompsen and Sharp's age, though. OK, that made sense.

He pulled up Fuller's picture. OK, not Pasha's type. He tended toward skinnier women. But he knew that her fuller figure – Ha! Her very name was Fuller. – was right up Sharp's alley.

Back to Ariel.

Admiral Jurgens had given Pasha access to Navy servers during the piracy operations, and extended it recently. He pulled them up now.

He watched the conversation between Chief Mulcahy of New Destin P.D. and Captain Amit Patel, the commanding officer of Ariel Station. Oh, Chief Mulcahy had been more than a little peeved about that.

He also saw the conversation between Patel and Sharp.

So Jurgens' delay on the cross-jurisdictional agreement was holding.

Ariel Station also had a record of FNS *Medea* leaving the station, accelerating to the envelope, and disappearing from normal space.

Where had Deke Sharp gone? Humphreys?

As the days went by, Pasha continued to check arrival and departure records for Humphreys Station.

There was no record for *Medea*. A week or more in, there was a record for FNS *Hera*, though. Could that be Sharp?

The timing looked too tight for that.

Then again, *Medea* was the fastest ship in space.

Pasha checked the list of aliases Jurgens had given Pasha for *Medea*, and there it was. *Hera*, so called, had been on Humphreys Station barely a day before departing the station and leaving the system.

Pasha pulled up the ship's docking record on Humphreys Station. One shuttle launch. One shuttle emergency launch. Two shuttle arrivals. Doctor visit for gunshot wound. Supplies, including reaction mass and food stores.

Hmm. Coloring books and crayons, but no marines on board. Also, the downloading of dozens of hours of children's movies.

Pasha opened the medical record, using a D Branch override on patient privacy. Lydia Thompsen. Calf wound, bone and artery not involved. Cause given as accidental discharge.

He went back to the Humphreys newsfeeds. The fugitives had been discovered, but, as police moved in, they escaped to space in two shuttles. They had help from what the news called 'armed terrorists.'

The times worked out for Sharp's shuttles to have extracted Thompsen, Camden, Fuller and the kids as the cops moved in.

More detail now showed three policemen killed, and two injured, in the melee.

OK, so who were Camden and Fuller? Camden first.

Hmm. Camden – Thompsen's spouse – was a senior red-team hacker/penetrator for a top-notch corporate IT security consultancy. Certainly someone Sharp could use in tracking down who was behind all this.

Now who was Fuller?

Oh, my. Oh, this was just too good. Fuller was a Senior Investigator for the New Denver D.A.'s office in the Humphreys Department of Justice. Specializing in financial corruption investigations.

Under the anti-piracy laws, she would have access to banking records across the Federation.

Pasha had been concerned about getting Sharp whatever help he needed to track all this down, but, together with Thompsen, he already had one hell of a team assembled.

About the only personnel he could use was a babysitter to help with the kids.

What about computer access?

Pasha switched to his own account and logged in with superuser status. He looked at the accounts currently active.

He knew that all his field operatives maintained multiple alias accounts. That, by his lights, was a good thing. The IT people thought D Branch had four times as many field operatives as it did, but that was OK with Pasha.

Two of those aliases – two that he thought were likely Sharp's – were burning up the CPU cycles right now. Sharp had likely given one of those accounts to Camden.

Without Pasha's permission, by the way.

Good. No sense making potentially dangerous contact if one didn't need to.

Pasha locked those two accounts' permissions and marked them to remain unchanged without specific authorization from himself.

He also bumped their privileges. No resource within D Branch would be unavailable to them.

Change Of Venue

Once he was granted access to the D Branch systems, Camden looked around the tools area. One interesting bit was the educational section. Looking there, he found beginning, intermediate, and advanced courses on system penetration, as well as tutorials on each of the D Branch tools.

Camden dug into the tutorials, running them on his virtual terminal at one and a half times normal speed.

D Branch had some nice tools, no doubt about it.

They also had access to interplanetary data lines, and had archived many things of interest.

As much as Paul Camden liked what he had been doing for a living, it was clear that, compared to analysts and system penetration teams at D Branch, he had been working with one hand tied behind his back.

Not anymore.

After working all day with the D Branch tools, Camden logged out. Before he did, he attempted the safety play of creating two more alternate IDs for himself.

Somewhat surprisingly, they went through. Superuser status? Really?

Nice.

He didn't feel this was an abuse of Sharp's trust. If Sharp was incommunicado for some reason, and the ID Sharp had given him was compromised, progress on the project might depend on his having another way in.

Now he did.

But how did he have superuser status?

"So how are things going?" Sharp asked Camden that evening after supper. "Are you making progress with the D Branch tools?"

"Oh, yes. In addition to the tools, which are great, there are extensive archives of interstellar communications. I'm trying to identify the interesting data streams in and out of the intermediate account location. I hope to nail down where the instructions came from.

"One question, though, Deke."

"Yes?"

"Did you mean to give me an account ID with superuser status?"

"Excuse me?" Sharp asked.

He got a blank look on his face as he accessed his virtual terminal processor. After just a minute or two, he was back.

"Well, that's interesting. Both of the accounts we were using today now have superuser privileges. That's new."

"That's new?"

"Oh, yes. New today, I think."

"What does that mean, Deke?"

"It means that Otto is watching, and trying to make things easy for us any way he can."

"Really."

"Yes. And since both accounts were active at the same time, he knows I gave you access. He's communicating back that he's good with that and is helping us out."

"All without direct communications."

"That's right, Paul. Direct communications are dangerous. But Otto and I don't need them anymore. Not often anyway. We know each other that well."

"Well, that's comforting, I suppose, but how does he know we've teamed up?"

"Oh, I imagine our little escapade on Humphreys made the news feeds. He knows of Lydia's work on the piracy issue. My shuttles leaving and coming back to Humphreys Station are in the Navy logs, which he can see. He knows *Medea*'s various aliases. And we ordered coloring books and crayons."

"Is there no other use for coloring books and crayons than for children?"

"Sure, but he knows we don't have any marines aboard."

Camden chuckled and Sharp continued.

"Otto knows I extracted you, he knows what we're about, and he's helping. That also means if I need backup, I can call for it."

"That could be handy."

"Yes, indeed. *Medea* is not the only ship of her type."

In his exploration of the D Branch tools, Camden found that D Branch had a large factoring engine. That would be handy. Very handy.

Encryption worked because of the difficulty of factoring the product of two very large prime numbers. If you knew one of the prime numbers, decryption was easy. That was the private key. The public key was the product of the two.

Someone could encrypt the message with your public key, and you could decrypt it. No one else could decrypt it, though, unless they could factor the public key.

D Branch could do just that. It took a long time on an expensive, special-purpose machine to do it, so encryption mostly still worked. After all, even D Branch couldn't decrypt everything.

But Camden didn't need to decrypt everything. He only needed to decrypt the message streams they were interested in. The ones that looked like they could be the instructions to agents on Humphreys and Ariel to enter the arrest warrants for Deke Sharp and his familiars into police records.

He submitted one of the suspect public keys for factoring while he worked on further tracking of the message streams.

After ten days of spacing around in circles, Sharp called a meeting to assess progress. It was evening, and the kids were in their shuttle, falling asleep in front of a movie after supper.

"OK, so where are we? Are we making any progress?"

"Oh, sure, Deke. At least I think so," Thompsen said.

She turned and raised an eyebrow to Camden.

"Yes. I think so, Deke. We've got the intermediary nailed down to a city and a planet at least. Gotham, on Elizabeth."

Gotham was the financial capital of the Federation. With big money behind the assault on them, that made sense for where the money might be. But...

"Would the intermediary be where the money behind this is?" Sharp asked. "Not more indirection?"

"Could be," Camden said, "but not necessarily. They could be using the same intermediary they always used. One local and convenient to them. They probably didn't expect someone with D Branch's resources to be after them when they set it up originally. With a factoring engine, for example. But now that's the source their agents expect."

Sharp nodded.

"So going to Elizabeth would help?"

"I think so, D.K.," Fuller said. "We can do some surveillance. Pick up some extra intel that way."

"Bear in mind, there's no access to the computers while we're gone."

"Won't slow me down right now, Deke," Camden said. "I have half a dozen public keys to factor now, and that'll take two or three weeks anyway. I can submit them as a queue and just let the machine run."

"OK, so now is probably a good time."

Sarah came in from the shuttle at that point.

"Our movie finished."

"What are the boys up to?" Thompsen asked.

"They fell asleep."

She looked around at them.

"What were you talking about?"

"We're thinking about going to a new planet," Sharp said.

"Which one?"

"Elizabeth."

"That's a pretty name."

"Would you like to tell the ship to take us there, Sarah?"

"Can I?"

"Sure. You just have to tell the computer what I tell you. Can you do that?"

"I think so."

"*Medea*, take your next two commands from Sarah."

"Next two commands from Sarah. Aye, Sir," the ship's computer voice came back.

"OK, Sarah. Say, *Medea*, set course for Elizabeth."

"*Medea*, set course for Elizabeth."

"Aye, Ma'am. Course laid in."

"*Medea*, depart for Elizabeth at ten gravities," Sharp said.

"*Medea*, depart for Elizabeth at ten gravities," Sarah repeated.

"Aye, Ma'am. Departing for Elizabeth. Ten gravities."

They all felt the ship rotate its nose out from pointing at the center of the circle they had been spacing in, and the ship's engines increase thrust until they felt one gravity.

"You did it, Sarah," Thompsen said. "The ship is doing what

you told it."

"Wow."

"Wow, indeed," Sharp said. "Thank you, Sarah."

"Daddy, I ran the ship!"

"You sure did, honey."

"OK, Sarah. Time for bed now," Thompsen said.

Sarah yawned and followed her mother into the kids' shuttle.

"All right, Paul," Sharp said. "You have a bit less than a day to the envelope. Get those factoring jobs queued up first thing tomorrow."

"Right, Deke."

At lunch the next day, Camden seemed relaxed and was joking around.

"All set?" Sharp asked.

"Yeah, Deke. I queued up a dozen public keys. It won't get through them all before we get there, but it'll get the most important ones."

"Excellent. We're just a couple hours away now."

"So what happens when we hit the envelope?" Thompsen asked. "I mean, we did it before, when we moved away from Humphreys, but that was just a few light-years. Elizabeth is dozens of light-years away."

"Over a hundred," Sharp said. "Basically, we won't notice much difference. We'll still feel one gravity of acceleration."

"How can that be, D.K? To get to Elizabeth at one gravity would take centuries, wouldn't it?"

"Yes. For that matter, getting to the envelope would take over a week at one gravity. One gravity is the part we feel. The engines are shielding us from the full acceleration effects."

"That doesn't make any sense."

"You're right, Lydia. It doesn't. But that's the way it works. Some pencil jockeys figured it out, and we just use it."

Thompsen shook her head.

"So how fast are we accelerating?"

"Right now? Ten gravities. The engines are shielding us from the full effect or we would be dead."

"That still won't get us to Elizabeth in our lifetimes, Deke."

"Nope. Once we hit the envelope, we are in a different environment than normal spacetime. We'll make more like two hundred thousand gravities. Something like that. Some huge number."

"And we'll still feel one gravity?"

"Yes, because we'll be in the envelope, and spacetime rules like inertia don't apply the same. Of what's left, one gravity is what the engines are letting through to us. I could as easily make it two gravities, or none."

"D.K., this makes no sense at all. How does it work?"

"We don't know, Lydia. The guys who discovered the envelope, the first time, hit a certain velocity, and then they just shot out into interstellar space. When they stopped, they were light-years away and thought they might never get home. They turned the ship around and did the same thing to get back. So we've learned how to use it, but we don't understand it."

"That's crazy."

"The cannon was invented in the eleven hundreds, but Newton didn't provide the basic equations for ballistics until 'Principia Mathematica' in the late sixteen hundreds. That doesn't mean they didn't work for five hundred years. Constantinople endured for a thousand years, but ultimately fell to cannon fire hundreds of years before Isaac Newton."

"Bottom line, though," Fuller said, "it's two weeks to Elizabeth. Is that right?"

"Something like that. Sixteen, seventeen days. For *Medea*, anyway. *Medea* is very fast."

"Why is *Medea* so fast, D.K?"

"You think of *Medea* as a small ship, because we have this one little cabin, plus the two shuttles. It's a one-man ship. In the main cabin here, four adults and three kids are really crowded.

"But *Medea* is the size of a frigate, which has a crew of over a hundred. Where did all the extra space go?

"*Medea* has the engines of an attack ship carrier, which is ten times our mass and has thousands of crew. They launch one-man and two-man fighters from that big of a ship.

"*Medea* also has the broadside of a heavy cruiser. Eight guns that can destroy any ship in space. Those are big and heavy, and the heavy cruiser that carries them also has a crew of a thousand or more.

"We have all that on *Medea*. It's the fastest ship in space, the most deadly, and the safest against attack."

"Why safest against attack, Deke?" Camden asked.

"Because the shields are generated by the engines, and designed to protect an attack ship carrier from anything but a direct hit at close range. When that powerful of a shield is shrunk down to the size of *Medea*, it's diamond-hard. A cruiser's heavy guns, even at close range, can't hurt us."

"Criminy," Fuller said. "And it's yours, D.K?"

"Permanently assigned to me. Same as makes no difference. She's mine."

"Which is why we can go from Humphreys to Elizabeth, across much of human space, in two weeks?" Thompsen asked.

"Instead of a month or more in a liner or a regular warship. That's right, Lydia. Nobody in their right mind would put engines and guns this powerful and expensive on a ship designed to move one guy around."

"And yet D Branch did."

"Yes, for two reasons. One, Otto Pasha isn't in his right mind and hasn't been for decades. And two, it depends on who that one man is. I basically took the piracy ring down myself, Lydia. One specific man, in this very special ship."

"OK. Now I get it. As much as I can, at least."

"You know now about as much as I know, Lydia. We can make it work, but we don't understand it. Not yet, anyway."

"And when we figure it all out? The envelope and all?"

"Then we'll be even better at using it. For right now, we make do."

The two weeks to Elizabeth was spent as people had spent long voyages since time immemorial. They entertained the kids. They played cards. They talked about the mission. Fuller even spent time coloring in one of the kids' coloring books.

The kids were impressed by how good she was at staying within the lines and worked to up their game.

Deke Sharp had adjusted the ship's clock by half an hour extra every day so that, when they got to Elizabeth, ship's time would match the time in the capital city of Gotham.

Medea decelerated enough to drop out of the envelope around noon on the sixteenth day in transit. There was still almost a day of deceleration to make dock with the Navy's orbital Elizabeth Station.

The kids were excited about being back on a planet after a month camping out in the kids' shuttle of *Medea*. They looked forward to wide open spaces again.

The adults were not so sure. The last time they were in wide open spaces, they were being shot at and fleeing for their lives. Getting to the shuttles on the beach on Humphreys had been their escape from evildoers. *Medea* had been a safe haven since.

And now they were going down to the planet where the evildoers were, they believed, headquartered.

Medea was transponding FNS *Hecate* when she dropped out of the envelope, and she docked with Elizabeth Station under that name. Checking Navy logs on the way in, Sharp found no orders to detain Deke Sharp and *Medea*, but he didn't want to advertise their whereabouts.

Sharp turned his supplies orders, prepared on the way in, over to the Navy supply department. He also ordered shipkeeping to come in and clean the cabin and the shuttle they left behind.

All seven took a single shuttle to the surface, with the kids in the command chair and jump seats, and the adults tethered to the pop-up handholds in the floor.

Sharp set the flight profile to delicate handling, and they set off for the Navy shuttleport outside the capital.

On far Ariel, Pasha had noted that the computer use had settled down to the factoring machine, and that the two individual users he associated with Sharp and Camden were not logged in. He concluded that *Medea* was in transit, and watched for it to pop up somewhere.

Pasha saw that FNS *Hecate* was inbound to Elizabeth, and knew that was one of *Medea*'s alias transponder settings. He checked his personnel roster for D Branch on Elizabeth and smiled.

He was covered there for backup or assistance, but he did not send any heads-up to the local agents.

One could never be sure just how tight-lipped people really were, and one thing Pasha would not do is put Sharp and his retinue at risk.

But if – when – push came to shove, Sharp could use local resources to assist.

Arriving at the Navy shuttleport, everyone exited the shuttle as a limousine pulled up. They were waved into the back compartment, then the driver and shotgun loaded all their luggage into the large trunk.

Soon they were off, heading into town.

"This is a nice ride, D.K.," Thompsen said. "You're going to spoil the children. We can't afford accommodations like this when we get back home."

She turned from watching the children playing with all the controls in the back of the limo to face Sharp. He shrugged.

"I can't either, Lydia. This is expense report stuff. And just wait until you see the hotel."

"Is it smart to be so high-profile?" Camden asked.

"Sure. For one, we can't possibly be here for another two weeks. Humphreys is just too far away. Second, no one expects a government agent to be limoing in, and sloshing it up in a luxury hotel. They won't even be looking for us for another two weeks, and they'll be watching lower-rent quarters."

"What are the accommodations going to be like?" Thompsen asked.

"Two connected family suites on the penthouse floor of the Gotham Astoria."

"That's billionaire territory, Deke," Camden said.

"Yup. We'll be safe there. The hotel has excellent security. The people they would likely send against us won't make it past the lobby. Maybe even the front doors. And the elevators won't even go to the top floor without a passcode."

TOO SHARP TO HOLD

One did not 'check in' to the Gotham Astoria. There was a concierge counter in the lobby, but no check-in per se. The porters who came out to the limousine to take their luggage included the bellhop, who led them into the hotel and up to their rooms.

He let them into their rooms, then handed out the code sequences on little cards, very elegant, with the Gotham Astoria logo on one side and the number on the other.

"Note these codes, please, then I will take the cards back. Dropping one outside your rooms would be a security breach that could be uncomfortable."

"And the children?"

"You can use your hotel login to create codes for the children that are limited in the manner you specify. In and out of the room, for instance, but not the elevators. That sort of thing. There is a snack center on this floor they may wish to visit, and which you may allow."

"I see. Thank you."

"Of course, madam."

Their luggage showed up, and it was split between the two suites, with Thompsen, Camden, and the kids in one suite and Sharp and Fuller in the other.

There was no tipping. The Gotham Astoria did not permit it. Their staff was, instead, very well paid.

"They assume anyone checking into this floor has a virtual terminal processor?" Thompsen asked.

"There are the keypads on the doors if not," Sharp said, "but I suspect it doesn't come up very often."

"Well, the kids don't have them. They'll have to use the keypads."

Sharp nodded.

"Now that we're here, there's something we need to do."

He produced a small pill bottle out of his jacket pocket.

"I need each of you to swallow one of these."

"What are they, D.K?"

"Homing beacons. If we get separated – any of us – I can find you."

"They're only good for two days?"

"Oh, no. These hang on inside until their battery is dead. I will be able to track any of you, if, say, something untoward happens. Kidnapping, say."

"Well, that sounds like a good idea," Camden said, taking one of the devices.

When everyone had swallowed one – including the children – Sharp logged into a device in his luggage with his virtual terminal. He could see all seven of the devices – he had taken one, too – from the next room. He labeled each of them as to who they were.

"That's better."

"You took one, too, D.K?"

"Of course. That way, you can find me, once I show Paul how to operate the locator system. Besides, you don't think I'm the only D Branch asset on Elizabeth, do you?"

They had dinner from room service in Camden and Thompsen's suite that evening.

The food, as one might expect, was exceptional.

Gotham

When the Federation of Human Planets was founded – and with Earth abstaining – no planet was willing to sign up for a central government that would be centered elsewhere. Governments had too much "spreadin' around" money, and it typically got spread around to the bureaucrats.

Whichever planet hosted the government would get rich. Others, not so much.

To make the Federation work, the government itself and its adjuncts were spread around. With QE radios, that wasn't a problem.

So D Branch was on Ariel, the Federation Navy was located on Meredith, the insurance industry on Juliet, the legislature on Christine, and so on.

The financial industry, including the stock markets and the big banks, was based on Elizabeth.

The capital of Elizabeth was named Gotham, the traditional nickname for New York City on Earth. As Earth wasn't then in the Federation, no problem. When Earth joined the Federation later, it was fait accompli.

When the founders of Elizabeth had named their capital, they had intended it to be a financial capital, like its namesake, and so it had become.

Many of the financial movers and shakers in the Federation lived in Gotham, including most of their suspects.

And Gotham was where the intermediary had tracked to.

They took it easy that evening, getting the kids settled in at the hotel and laying down some ground rules. The kids loved the snack shop – where all the snacks were free; they didn't nickel and dime you on the penthouse floor of the Gotham Astoria – and it was within their permitted roaming radius, whereas using the elevators was not.

They all went to bed early, worn out by the excitement of arrival and the shuttle trip down.

When Fuller and Sharp got into bed, she sighed.

"A real bed again. It's been too long."

"First time in a month," Sharp said.

"A real bed with you in it again? It's been over a year."

"True enough."

"C'mere, you. Suzie needs some lovin'."

"I live to serve."

She laughed and pulled him to her.

The next morning after breakfast, they got the kids settled in one suite and hit the ground running in the other.

First up for Camden was decrypting a number of message streams using the factored public keys from the D Branch factoring engine.

He hit the jackpot.

Camden forwarded the results from those decryptions to Thompsen and Fuller, and they started tracking the accounts and working the financials.

Then, after lunch, another factoring solution came in.

It was Sarah who discovered they had more room service options than they had thought. She was coming back from the snack center where the attendant had made a bowl of popcorn for her and the twins. She saw someone was getting a mid-morning breakfast of huevos rancheros, which she did not remember from the menu.

Sarah hung around in the hallway and asked the bellhop about it when he headed back to the kitchen.

"Oh, you can order room service from some of the restaurants here in the downtown area," he said. "The room service menu lists them at the end of the menu."

She thanked him and went back to the room to join the twins in watching a movie.

When it came time to order lunch, she told the adults.

For lunch that first full day they ordered Chinese food. Sarah and the boys loved spring rolls and crab Rangoon, finger food the adults didn't object to on nutritional grounds. The adults got wild rice and split two large entrees among them.

For supper, they ordered Italian food. The adults had traditional Italian dishes like veal parmigiana and rotini Bolognese, while the kids ordered a pepperoni pizza.

After supper, the kids headed back to the other suite to color for a while before bed.

"Oh, that was good," Fuller said. "I wasn't looking forward to continuously eating from the room service menu."

"Yeah," Thompsen said. "That makes all the difference in the world."

"Aren't the prices pretty steep, though, Deke? How's that going to play with your expense report?"

"Doesn't matter, Paul. It's more important we stay secure and out of sight. Two couples with three young children, including male twins, is too specific. And I never get any grief about expense reports. It's my call. Besides, room service is getting the food as takeout and then prepping it on heated plates and all before bringing it up here."

"Well, then, I agree with the ladies. Very nice."

Sharp nodded.

"So how did we do today?" he asked. "Report time. I guess I can go first.

"I went into my copy of D Branch field assets to see who was here on Elizabeth. Who we might use. I found that the Elizabeth entries had been sorted to the top of my list, and the order of assets on the planet rearranged. It wasn't in alphabetical order anymore."

"What does that mean, D.K?" Fuller asked.

"It means that Otto Pasha knows we're here. He knows *Medea*'s aliases, and he saw the arrival record of one of those aliases, FNS *Hecate*, at Elizabeth Station. Not only that, but he's sorted the local assets for me in terms of their capabilities, with an eye to what we might need."

"Are we that easy to track?" Camden asked.

"No, not by most people. But Otto has super-access to both D Branch and Federation Navy records. The only person who does, I think. For him, it's easy."

"All that, from resorting your list," Thompsen said.

"Yes. But Otto and I have been working together for fifteen, sixteen years, and are friends besides. We can read each other pretty well by this point. He didn't have to do it, but he's letting me know he's got our back."

"Well, that's good," Fuller said. "Just knowing we're not, you know, running open-loop out here."

"And all without sending a message," Camden said.

"Yes. In an investigation like this, the less communication the better. We don't know who's been subverted. Not yet, at least. When there's a lot of money involved, some people are vulnerable."

Camden nodded. As far as communications with Ariel was concerned, less was more.

"So where have you guys gotten to?" Sharp asked. "Make

any progress?"

"Oh, you might say that," Fuller said, rolling her eyes.

Thompsen and Camden laughed.

"I should probably start," Camden said.

The women both nodded, and he turned back to Sharp and continued.

"When we got here yesterday, I checked, and eight of the public keys I had submitted to the factoring engine had been solved while we were in transit.

"This morning, I applied those solutions to the message streams with which each was associated. They all decrypted, and I sent those results on to Lydia and Suzie."

"And we were drinking from a fire hydrant," Thompsen said.

Fuller nodded.

"That's for sure," she said. "We found the money stream, and we found the instructions. Orders. Whatever you call them. The messages to their agents to carry out the plans by putting us in the arrest pending lists of the police departments on Ariel and Humphreys."

"Was it all of us?" Sharp asked.

"Not Paul. But you, me, Lydia, Otto Pasha, and Daphne Duplay. The five of us."

"Oh, by the way, I found out what happened with Duplay," Sharp said. "The Chairman of the Judiciary Committee of the Ariel Senate showed up personally to bail her out. He demanded the chief of police be there to oversee the process, and he read him the riot act at the same time."

"Ouch. That's satisfying."

"Oh, yes. Daphne has friends in high places. It was a huge mistake to go after her. That's what convinced me it had to be an off-planet scheme. Anyone on Ariel with any power or money would have known better."

"It's definitely an off-planet scheme, D.K.," Thompsen said. "The money and instructions came from here. From Elizabeth. And we now know who the intermediary is."

Sharp raised an eyebrow, and Thompsen continued.

"It's an attorney. W. Cameron Flannery."

"W?"

"William Cameron Flannery, but he goes by Cam Flannery. For some reason, attorneys often use their middle name, with their first name just an initial."

"OK. What do we know about Mr. Flannery?"

"Financial attorney. Works mergers and acquisitions, initial stock offerings for companies going public, that sort of thing. Very high priced. Thousands of credits per hour."

"And that's the guy who's sending criminal instructions and payouts to corrupt officials?"

"We don't know that he knows what he's sending, D.K.," Fuller said. "In corruption investigations, we often find people are forwarding things without looking at them. Attachments. Money transfers. They don't know what they're sending. They make it a point not to read them."

"So they can claim ignorance. They're just a cutout."

"That's right."

"What kind of person uses such an expensive cutout?"

"A lot of people do, actually. The expensive lawyers are harder to prosecute, and they won't talk when they're arrested because they know they'll get off."

"Ah. So who does he work for? Do we know?"

"Not yet," Thompsen said. "But he's most often associated with Dominic Trask."

"No shit."

"Yeah."

"Damn," Camden said. "Even I know who Dominic Trask is. Serial entrepreneur. Had some big successes early. Venture capitalist. Investment banker. One of the richest people around."

"Or *the* richest," Sharp said. "He's our big money man?"

"Careful, D.K.," Fuller said. "We don't know that."

Sharp turned to her, and she continued.

"These people often invest in groups. Someone has an idea for a big play. They bring it to the group. They bounce it around and decide whether to do it or not.

"If they do, they all pitch in to a fund to finance it. One guy is named as the managing partner for that effort. That may or may not be the original idea guy. Sometimes the big ideas guy is no good on execution.

"Then they carry out the plan. If something needs to get done, and the managing partner isn't the right guy to do it, he may assign that to someone else."

"So we don't know if Trask was the idea guy or not, or the managing partner or not," Sharp said. "He may just have been the guy with the right resources on Humphreys and Ariel."

"Or he may have had the best cutout. Exactly. And he may not know what he forwarded, either. The only thing we do know for sure is he is one of the group that's striking back at us, and that's probably the group that funded the piracy operation in the first place."

"He may not even know the group was involved in something illegal," Camden said.

"Oh, I don't sign up for that, Paul," Thompsen said. "He knew it was illegal. What exactly the managing partner was doing – what specific illegal acts he committed – he might not know, but he knew the project was illegal. That's why they keep cutouts."

"OK, I got it," Sharp said. "For that matter, while Flannery is often associated with Trask, we don't know these came through Trask anyway."

"We do now, Deke," Camden said. "I got one more factoring solution this afternoon. Flannery's public key. So we now know that the money and instructions came to Flannery from Trask. Or through Trask, anyway."

"Wow. So we do know Trask's involved now?"

"Yes, D.K.," Fuller said. "We now know he's one of the group."

"I think it's time we started focusing in on Mr. Trask."

"Yes, Deke," Camden said. "But very, very carefully."

"Oh, of course," Sharp said with a smile.

Thompsen and Fuller rolled their eyes.

Before they went to bed, Sharp logged into his main account in D Branch. He created a new file – 'Project Notes' – in his top-level directory.

The only content was Dominic Trask as the primary suspect in his investigation thus far.

On Ariel, Octavius Pasha had set an alarm on Sharp's account. Any changes to the account would be noticed to him.

Receiving such a notice, Pasha looked at the new file, and saw the notation about Dominic Trask. He nodded. Not a surprise.

Pasha set a track-and-trace flag on Trask's communications, including a three-deep archiving bot. The system would record all of Trask's communications, as well as those of anyone he contacted – and anyone they contacted – for three jumps out from Trask.

Pasha also set the bot to forward the public keys of those

individuals to the factoring engine, with the priority set by how close they were to Trask.

Time to unearth this whole thing and see where it went.

All that done, Pasha sat back in his office task chair and stared sightlessly out the window of his office.

Pasha and the analysis section of D Branch had long suspected Dominic Trask of being less than honest in his business dealings.

At the same time, Pasha was not a fan of Lavrentiy Beria's methods. 'Show me the man and I'll find you the crime.'

Nope. That wasn't how justice worked. It was completely legal to invest in opportunities and make money – even lots and lots of money – thereby.

But here they had the crimes first. Someone had financed the setting up of the piracy operation over twenty years ago. Someone had targeted Sharp, Pasha, Duplay, Thompsen, and Fuller for legal harassment just a month or two back.

If those crimes traced back to Dominic Trask, investigating Trask wasn't an abuse of justice.

It was the operation of justice.

Pasha nodded and turned his attention to other matters.

The next morning, they were back at it.

When Camden saw Sharp take a break at mid-morning, he caught his attention.

"Hey, Deke. My factoring problems got bumped down in priority. Something else is running."

Sharp logged into D Branch to look into it. When he did, he noticed that his Project Notes file had been updated. He opened it.

Under the single notation about Dominic Trask being a suspect, the following cryptic line was new:

T&T +3; Q to FE.

Sharp logged back out and turned to Camden.

"Looks like Otto put a track and trace on Trask and his contacts, and anyone they contact, within three hops of Trask. D Branch is recording all of their communications. Any public keys in those communications are going to the factoring engine."

"Oh, good. That's what I was going to try to do anyway. Did you send him a message?"

"No. I planted an Easter egg, and he found it. He's following along with our progress."

"There's gonna be something of a wait on those factoring solutions. What do we do now, Deke?"

"I'm going to go poke around a bit on Trask. You guys could do some sightseeing. Take the kids to the zoo or something."

Camden raised an eyebrow.

"The six of us? Together?"

"Not exactly."

Camden brought it up during lunch. Lunch today was from a local Greek restaurant, primarily gyros and souvlaki. The kids got chicken kabobs, which they ate as finger food.

"So how would you kids like to do some sightseeing? Maybe go to the zoo or something?"

"Yay!"

"We'll probably do that tomorrow. But there's one thing. We can't all go together. We're playing hide-and-seek with the bad guys, and they're looking for three adults and three children, two of whom are twin boys. So we have to be disguised."

"Disguised?" Sarah asked. "Like wear costumes?"

"No, but we can go in two groups. Sarah can go with Aunt

Suzie, and the boys can go with Mom and me."

"We're still twins, though," Matt said.

"Yeah," Mike said. "We look alike."

"I think we can hide that, too," Camden said. "If one of you gets a shorter haircut, more like me, and wears long pants, he'll look older. You'll still look like brothers, but not twins."

The two boys looked at each other.

"Zammers," Mike said.

Matt nodded.

"Glass," he said.

They turned back to Camden and nodded.

Camden knew some of the words in their private language. Zammers was something like 'sounds good' or even 'sounds great.' From 'Shazam!', he thought, which had been in a kids' movie. 'Glass' was basically yes. Maybe from 'I can see it' or 'it's clear.'

"OK, so I think one of you should get a haircut in the hotel today, so we can go tomorrow. Who gets to look older?"

The boys turned to look at each other, then back.

"Matt," Mike said. "He looks a little older anyway."

"What's Uncle Deke gonna do?" Matt asked.

"Oh, I'm going to be playing hide-and-seek with the bad guys, too," Sharp said.

"You are?"

"Yes. But in my case, I'm 'it'."

"Wow," the twins said together.

"I think the other thing we should do this afternoon is hit some clothing stores here," Thompsen said. "Get something a little more updated than what the Humphreys Station exchange had. Something a little more Gotham. I think we'll stand out right now."

"There's a lot of boutiques in this neighborhood," Sharp

said. "They'll be expensive, but let's stay close until we get wardrobe sorted out. Don't worry about cost. Just send me the bills."

"Are you sure that's OK, D.K?"

"Absolutely."

Dominic Trask

That night at dinner, Sharp paid particular attention to Matt and Mike. Thompsen had been gone with the boys most of the afternoon, while Suzie had gone out with Sarah. Camden had gone out on his own.

All were now sporting clothes much more suited to being downtown in the big city.

As for the twins, Matthew and Michael were not identical twins. As fraternal twins, there were the normal similarities between brothers, but not to the level of identical twins. Matt was a little taller, and his face had matured a bit more. Mike still had something of a baby-face, and was a little smaller than his brother.

Those differences were magnified now by the clothing choices Thompsen had made. Mike was wearing shorts and a knit shirt with an embroidery of a cartoon character on the left breast. Matt was wearing long pants and a buttoned shirt more like an adult.

Their behavior was different, too. With long pants and a buttoned shirt, Matt felt more dressed up, as if for some occasion. His behavior was more restrained – more grown-up – than Mike's.

Finally, Matt's hair had been cut shorter, more in the style of a child already in school, rather than Mike's longer, pre-school look.

The combination created an apparent age difference between the two of maybe a year to eighteen months. Brothers, yes, but not twins.

Thompsen noticed Sharp's weighing attention on the boys.

"What do you think, D.K?"

"It's perfect, Lydia. Clearly brothers. Clearly not twins. Nice job."

"Thanks."

"So we're clear to go out to the zoo tomorrow?" Camden asked.

"Sure, Paul. Just go as two parties. Have separate fun, then talk about it when you get back."

"What about you, Deke?"

"Oh, I'll be out of here early. I have some reconnaissance and surveillance to do. You guys go ahead and get up at a normal time, have breakfast, and set off on your day. I'll see you for supper if not before."

Sharp's virtual terminal processor woke him at five in the morning, the time he had set. He extricated himself from being tangled with Fuller.

"Mm-mmf?"

"Back to bed, Suzie. Wake up when Sarah gets up."

"Mmf."

Fuller rolled over and went back to sleep.

Sharp showered, got dressed, and left the suite, heading down to the restaurant on the first floor for breakfast.

Unlike the others, he had a varied wardrobe along from *Medea*, including some disguise and cosmetic items. Wearing a blond wig and business suit, he looked like just another successful businessman in the busy downtown of Gotham.

Sharp knew – or thought he knew – where Dominic Trask lived and worked when he was in Gotham. He also had a country estate elsewhere on Elizabeth, but downtown Gotham was his most common location.

TOO SHARP TO HOLD

Sharp had gotten up so early because he knew, as many people perhaps didn't, that the self-made men among the very rich were usually workaholics, and would be early into the office in the morning.

As it was, he was almost not early enough. Sharp arrived at Trask's downtown condo building just as Trask's morning limo was pulling up. Trask – with four security people, two in front and two behind – crossed the sidewalk to the limo and got in. One of the security men got in the shotgun's seat, and one got in the back with Trask. The other two disappeared back into the condo building.

Sharp zoomed in and photographed the driver with his electronic eyes.

The limo then pulled out and headed to Trask's office. As it did, Sharp got the angle and zoomed in on the limo's tag number and photographed it.

Sharp walked across the street, then across the front of the condo building, around the corner, and down the side of the building. Plenty of handholds. The dog suit would have no trouble scaling the building if it came to that.

Sharp had looked at the building's plans yesterday. Trask's condo was on the top floor, with a garden area on the roof of the larger-footprint floor below. Not a problem for Sharp with the dog suit.

Sharp flagged a cab and took it to the building containing Trask's office, two miles away.

Unlike his condo, which was in the tony north side by the large city park, Trask's business office was in one of the more desirable buildings in the financial district.

It was Trask's building, of course. The Trask Building, in fact.

The lobby opened to the public at seven, though Trask had gotten there earlier. Just a bit after seven, Sharp walked in through the front doors to the lobby and looked at the directory there.

'Trask Investments, LLC' was listed in the directory, located on the sixtieth floor. The top floor, of course. Sharp had pulled the plans for this building yesterday as well. Again with the garden outside the smaller top floor, but this one went all the way around the top-floor suites.

Sharp walked back outside and looked at the side of the building. This one would be a harder climb. Not much in the way of handholds.

Ah, well. One couldn't have everything.

Sharp went back into the Trask Building and got a large coffee at a coffee shop in the expansive lobby. The coffee shop was just one of the food vendors in the lobby, but it was the only one currently open. The others were more geared toward lunch.

Once seated with his coffee, Sharp opened his virtual terminal processor and logged into one of his alias accounts in D Branch. He drew up the requirements for a set of suction-cup feet, with vacuum, for the dog suit. They would be swappable with the other feet.

Such feet would have to be 'suitable for climbing a smooth, vertical glass or steel surface, such as the outside wall of a building.'

Hmm. Climbing up the outside of a building secretly, in the dark, probably wouldn't be an issue. Getting away afterwards, if there were some foofaraw or other, could be a problem, though. Climbing down the building would take too long, giving hostile forces time to gather at the bottom.

How to solve that?

Sharp added another requirement: a paraglider attachment of some sort, allowing him, in the dog suit, to fly away from the site of the action. That would do it.

Once drawn up, he logged into one of his alias accounts with super-user privileges, and added the requirements to the Project Notes file in his top-level directory. He marked them, 'Need to send these requirements on to Dr. Fiona Weatherly for prototyping.'

He included instructions to ship the prototypes to Elizabeth, care of Dick Harper, Gotham Astoria Hotel, Gotham.

That should do it.

Pasha would see it and send it on.

Sharp hung around the food court of the Trask Building through lunch. He could see the elevators from where he was sitting, but Trask did not leave the building for lunch.

Why should he? He was wealthy enough to have a kitchen and dining room, with chef standing by, in his offices on the top floor, or at least to send out for anything he wanted.

Again, self-made wealthy men were typically workaholics, and such an arrangement would allow him to work through lunch.

Sharp walked several blocks west in the downtown, to Cam Flannery's office. Another big office tower.

Sharp walked into the lobby and looked at the directory. Here it was: 'Halligan, Flannery, Cohen, and Levy, LLP.'

Named partner. Nice.

Twenty-eighth floor.

Sharp went over to the elevators, got in one, and pushed the button for the twenty-eighth floor.

When he got to the twenty-eighth floor, there was a door at either end of the elevator lobby. One was a solid door with a bio-lock marked 'Staff Only.' The other was a fancy glass-door entrance, with 'Halligan, Flannery, Cohen, and Levy, Attorneys at Law' in gold lettering on the glass.

Hmm. They had the whole floor.

Sharp walked through and looked around the lobby. There was a reception counter with a young woman behind it.

"May I help you, sir?" she asked.

Sharp looked around as if confused, but he was taking in the details.

"Is this twenty-seven?" he asked the receptionist.

"No, sir. Twenty-eight."

"Oh. I'm sorry."

"No problem, sir."

Sharp went back out to the elevators and pushed the call button for down.

When the elevator came, he entered the car and pushed the button for the first floor. Arriving back in the lobby, he exited the building.

Walking down the sidewalk, he looked up at the side of the building. Plenty of handholds.

Trask's office was the only one so far that would require his new climbing gear.

If it even came to that.

Sharp walked back to the Trask Building. He had plenty of time and he could use the exercise after the forced inaction of the trip from Humphreys.

He looked around as he walked, getting the flavor of the city. Much like in its namesake, people walked around in the downtown largely ignoring each other, except as obstacles to progress. The anonymity of crowds. People distancing themselves from the overwhelming mass of people around them.

That could work to Sharp's advantage. He was as anonymous and faceless in the crowd as if he had donned a disguise. No one would interfere, no one would get in his way. They did not want to be involved.

Back at the Trask Building by late afternoon, Sharp staked out the coffee shop again. It was a different shift on at the counter now, and they did not recognize him.

The door guards, too, were different.

Sharp settled in to wait for Trask himself to come down and go home. He expected the wealthy investor would wait until five-thirty or six o'clock, when the traffic of people departing work at five had died down a bit.

A limo pulled up at quarter to six. It was ten to six when Trask came out of the elevators with two guards and headed for the front doors. The guards were different from the guards that had come in with him this morning.

Sharp got up and followed, about thirty seconds behind. He zoomed in on and took a picture of the driver as he walked toward the front doors. It was a different driver than this morning.

Passing through the right-hand set of doors as Trask was getting into his limo, Sharp headed down the sidewalk in the direction the limo was pointed. He zoomed in on the tag and photographed it as the limo passed him.

It was the same car as this morning.

Sharp hailed a cab and took it back to the Gotham Astoria.

When Sharp got to the penthouse floor, he went into his and

Fuller's suite. The communicating door was open to Camden and Thompsen's suite, and he could smell pizza. He had a pang of guilt about being so late.

Sharp removed the blond wig and dressed down from his business suit to casual clothes. He then went through the communicating door to the next suite.

"Hi, everybody."

The kids were just mopping up the remains of a pizza, while the adults sat in the living room area.

"Uncle Deke!" Sarah shouted and came running to hug him.

"Uncle Deke, we went to the zoo."

"You did? Wow. Was it fun?"

"Oh, yeah. We saw all the pretty birds with colored feathers."

"But we saw the cats," Mike said.

"*Big* cats," Matt said.

"They were awesome," Mike said.

Sarah went back to the table to finish her pizza, and Sharp sat with the three adults in the living room area.

"Sounds like everybody had a good time."

"Yes," Fuller said. "We passed them when they spent so much time with the big cats, and they passed us in the bird area. Sarah was so interested in all the tropical birds."

"Everybody ignore each other?" Sharp asked.

"Oh, yes," Thompsen said. "The kids thought it was great fun to be separate for a while."

"We had to feed the kids, but we held dinner for ourselves until you got back. We were starting to get concerned."

"Sorry about that. Trask is a workaholic, and I wanted to see him leave the office."

"Well, let's let the kids have the display in this room, and order dinner to our suite," Fuller said.

"Sounds good," Sharp said.

During dinner, Sharp told them about his day. After dinner, they sat over coffee and talked plans.

"What's the status of the factoring so far?" Sharp asked. "Any news?"

"No, nothing yet," Camden said. "It's probably going to take a couple weeks."

"Hmm. Maybe we should go to the beach or the mountains or something."

"Could we?" Thompsen asked. "I mean, without giving ourselves away?"

"I think so. We separately book adjacent cabins. You know, so we don't show up in records as a party of seven. Then the kids play together, we all eat together, as we might if we just met on vacation. I don't think that's a problem."

"Well, that sounds like fun," Fuller said. "I don't look forward to weeks here just waiting."

"Yeah. And even if the factoring comes in, I'm sort of waiting on that extra equipment."

"Climbing equipment, you said. For the dog suit?" Camden asked.

"Yeah. That might come in handy."

"But how do you get down?" Thompsen asked. "That could take a while. Too long, I would think."

"Paraglider."

"For the dog suit?" Camden asked.

"Yeah."

"This I have to see."

Dominic Trask was not happy. The sixty-year-old businessman called in his chief of security, who worked six in the evening until two in the morning at his residence. The

Trask Building had its own security staff.

"Yes, sir," Gary Jones said.

"Something's going on."

"What's that, sir?"

"I don't know, but I've felt like I had a target on my back all day. I think someone is following me."

Jones suppressed a sigh. This sort of thing had happened before. That didn't mean it wasn't true this time, but....

"I see, sir."

"Yes, yes, I know I've said the same thing before, but today it was so strong it was almost tangible. Something's going on."

"What would you have me do, sir?"

"Go through the security videos from the Trask Building. See if you see anything. Humor me if nothing else."

"Very well, sir."

Jones left and Trask fumed. Was he being paranoid? It had been a month since the people he had targeted for arrest had mostly escaped his grasp. They could be anywhere by now.

Worse, he had attacked D Branch. He had hoped to scare them off. Discredit the people involved. Get them fired. Something.

That hadn't worked, and D Branch had operatives everywhere. Quantum-entanglement communications meant they didn't even have to move agents around. They could just tell someone else what to do. Someone here on Elizabeth, for example.

He should have let sleeping dogs lie. Still, their actions last year had cost him big money, and he seldom let such things go.

There was another motive as well. Perhaps he could get them to look deeper into the piracy issue. Find out who had really been behind it all. Remove a threat that had been hanging over his head for over a decade.

D Branch, though? Perhaps it had been foolhardy. Like that Emerson quote: 'When you strike at a king, you must kill him.' He now regretted acting out on his peeve with them.

Still, it could be nothing. Just a bad feeling.

That's what he hoped, anyway.

Gary Jones called up the security videos from the Trask Building. Trask had asked him to review them, and he would.

Jones liked his job, and, despite Trask being a bit paranoid, it was mostly a sinecure. There had never been any serious risk to Trask. The minor annoyances occasionally aimed at any wealthy man, sure, but nothing serious. Mostly weirdos. Nothing not easily dealt with.

So he was going through the motions when he noticed something curious. This guy who walked out of the lobby after Trask as he got in his limo for the trip home tonight. Where had he seen him before?

There he was. In the morning videos of the lobby. He came in about seven, after Trask, and got a coffee. Then he sat at a table in the food court area and apparently worked all morning in virtual terminal.

OK. Not that common, but not unknown.

Sometime after one – six hours later – he left the building, then returned around four to take up his post again, in the food court area.

And always facing out into the lobby, so that he could watch the elevators.

When Trask had come down just before six, this fellow got up and walked out one of the front doors a bit after Trask – and through a different door – but it was as if he had been waiting for Trask to leave.

Jones tagged the videos – and tagged the fellow in them –

and sent them to his data boys to see if they had prior images of this guy, and to make sure, if he came back, that they kept an eye on him.

The Beach

On Earth, small cities had originally grown up almost everywhere. Which ones became large cities over time was a function of their utility, often due to their location. When ninety percent of the human population worked at farming, cities near the best farmland grew larger. Cities on the coast, especially those with sheltered harbors, grew larger. Cities that spawned empires grew larger.

As a result, cities were often located in areas where the weather was often less than ideal. It was necessary, because the ability to survive – meet the needs of food and fresh water – was paramount.

When Man moved into space and settled colonies, issues of food cultivation and transportation, issues of water collection and piping, had largely been solved with technology and infrastructure. The location of the colonies' capital cities was therefore chosen more for the quality of life than raw survival, and weather was a big factor.

Gotham was no exception. It was in a coastal location, in a semi-tropical area, and, unlike that of its namesake, the climate was wonderful.

Its location also meant the beach was nearby.

It was barely a two-hour drive to the best resorts.

They did not check out of the Gotham Astoria, but kept their rooms, at least for the time being. They took separate hired cars out to the resorts along the coast. They left at different times, so as to appear to be two parties, Camden and Thompsen with the boys and Sharp and Fuller with Sarah.

Arriving at the resort at separate times, they checked into adjacent bungalows along the beach at one of the better resorts.

"I think this is better than the mountains idea," Sharp said.

He lay back in the beach chair and sighed, basking in the warm sun.

"Agreed," Camden said. "And the kids are having a blast."

Sharp opened an eye to see the twins building yet another sand castle, and Sarah walking the beach looking for shells. Thompsen and Fuller, in bikini bottoms only, were in a couple more beach chairs closer to the kids.

If it wasn't quite heaven, for Sharp it was very close.

"Deke?"

"Hmm?"

"I had a question. Didn't the Navy take credit for ending the piracy operations?"

"Yes. We let them. We'd just as soon avoid the publicity, and it helped them out a lot. Part of their charter."

"Then why did Trask go after you, Pasha, us, and your girlfriend Daphne?"

"That's a good question, actually. He must have found out, somehow, that it wasn't the Navy. That it was D Branch."

"That's what I figure, but how did he know that? And how did he know that it was you? Or that we were involved in it? That's pretty specific information, if you think about it."

"He must have a source – or one of his investment group has a source – within D Branch."

"Right. So what do we do about that, Deke?"

"Right now, nothing. Except we need to make sure we don't have knowledge of our current mission disseminated very widely within D Branch. Keep it very restricted."

"I hope Pasha knows that."

"I'm sure he does. That's his reflexive position anyway, as far as active field operations go. He's pretty close-mouthed about all that stuff."

"All right. Another question."

"Go ahead."

"You hung out in the lobby of the Trask Building most of the day?"

"Yeah. Except in the afternoon I left to check out Flannery's office."

"How do you know you didn't get made?"

"Oh, I probably did. That has to be my working assumption, anyway. No more blond wig this trip."

"So you were disguised a bit?"

"Yeah. Blond wig is best for that. People fixate on the blond thing."

"Yeah. That and bald. When they look for somebody, they start rejecting possibles on the basis of the hair, or lack of it."

Sharp, of course, was bald and clean-shaven. He had so much scar tissue and new-growth skin on his scalp and face as to make any kind of hair or beard growth very patchy.

"Exactly. Besides, I want him to know he's being watched."

"You do?"

"Sure. He'll likely change his habits a bit, from the ones that have been working for years to something a little less well thought out."

Fiona Weatherly was surprised when she got the request for the modifications for the dog suit from D Branch. She had not heard from D Branch or Deke Sharp in over a year, since the water modifications they had made to his prosthetics.

She well remembered the handsome young man Sharp had been in the pictures of him from before the explosion that had so severely crippled him. They had managed over the course of a year of surgeries and prosthetics and implants to restore him to an amazing degree, even returning him to some measure of his original good looks.

Weatherly had been proud of her role in that process. Pleased that they could do such a thorough job, given what they had started with. 'A freezer full of parts,' someone had said.

Worse, a lot of the parts had been missing.

But they had slugged it out for over a year. And the irrepressible Sharp had been with them all the way, working hard at it, fighting his way back to function. Motivated by his need for vengeance. Refusing to give up.

Now this new request, for climbing gear and a paraglider capability for the dog suit.

Weatherly started off by researching different types of climbing gear. Specifically, gear with which to climb buildings.

The specifications mentioned suction cups, but Weatherly's research indicated suction cups weren't the best method. There were too many ways to defeat them, such as with a grooved or pebbled surface. The better method was to use some sort of sticky compound.

Interesting.

As for the paraglider, that was easier. Yes, they existed. It was a standard thing, even for the weight of Deke Sharp in the dog suit. She homed in on a larger, two-man unit.

The controls were harder. She assumed Sharp's hands might be otherwise occupied, such as with weapons. The controls were simple, though. Pull down on this side or pull down on the other. She could do that with motors and cable drums.

Of course, a paraglider was only useful if you had altitude. How did you get to altitude if you couldn't climb a building?

Hmm. Some options there.

Weatherly bent to her work.

One thing: Working for D Branch was never boring.

The first few days on the beach were carefree and relaxing.

Then the factoring solutions began showing up, and Camden, Thompsen, and Fuller were all busy tracking down new correspondents, additional cash flows, and more mail communications.

The case started to go wide.

"I heard what you said," Sharp said, "but what does it mean to 'go wide'?"

"Whenever you investigate a case, D.K.," Fuller said, "you're following a lead, and it leads you on, leads you on, and then the evidence sort of fans out. You end up with multiple leads, going off in different directions."

"OK, that I get. So things have fanned out? Shot off in all directions?"

"Not all directions, but a bunch of them," Camden said. "We have multiple threads of communications now. To the other people in the investment group. To other people within Trask's own companies. Lots of communications."

"It's taking quite a while just to read them all," Thompsen said.

"Would it be easier to search on them?" Sharp asked.

"That's what we're doing right now," Fuller said. "With some success. But there's more factoring solutions coming in, and for each new solution, we have a huge bunch of stuff that decrypts."

"It's growing faster than we can get a handle on it," Camden said.

"Well, just keep after it. We seem to be pretty secure here for the moment. It takes as long as it takes."

"Wouldn't we be more secure on the ship, Deke?"

"Sure. You wanna spend a month in zero-gravity eating meals out of tubes?"

"Uh, forget I said anything."

"Is it always like this, D.K?" Thompsen asked.

"You mean, in terms of taking time?"

"Yes."

"Oh, sure. It can take months to figure out what really happened. And once the decision is made, say, to take someone like Trask down, it can take months more of surveillance to figure out how to do that while ensuring first that it's successful, and second that I can get away. I like getting away."

Camden chuckled.

"Yeah, I can agree with that."

"So it takes as long as it takes. Just keep at it."

Deke Sharp had never been in the analysis section. He had been hired into field operations and remained there during his time in D Branch.

But he had some familiarity with the tools and methods of the analysis section, and something hovered just out of his mental reach. How would they handle this situation, with way too much data to take in easily.

He remembered once he started thinking not in terms of limiting the data, but organizing it.

The next morning after breakfast, he brought it up with Camden.

"Paul, is your virtual terminal processor 3D capable?"

"Sure, Deke. It's pretty high-end."

"OK, good. I'm going to put a call into you, then I have

something to show you."

Sharp called Camden with his virtual terminal processor. They were in a face-to-face call.

"I'm going to split-screen another system in here, then switch to that screen."

"OK, Deke."

They were apparently standing in an open space, the channel being full three-dimensional and total-globe surround. This wasn't the usual mode for using one's virtual terminal processor, because it needed a lot of bandwidth, bandwidth one didn't necessarily have.

The connections here at this high-end resort, however, were very capable, there was huge bandwidth from Elizabeth to Ariel, and D Branch's central server facility had big pipes as well.

"OK, Deke. What do we do with this?"

"This is D Branch analysis section's data visualization engine. So let's import your database of all the encrypted communications."

"All right. I can do that."

They were suddenly faced with a rat's nest of data and connections. Entries for all the players, and entries for all the communications between them. It looked like someone had taken an egg beater to a box of string.

"Whoa," Sharp said.

"You see what we're dealing with, Deke?"

"Yup. I haven't used this much, but I know a little. Let's try something."

Sharp addressed the software.

"DV. Collate communications between people. Arrange people entries by the bandwidth of communications between them, rubber-band style."

The three-dimensional map sorted itself out over the next thirty seconds into a couple of dozen major entries – one for each person in the investigation – each connected into one or more of the others by lines varying in thickness. The people entries with the heaviest lines between each other were closer to each other than those connected with lighter lines.

It was a much simpler map, and the members of Trask's investment group stood out clearly.

"Geez, Deke. What did you do?"

"All the communications between people are now in these lines. Select a line – like this – and you get a sorted table of the communications between those two individuals."

One line generated a drop-down with the communications in a table, currently sorted by date.

"Each communication is like a rubber band between those people. The rubber bands pull people toward each other. Lots of communications is like lots of rubber bands. That makes more tension and pulls those people closer to each other in the display. Can you see Trask's investment group now, Paul?"

"Sure, Deke. It's this bunch with the heavy lines right here."

Camden waved his pointer around a dozen people in the center of the map with thick lines between them.

"Right. Does this help at all?"

"Oh, this helps a lot, Deke. Is there a manual or on-line training for this app? It must have other tools we can use."

"Sure. Should be here in the banner...."

Sharp pulled an icon down from near the ceiling of the room.

"Yup. Here it is."

"Excellent. And we all have access to this app?"

"Yeah. With the permissions you have now, all three of you should have access."

"Great. Thanks, Deke. This is going to help a lot. It actually lets you see what's going on in all that mess."

That night at dinner, they all seemed much more relaxed. They had all been pretty frazzled and distracted yesterday.

"Things go better today?" Sharp asked.

"Oh, D.K., you've no idea," Fuller said. "We had tools like that in the DoJ back on Humphreys, but not as sophisticated as D Branch's. And I was afraid to use those, because they could track my login."

"Yeah, D.K.," Thompsen said. "It's working out great. With the big picture so obvious, we're now looking at the little things, picking up on nuance, sifting details. It's a tremendous tool."

"And the new factoring solution that came in today?" Camden asked. "All those decrypted communications fit right into the existing construction. The players moved around a bit, but not much. Our picture of what was going on is pretty stable now."

"Anything you want to share yet?"

The others looked back and forth at each other.

"Not quite yet, Deke. Soon."

Their relative relaxation became apparent to Sharp later that evening, as Fuller's appetites had returned in their full strength.

And Fuller could get noisy.

He worried, with Sarah in the other bedroom of the two-bedroom bungalow, that the six-year-old would think Sharp was mistreating Fuller somehow.

Geez, it sounded like a vivisection.

Sharp looked around, and finally pulled a pillow case off

one of the pillows and jammed the end of it in Fuller's mouth.

She got even more excited with that, but at least she was quieter.

Afterwards, he apologized.

"Sorry about that, but I was worried about waking Sarah."

"Oh, D.K. It was dreamy."

Huh.

People are weird, Sharp thought. *Women no less than men.*

During the day, the adults took turns being in charge of the kids at the beach while the rest were in their virtual terminals. They were all on the beach, but those working were out of contact with the reality around them.

At lunch one day, Thompsen brought up a new scenario.

"The investors who funded piracy, D.K? What is to be their fate?"

"Aiding and abetting piracy is a capital crime, Lydia. And I am still the captain of FNS *Medea*."

"Yes, but what if they didn't know that was what they were doing?"

"What?"

"What if they didn't know, D.K? What if they were investing in someone else's project idea, but didn't know any of the details?"

"Do they do that, Lydia? Invest hundreds of millions of credits – perhaps billions of credits – in some project without knowing what it is?"

"Let me show you something, D.K."

She sent him a pointer to the app so he could piggyback on her view, then went into virtual terminal. He joined her there.

"This all looks like it did before, Lydia, except more so."

"Right. Now watch this."

She spoke to the app.

"DV. Lock people locations. Filter messages on words 'pirates' and 'piracy.' Show only hits on either."

Lots of links to various people went away, and most links got thinner. Some got much thinner.

"Trask's investment circle looks intact in this view, Lydia. They were all in on it."

"Yeah, at the end. But watch this, D.K."

She spoke to the app again.

"DV. Retain previous filters. Add additional filter. Show only messages older than ten years."

A lot of connecting lines got thinner yet. Many disappeared. In particular, many of the lines between members of Trask's investor group disappeared. Trask had no connections at all.

"No shit," Sharp said.

"He didn't know, D.K. Not initially. He only found out later that he was an accessory to a capital crime."

"And kept his mouth shut lest his partner drag him down with him."

"That's what I think, D.K. We're still working it through to be sure."

"No matter how long you've been in this business, Lydia, you can always get surprised."

Trask's Move

D Branch's IT department got in touch with Octavius Pasha over the amount of computer time being used by field operations in the past week.

In particular, there was a lot of use of the analysis section's data visualization engine by the field operations department, which was unusual. Further, this use was coming in from off-planet, from Elizabeth, a strange use of that app.

"We just wanted to make sure this was authorized use, Mr. Pasha, and not an indication that our servers have been compromised in some way. We request that you look into it."

"I don't need to look into it," Pasha told the IT manager. "I'm aware of the circumstances, and this is a critical part of an important project. You don't need to worry about it."

"All right, Mr. Pasha. Just checking. Unusual use is one of the things we keep an eye out for."

"I appreciate your vigilance against outside hacking. In this case, it's our own people, but we do have to keep an eye out. Thank you for that."

Having satisfied IT, Pasha logged into the data visualization engine and looked at the data map of Sharp's group.

Impressive.

Pasha then ran some of the previous filter settings against the map. One caught his eye, and he looked at the filters.

Hmm. This one showed no links to Dominic Trask at all containing pirates or piracy for the period when the piracy group was put in place.

That was interesting.

Later that day, Pasha received a call. It was from off-planet – from Elizabeth, in fact – but the caller was not identified. He expected it was Sharp.

Pasha took the call, but it wasn't Sharp looking out at him. The sixty-year-old businessman behind the desk in his office certainly wasn't Sharp.

"Good afternoon, Mr. Pasha. My name is Dominic Trask."

"Hello, Mr. Trask. How can I help you today?"

"Someone is doing surveillance on me, Mr. Pasha. I believe it is one of your people. Perhaps Mr. Sharp."

"Why one of my people, Mr. Trask? Surely you have competitive interests who might wish to surveil you."

"Yes, Mr. Pasha. But this person was surveilling me in a most obvious way, then disappeared. Despite having very clear video of him, my considerable assets on the planet cannot find him or even identify him. That sounds like one of your people to me."

"For the sake of argument, Mr. Trask, let's suppose it is a D Branch operative. Where does that take us?"

"I should like to meet with him, Mr. Pasha. Particularly if it is Mr. Sharp. I believe I may have needlessly— irritated him recently."

"A meeting? For what purpose, Mr. Trask."

"I believe I have intelligence he would find interesting."

"Interesting and probably extremely dangerous, Mr. Trask. If D Branch were to have you under surveillance, that puts us at some sort of odds with each other, does it not?"

"Not necessarily, Mr. Pasha, but I take your point. Then again, I believe I am actually in much more danger from Mr. Sharp than he is from me. I am aware of his involvement in certain extra-judicial proceedings a year or so ago. He seems quite competent in that regard.

"However, I am prepared to guarantee Mr. Sharp's safety if he will in fact guarantee mine. Let's say for the meeting day and the two days following. After that, we will see how things play out."

"The venue for this meeting, Mr. Trask?"

"Oh, it would have to be a place we can mutually agree on, Mr. Pasha. It could even be at my offices or my home. There is some additional risk from my 'competitive interests,' as you called them, if I were to depart from my normal activities."

"An interesting proposal, Mr. Trask. Can I consider it and get back to you?"

"Of course, Mr. Pasha."

"And this address will work, Mr. Trask?"

"This address will work fine, Mr. Pasha."

"Until then, Mr. Trask."

Trask waved a hand and cut the connection.

Pasha put a file containing the video of the conversation into Sharp's top-level directory, and put a pointer to it in Sharp's Project Notes file.

"Dominic Trask wants to meet with me," Sharp told them after dinner, once the kids were in bed.

"What?" Camden asked.

"That's what *I* said. He called Otto Pasha and said he wanted to meet with me. Watch the call."

Sharp sent them the pointer and then waited while they all watched the video call in virtual terminal.

"OK, that's completely nuts," Thompsen said when they dropped out of virtual terminal.

"Maybe not," Fuller said.

They all turned to her.

"Consider this. If Trask kills you once he has guaranteed

your safety, it really hurts him with his own crowd. His word can't be trusted. That's the coin of the realm for somebody like him.

"Second thing, it's still murder for him, whereas for D.K. killing him, it's not. He knows about last year's 'extrajudicial proceedings,' as he called them, He knows D.K. walked after those, and would walk again, whereas Trask wouldn't.

"And third, he knows D Branch went after the Ariel police department over jailing Pasha. They went after the *police department*. He's got to figure that if he kills you, he's signing his own death warrant with D Branch.

"So I think D.K. is safe taking this meeting."

"That actually makes sense when you put it that way," Thompsen said.

"But why does he want a meeting?" Camden asked.

"Remember what we saw with those filters in place. The subject of piracy and pirates never came up with Trask. Not at the beginning. He may not have known anything about it. Not until it was too late, anyway."

"Why too late?" Camden asked.

"Because, by then, he had been implicated in funding the whole scheme by his partners. Some subset of them, anyway. He was at risk of prosecution. Execution, for that matter."

"He was trapped," Fuller said. "And open to blackmail."

"Well, not from his partners," Thompsen said. "If they took him down, they would be sucked in as well. But they all had to keep it quiet. If one went down, they all went down."

"So why the meeting?" Camden asked.

"Potentially, to make sure D.K. understands all this. Assuming we're right in our conjectures here. To get his case in front of D.K. before he starts some more 'extrajudicial proceedings,' potentially against Trask and the others."

"And the benefit to us?"

"To get the inside story from someone who knows."

"Can we trust him, though?" Sharp asked.

"No. Of course not," Fuller said. "But it's much easier to confirm or disprove a given story than it is to build up what happened from messages alone. Whatever he tells us, we check against the record. But his story will give us a starting point."

"Yeah," Thompsen said. "That will be much easier."

"So you all think I should meet with him?"

Fuller nodded. Camden thought about it, then nodded.

"If you can do it safely, D.K.," Thompsen said. "If you're careful, and on alert for the double-cross. I don't think it will happen, but you have to be aware it could, and be prepared."

Sharp nodded.

"All right. Let me think about how to pull this off."

The next day, Deke Sharp lay out on the beach on one of the big beach blankets provided by the resort and considered his options.

Of course, one option was not to meet with Trask. They had enough evidence now that he had provided part of the funding that had enabled the setup of the piracy operation more than twenty years ago.

On that basis alone, Sharp could execute him and move on.

They also suspected, however, that he had had no idea what his investment partner's new project was. There was evidence for that, in the form of the dog not barking. There was no evidence he was aware of his partner's plans when he provided the money.

Mostly, though, it was because Sharp wanted to know. Know how the whole thing got started. Know whose idea it was. Know how to prevent it from happening again. That was part of his job, after all. To know.

There was another factor. Like all other field operatives in D Branch, Sharp was an adrenaline junkie. With other interests, he may have been a race car driver, or a test pilot for new starship engines, or even a litigation attorney. Adrenaline junkies all.

That's why the field operatives between assignments on Ariel had gone after the New Destin police department when they had imprisoned Otto Pasha. They weren't afraid of going after the cops. They enjoyed it. They knew they wouldn't be caught. Just as they knew they wouldn't be killed on assignment. It was impossible – until it happened.

Pasha had made it clear to all the field operatives that they could transfer to the analysis section whenever they lost 'the edge' – whatever it was that made them go out into unknown situations and poke the bear to find out what it would do.

Sharp wasn't there yet. Despite getting caught out in *Circe* and being so horribly injured, despite the long recuperation, despite how much of him was now artificial or assisted, he had been eager to go out again and take on the pirates. Deliver vengeance for his dead crew.

He had been just as eager this time. When the police had smashed their way into his apartment, he had jumped right into what had become this new assignment.

Follow the money. Find the funders.

He had one now – one of the funders – that wanted to meet with him, and he knew he would do it. Would go and listen to Trask's story. Oh, sure, it would be self-serving. Of course. Trask didn't want Sharp to execute him, and, from what he said on the phone call to Pasha, he knew that was a good possibility.

Still, it was an opportunity for Sharp to learn more.

How to go about it was a different question.

Fuller had made good points about why Trask would likely honor his guarantee of safety to Sharp. How could Sharp make it even more likely?

On the surface, meeting at a third-party location seemed safest, but that was too easy for Trask to sidestep. Being in a public place, Trask was not in full control.

'It must have been one of my competitors. Mr. Sharp insisted on a public place.'

No, that was the wrong move. If Trask was guaranteeing his safety, make him own it completely. Trask's car could pick him up at some location, communicated at the last minute, and take him to Trask's home. Not his workplace, his home. The private penthouse in a building Trask owned. Trask's car could deliver him somewhere of Sharp's choosing when it was over.

No sidestepping that.

If any harm came to Deke Sharp, Trask would own it.

"I'm going to meet with Trask," Sharp told everyone that night after dinner.

"Third-party location?" Camden asked.

"No. His penthouse. I want him to own whatever happens."

"And if something happens to you, D.K?" Fuller asked.

"Then Mr. Trask will meet some of my colleagues. I am not the only field operative within D Branch, though my responses are usually more, um, measured than some others'."

"Oh. Oh, my. Yes, he won't want that."

"No. He won't."

The avatar was of a good-looking man in his mid to late thirties, with blond hair.

"Good morning, Mr. Trask. My name is Deke Sharp."

"Good morning, Mr. Sharp. Do you have an answer to my request?"

"Yes, Mr. Trask. I'll meet with you."

"Excellent. And your choice of location, Mr. Sharp?"

"Your penthouse home, Mr. Trask. I want to simplify things for my colleagues. If anything does happen to me, there will be no doubt as to who is responsible."

"Meeting with you at my request and with mutual guarantees is my preference, Mr. Sharp. I have no desire to meet with any of your colleagues under, shall we say, less favorable conditions."

"A wise choice, Mr. Trask."

"No doubt. And the arrangements, Mr. Sharp?"

"The timing of our meeting is at your convenience, Mr. Trask. Your car will pick me up for the meeting at a location in downtown Gotham, and will deliver me to a different location in downtown Gotham after we have concluded. I will communicate those locations at that time."

Trask nodded. Careful, yet completely under Trask's control. All well and good. Trask had no intention of double-crossing Mr. Pasha in any case. Life expectancy after such a move would likely not be high.

"Will you be my guest for dinner this evening, Mr. Sharp? A six-thirty pickup with dinner at seven?"

"Why, thank you, Mr. Trask. I'm looking forward to it. I will call this address at six-twenty to let you know my location."

"I'll see you then, Mr. Sharp."

Dominic Trask was explicit with Gary Jones, his head of security, as he finished his instructions.

"Understand me that absolutely nothing adverse is to happen to Mr. Sharp. You are to protect him as you would protect me, because if anything happens to Mr. Sharp, I am as good as dead. You could do nothing to protect me from the vengeance of D Branch. Their operatives are extremely capable at any sort of violence, up to and including bombardment from space. They would go through your people like crap through a goose to get at me, and I would not survive."

Jones didn't object. Keeping Mr. Sharp safe for this meeting was high in his priorities. He had no desire whatsoever to tangle with D Branch. If even half of what he'd heard were true, his people would stand no chance.

"Yes, Mr. Trask. Absolutely. If you had suggested otherwise, I would do my best to talk you out of it."

"Excellent. He should be calling soon. I want you in the car when picking him up and dropping him off so there are no screw-ups."

"Yes, sir. That's my preference as well."

The armored limousine pulled up in front of the Wilmott Downtown Hotel in downtown Gotham. A handsome, blond-haired man in his mid to late thirties, wearing a suit, walked up to the car from where he had been leaning against the front side wall of the building.

The shotgun got out and opened the rear door, the man got in, and the shotgun returned to his seat and closed his door. The limo edged out from the curb into traffic.

"Good evening, Mr. Sharp. My name is Gary Jones. I am Mr. Trask's head of security."

Sharp looked at the other man in the back of the limo, facing him from the rear-facing seat. He was a bit older than Sharp, also wearing a suit. By the cut of the suit, he was armed with a pistol in a shoulder holster, as was Sharp himself.

"You're his head of security, and you're here with me instead of with him?"

"Mr. Trask was most concerned that there be no issues with your safety, Mr. Sharp."

Sharp nodded. Nice.

So far, so good.

It was just a few blocks to Trask's downtown condominium building. Jones led Sharp into the building and across the lobby, while the shotgun from the limo followed.

When they got in one of the elevators, Sharp could see there was no destination button for the penthouse floor, just an indicator. That light lit when they got in.

Access to the penthouse floor via virtual terminal only. Nice.

Jones walked across the small elevator lobby on the penthouse floor to a set of double doors and put his hand on the knob of one of them. There was a soft click as the lock unlatched, and Jones opened the door to let Sharp pass through.

Jones closed the door behind Sharp, remaining in the elevator lobby.

The Meeting

The living room beyond the doors from the elevator lobby was a big room, set up for entertaining. The room contained several seating arrangements, with large spaces between. There was a bar on the left, and a large display and speaker system on the right. On the far side, a glass wall opened out onto an exterior terrace, decorated with live plants.

Trask stood a few feet inside the doors. He was sixtyish, with salt-and-pepper hair. He was in good shape, as one who worked out regularly, if gone a little soft with his age.

"Ah, Mr. Sharp. Good evening, and welcome to my home."

Trask walked toward him, holding out his hand, and Sharp shook his hand.

"Thank you for inviting me, Mr. Trask."

Trask nodded.

"It seemed to me that we should speak. I know that you are looking into some things about which I have first-hand knowledge, and I can be of service in informing you about what I know."

Trask waved a hand toward the far wall.

"Please join me out on the terrace where we can enjoy the pleasant evening."

Sharp followed Trask across the big room and through open patio doors out onto the terrace. Trask waved him to comfortable captain's chairs at a table.

"Please, Mr. Sharp."

They both sat, and Trask motioned to a humidor on the table. Sharp enjoyed the occasional premium cigar – though not possible aboard ship – and Trask's cigars were likely to be the best available. Indeed, there was a group of Gran Pedro cigars from the planet Hidalgo, gleaming in their glass tubes.

Sharp selected one of the Gran Pedro cigars, as did Trask.

"A discerning palate, Mr. Sharp."

"An occasional dalliance, Mr. Trask."

Trask nodded, decanting his own cigar from the glass tube and cutting the end, then passing the cutter to Sharp. They both lit their cigars with the large lighter on the table and enjoyed the first puffs. Trask sighed.

"Such a civilized vice. Yet I always smoke on the terrace, so as not to draw the ire of my family."

His wife and their daughter, Sharp knew, both likely out for this potentially dangerous evening.

"As we are now smoking acquaintances, please call me Dominic, Mr. Sharp."

"And you must call me Deke."

Trask nodded.

"Very well, Deke. I propose we let substantive discussions wait until after dinner, which, with your permission, we can enjoy here."

"A splendid suggestion, Dominic," Sharp said, looking around. "You have an excellent view of the city from this terrace."

"Yes. I had to add five stories to the building plans when I saw the design for the neighboring building, in order that the view not be spoiled. It worked out well for me."

A waiter with a cart came out onto the terrace. He set the table as they smoked, then moved the ashtray with their cigars to an adjacent table and set out the food.

Dinner tonight was duck à l'orange, each of them receiving an intact half of duck served on orange slices, with duck-fat mashed potatoes and an arugula almond salad on the side.

"You have an excellent kitchen, Dominic."

"Yes, Deke. I asked them to push the envelope a bit for my important guest this evening."

They ate in silence, neither gourmet wishing to slight the excellent meal through his inattention. The entrée was followed by a lime sorbet, continuing the citrus theme, with a plate of chocolate biscotti presented mid-table.

When dinner was cleared, the biscotti remained, coffee was served, and the ashtray was returned. The staff departed.

"And so, Deke, we come to the substantive portion of the evening. I am aware, of course, of your activities of perhaps a year ago. It is to avoid becoming another of your objets d'exécution that I invited you here tonight."

"Aiding and abetting piracy is a capital crime, Dominic."

"Indeed, Deke. Indeed. And had I known of such activities, I would surely not have funded such a project."

Sharp raised an eyebrow, and Trask waved a hand.

"I must take you back some twenty-five years in the relating of this tale, Deke. I was in my mid-thirties, perhaps your age, perhaps a bit younger. They were heady times.

"My investment partners and I had, unusually, scored early successes. When financing various projects, one expects most of them to fail. That risk is counterbalanced by the tremendous payoffs enjoyed from the occasional project that succeeds. One might fund ten projects, and have one or two successes. Or not. There are no guarantees.

"This is why we formed an investment group, Deke. A capital management firm. To spread the risk. To increase the chances that we might hit the big payoff on one or more projects. A single investor cannot – at the stage of our careers we were then, at least – fund enough projects to have a reasonable chance of success.

"We had each had moderate success with starting our own companies, and selling them off to generate our stake. Looking for investment opportunities, we became aware of each other and pooled our resources. We selected our first projects to fund with a great deal of care and no small amount of trepidation, agonizing over each decision. We could lose it all were we not to hit with at least one big success.

"Imagine our surprise and delight when no fewer than four of our first dozen projects hit it big. Eight of them failed, of course, as one expects. But four of them spun wildly out of control, and we made a great deal of money.

"The tax treatment we had chosen allowed us to shield this income for a time, but only if the funds were reinvested within the tax reporting period. There was a great deal of money coming in, and, in the struggle to invest it all in a timely way, we became much less circumspect about what we funded.

"You must understand this, Deke. This is the critical point."

Sharp nodded.

"Go ahead, Dominic. I'm with you so far."

"Good. Good. So. We have this tremendous cash flow coming in from our unprecedented success with our first dozen projects. Our tax liability, were we not to reinvest it immediately, would be enormous.

"In such circumstances, one needs even fewer projects to succeed in order to come out ahead, because one must consider the tax implications. Additional failures within a group of investments would be offset by avoiding the taxes.

"In that environment, we each brought investment opportunities to the group. We accepted them without a great deal of oversight by the whole group. One of us had done his due diligence, the rest of us acceded and made the funding decision. We funded a number of things which I had little information about. No vision into the project.

"Unusual? Yes, of course, but we had to keep the money moving or divert a large part of it to the government. Such expenses were to be avoided, if possible, and we funded a lot of projects with the spiraling cash flow.

"One of the projects we accepted, alas, was the piracy project. It was actually an investment play into the large interstellar shipping insurers and military contractors. That's where the bulk of the money went.

"A smaller portion of the funds went to what were called lobbying and marketing expenses. To build the demand for interstellar shipping insurance and military expenditure. It was these funds that were used – without my knowledge or that of most of the investment group – to fund the startup of the piracy operation.

"The insurers and military contractors did end up doing very well once piracy emerged as a problem, but those were large, established businesses. Our profits on that project were not as high as they would be on startup businesses, but they were sizable.

"Imagine my horror some years later when I discovered what had been done with the money we had set aside for marketing and lobbying."

"You had no knowledge of the piracy operation, Dominic?"

"Of course, I knew that piracy had become somewhat endemic, Deke, but I had no idea that we had funded its growth. I considered it a perverse sort of luck that piracy had grown so while we had outstanding investments in the firms most likely to benefit.

"When I did become aware of our involvement, I was stuck. Were I to go public with what I knew, identify who had actually been involved, I would be swept up as well. I was one of the investors who had funded the setup of a piracy operation. My life was forfeit on that basis alone.

"This was something one of my erstwhile partners reinforced to me, Deke. Were I to blow the whistle on them – those who knew all along – they would drag me down with them. They would not go alone to the gallows.

"And so I kept my mouth shut. All this time, I knew. All this time, I have been waiting for it all to blow up in my face.

"Ultimately, our investment group broke up. Even after taxes, we were all wealthy enough now to go our own way. Fund our own deals.

"But always in my mind I knew I had exposure on this issue. That it might someday come out. I strove to keep it a secret, Deke. Obscure what had happened. Certainly to obscure my own involvement.

"And then you came along. Twenty years later. People started dying, in messy and sudden and very public ways. People connected to the piracy operation. Military contractor executives. Insurance executives. Even some military people, whom I hadn't known about.

"I began to expect you to show up here, Deke. You or one of your associates. I just hoped those actually responsible went down first, that I would be able to see them at last face the consequences before I, too, fell."

A waiter, apparently called in virtual terminal, came out to replace the empty French press with a fresh one full of coffee. He also replaced the ashtray with a clean one and departed.

Trask refilled both of their coffee cups. Sharp relit his cigar and considered.

Trask's story was internally consistent. It held together. It also jived with what Sharp knew from the analysis of the communications they had decrypted thus far. Whether the story would hang together under closer inspection of those communications was, as yet, unknown. Corroborating or disproving a story was easier once you had a story to work with.

It also jived with Sharp's own experience. How much did Otto Pasha actually know about what Sharp was up to, day to day? Claude Allard knew even less of what went on within his organization. That was the nature of management, and of delegation.

There were the more recent issues, though.

"And going after me now, Dominic? The attempted arrests?"

"Yes. Clumsy of me, to be sure, and the police made a complete hash of it. I was happy none of you was injured. You see, I had expected that, after a period of analysis of the data taken from the pirate ships and space stations, that you would resume your mission, Deke."

"You thought to dissuade me by intimidation, Dominic?"

"No, Deke. Clearly, that would not work. You live for the chase. No, I had hoped to inspire you."

Sharp raised an eyebrow, and Trask chuckled.

"I had hoped to inspire you to find out exactly where that initial money for the pirate operation had come from. I was hoping that you would track it to my erstwhile partners. I still have an overhanging danger from them, which you might mitigate. But, instead, you tracked the arrest attempts to me, and I found myself under observation."

"Which is when you called Octavius Pasha and requested this meeting."

"Yes, Deke. I hope to turn state's evidence, as it were, and avoid the long drop. I've made my mistakes, but I did not *knowingly* aid or abet piracy."

"Your part of this deal, Dominic? I know what you want

from us."

"My part of the deal – my penance, as it were – is first that I will provide you with all my notes and communications on this matter, which will allow you to see what happened with clarity. The second portion of my part of the deal is that I will provide tax-free, to the heirs of all those killed by pirates, the sum of one million credits per victim."

"You're talking twenty to thirty billion credits, Dominic."

"I am aware of that, Deke. A large sum, to be sure, even to me. Yet I can pay it, and it is only fair, after all. They suffered their loss, in many cases, at least in part due to my self-serving silence. I can also communicate with the other investors who were taken unawares in this perfidy, and see if I can prevail upon them to increase that sum, though most, perhaps, have not done quite as well as I have done."

The recipients would include the heirs of Sharp's own crew on *Circe*, killed by the pirates in the attack that left Sharp little more than a husk.

"Any conditions on these terms, Dominic?"

"Only that I and my fellow investors who were unaware of what was truly going on are forgiven for our parts, and that those who were the actual perpetrators get their just deserts at last."

"This is not a deal I can agree to on my own, Dominic."

"Oh, I am aware of that, Deke. Yet your opinion will count heavily, I am sure, as will your evaluation of how forthcoming I have been with the materials I will provide you. I suspect your superiors will approve any deal with which you are satisfied, in no small part due to the extent you and your own familiars were victimized. I am truly sorry for the loss of your crew aboard *Circe*, and your own terrible injuries, but it gives your opinion extra weight in this matter."

Sharp nodded. Trask had certainly done his homework to know as much as he did, and Sharp was surprised Trask's apology meant as much to him as it did.

"Thank you for that, Dominic. I appreciate it. I did recover, mostly, to the extent it was possible. More than my poor crew."

"And I'm glad to see it, Deke. Truly."

Sharp nodded. He had his vision enhanced into the infrared, which allowed him to see many things, including that Trask was not lying. Had not been, in fact, during the entire conversation.

Whether his story was true or not, Trask believed it.

"And now," Trask continued, "With our business concluded for the moment, can I interest you in a digestif, Deke? I have a bottle of the Dufort *Esprit* I've been dying to open, but it would be a shame to drink it alone."

Sharp waved his acceptance and the waiter appeared with warmed snifters and an unopened bottle of the finest cognac ever made.

Sharp and Trask spent another hour enjoying the pleasant evening with their cognac and their cigars before Sharp took his leave.

"I'll be in touch, Dominic."

"If there are any questions – any questions at all, Deke – you and Mr. Pasha know how to get in contact with me."

Jones rode along in the back of the limo as Sharp left the meeting. He asked to be dropped off in the Gotham financial district, at the Hotel Belvidere, a middling hotel for business travelers.

The limo pulled into the curb at the entrance, and the shotgun opened the door for Sharp to exit.

"Good evening, Mr. Sharp."

Sharp nodded.

"Mr. Jones."

Sharp walked into the hotel and watched as the limo pulled away from the curb.

He waited five minutes, then crossed the street and walked down the block to the Hotel Girond and booked a room for the night.

No sense being predictable.

In the morning, Sharp took a cab to the train station. He took a suburban train toward the coast, then called the beach resort for their car to come pick him up.

He arrived in time for a late breakfast on the beach.

"So how did it go?" Fuller asked.

"It went well, I think."

Deal Or No Deal?

Sharp got up from the table on the lanai after breakfast and limped to the patio doors into the bungalow.

"D.K., are you OK?" Fuller asked with concern. "You're limping."

"I haven't washed and salved my prostheses yet. I need to go do that, then I'll be all right."

"You should have left them off last night."

"I know, but I wanted to be able to make a quick exit if required."

"Ah. Well, if you need help, D.K., give me a call."

Sharp nodded and went inside.

When Sharp came back out in beach wear, they all lay on one of the big beach blankets while they watched the kids playing in the sand.

"What happened at the meeting, D.K.?" Thompsen asked.

"What was his place like?" Fuller asked.

"What did you have for dinner, Deke?" Camden asked.

"Is he coming after us, or was it friendly?" Thompsen asked.

Sharp held his hands up in defense against the onslaught of questions.

"OK. OK. I'll get to it all, I promise."

"Sorry, D.K., but it's exciting," Thompsen said. "We've read so much of this guy's mail by this point, we feel like we know him."

"OK, first, his place is very nice. Rich-guy penthouse stuff. The whole top floor. I only saw the living room, but it's big enough to have two addresses. Sleek modern furniture all over the place, like a furniture store, but with plenty of room to stand, like at parties or something. We could probably all be in there and none of us be within twenty feet of another."

"Wow," Fuller said.

"Yeah. And the terrace is very nice. That's where we spent all our time, because he doesn't want his wife mad at him for smoking cigars in the house."

"Well, that says something about him," Thompsen said.

"Yeah," Fuller said. "Not just a big meanie."

"We smoked a bit first, then dinner. Duck à l'orange. Very nice, actually. Among the best I've had. A sorbet for dessert, with biscotti. Then it was coffee and cigars and we got down to business."

"No business during dinner," Camden said. "Not a boor, then."

"No, not with a meal like that," Fuller said.

Sharp nodded.

"It was all very friendly, all very above board, all very pleasant, actually."

"What about business, D.K?" Thompsen asked.

"It's as you surmised from your communications map. Trask didn't know what that project involved. That it involved piracy. At least, that's his claim."

"But how could he not know?" Fuller asked.

"Trask and a number of other people who had built and sold off their first businesses formed an investment group. They all pitched money in, then researched their first investments. They went through them with a fine-tooth comb, wanting to make sure they hit on at least one or two winners. They hit on four."

"Oh, my," Thompsen said. "They got lucky. Really lucky."

"Or were really good. Yes. And the money started to roll in. Big money. That was the problem. They had organized in such a way as to avoid taxes, as long as they reinvested the money within the tax period."

Thompsen nodded.

"Must have been a capital re-investment fund. The Federation tax code provided that loophole to make it easier for startup companies to get funding."

"Right. So they were scrambling to get the money back out the door, and they didn't do the individual research they had initially done. Someone brought in a project, and they jumped on it. Again and again. They made a great deal of money, but they didn't look at things in anywhere near the detail they originally had."

"How do you not know the project is piracy?" Camden asked.

"But that's not what the project was, Paul. The project was to invest in interstellar shipping insurance and military contractors. A smaller part of the investment was set aside for marketing. In this case, creating the market. That's what they didn't look into."

"And the way they created the market was financing the setup of the piracy operation?" Camden asked.

"Yes, but Trask didn't know that. At least he says he didn't."

"Was he lying, D.K?" Thompsen asked.

"I don't think so, Lydia. I was watching him in infrared, and I didn't see any of the physiological effects of lying."

"Wait," Fuller said. "You can tell when we're lying?"

"I don't use that on my friends, Suzie. But I don't think Trask was lying. Once he saw the investments take off, largely on the basis of the piracy that was by then being widely reported, he figured it out, but by then he was stuck."

"Because if he fingered the partner that did it, he was implicating himself as well," Fuller said.

"In a capital crime. Yes. So he kept his mouth shut. And he made a great deal of money, off that investment and many others, before the group split up."

"Why did he go after us, D.K? You and Otto and us? And Daphne?" Thompsen asked.

"He figured the analysis section would use the pirates' records to identify the original money man. The guy who funded the piracy and trapped him in this scenario. He was hoping to inspire D Branch to go after his one-time partner."

"By getting us killed?" Camden asked.

"He says the police botched it. They were supposed to be simple arrests. To get our attention. But instead of the analysis section fingering the original financier, we followed the bribe money on the arrests to him."

"Did the analysis section not track the pirates' original financing?" Fuller asked.

"It can take them a while to come up with stuff like that, Suzie. I think Trask underestimated how long it would take them."

"Well, it all holds together, D.K.," Thompsen said. "And you say he wasn't lying…"

"Not that I could detect, Lydia."

"So that's probably the real story. So what's the deal?"

"Deal?" Camden asked.

"The reason for the meeting, Paul," Fuller said. "He wants a deal of some kind."

"Well, he obviously wants you not to execute him, D.K.," Thompsen said.

"Yes. Clemency for him and his other partners in the same situation. Because they did not knowingly aid or abet piracy."

"Except through their silence," Fuller said. "What's he offering, D.K?"

"His complete records of the whole thing, from the beginning, and through the present, including his finding out about the piracy. The threats to take him and the others down if they ratted. And the identities of the partners who brought the deal to the group and did the dirty work."

"And?" Fuller asked.

Thompsen raised an eyebrow at her and Fuller went on.

"That's not enough, Lydia. We will probably get most of that on our own, and he knows it."

Sharp nodded.

"He will also give one million credits to the heirs of every person killed by the pirates."

"That's twenty-some billion credits, Deke," Camden said.

"He's aware, Paul. He also offered to talk to his other partners and try to sweeten that number."

"OK, now that's starting to look like a deal," Fuller said.

"Buying his way out, Suzie?" Camden asked.

"Compensation to the victims," Fuller said. "That's got to be part of any deal. Information alone is merely cooperating with an investigation. There's no admission of wrongdoing there. No acceptance of any responsibility for one's actions. Compensation, though, that's different."

Sharp nodded.

"That's right. It's admitting he screwed up, even if he didn't originally know what was going on. Didn't knowingly fund the piracy."

"So is that a deal or not, D.K.?" Camden asked.

"I don't know, Paul. I have to talk it over with Otto. He may have to get his boss, Claude Allard, involved. Maybe even the Federation Justice Department. But I wanted to ask you guys first."

"That sounds good to me, D.K.," Thompsen said.

"We did deals like this with Humphreys DoJ all the time," Fuller said. "The issue here is, What is his crime? The usual standard is 'knew or should have known' that the funds were being used to support piracy.

"Trask told you he didn't know, and the mail evidence we've seen so far is corroborative of his position. If you pursue the 'should have known' part, you have to consider that the partner financing the pirates was keeping it from him.

"So it's very difficult to get a conviction on that basis, and such a conviction seldom results in prison time. It's usually just a fine and compensation to the victims. The amount he's offering is already well above anything I would hope of getting at sentencing, even if we got a conviction."

"The deal with Trask sounds OK to me, Deke, but what about the actual perpetrators?" Camden asked. "The guys who financed the pirates with Trask's and the other partners' money. They knew what they were doing."

"Aiding and abetting piracy is a capital crime," Sharp said.

"So you'll execute them?"

"Once we have the evidence, sure. That's my job."

"And then the money they made off of piracy goes to their heirs?"

"Not necessarily, Paul," Fuller said. "We didn't do it often at Humphreys DoJ – only if there was a lot of money involved – but the Federation DoJ can garnish the estate. Lock it up until they've worked out the numbers, then seize the illicit profits."

"Which would be the increase in value of the stocks of the insurance companies and military contractors?"

"If we can prove that those stocks were part of the plot, yes."

"OK, I worried about that last part," Sharp said. "It seemed like the guys who got sucked into this were footing the bills, but the families of the guilty would reap the rewards. That last bit clears up the part I was worried about."

"Yeah," Fuller said. "FDoJ can go after that money."

Sharp nodded.

"Can you guys write this up for me? The whole package, including that last part?"

"Sure, Deke," Camden said. "We got it."

Octavius Pasha got a notice that there had been an update to Deke Sharp's account, and he checked Sharp's top-level directory. There was a new file, there, right after Project Notes: Project Plan.

It was encrypted.

Now if Sharp intended him to see it, the file should have been encrypted with his public key, and should decrypt with Pasha's private key. It did.

The result was another encrypted file.

Hmm. Sharp wanted him to see it, that's why the original file decrypted with Pasha's public key. Then again, Sharp and Pasha had worked together a long time. Pasha tried to decrypt it with his last private key. The one from before the current one.

Nope. Hmm.

Pasha tried to decrypt it with his private key from the year Sharp had joined D Branch.

There it was.

What the hell was so secret to double-encrypt the file, using for the inner encrypt a seventeen-year-old key, when the file was on D Branch's secure servers?

Pasha started to scan the document, then whistled under his breath. Yeah, that would do it.

He settled back to read it in detail.

When he had finished, Pasha stared sightlessly out the

window of his office as he considered the plan. Discussion had been included, to bolster each of the points made.

He had initially found it difficult to believe that someone could invest tens or hundreds of millions of credits into some investment without knowing what it was. But when Pasha read about the amounts of money they had coming in from their wildly successful initial round – money that had to be reinvested to avoid income taxes – it made more sense. He had never been so wealthy himself, and was unlikely to ever be, but the tax avoidance implications resonated.

Pasha had to agree with Fuller that the conviction of Dominic Trask or the other partners who had been kept in the dark was unlikely, and, even if successful, would result in financial penalties only. Those penalties wouldn't be anywhere near as large as Trask had volunteered, which is likely why he had chosen such a high value. It was a major benefit to him to remain unindicted and unconvicted. It was in his best interest to offer such a deal.

Complete access to his records on this deal was also good for D Branch and the Federation as a whole. While the team already had their suspicions as to which of the investment partners were the guilty parties, for the resolution Sharp proposed, certainty was required. One couldn't go executing famous decabillionaires without evidence, after all.

As for Trask and the other, less guilty, partners, they were unlikely to be convicted and executed by the courts, but if Sharp did execute them under the captain's exemption for piracy, Sharp was unlikely to be convicted of murder either.

The criminal burden of proof – beyond a reasonable doubt – favored Trask and his partners at trial, but, if Sharp acted against them, that burden of proof inverted to protect Sharp. Prosecutors would have to prove Sharp guilty beyond a reasonable doubt as well, and that was unlikely given the evidence they had of Trask's funding of the piracy scheme.

But was executing someone because someone else used their money to fund a vastly illegal scheme what one could properly call justice?

At length Pasha nodded. He liked the deal. He also liked reminding the investment community that playing too fast and loose with the rules would not be tolerated, and, sooner or later, the chickens would come home to roost.

As for approving the plan, that was clearly above his pay grade. Claude would have to be involved, and Mr. Dearborn as well. The Federation Attorney General and head of the Federation Justice Department would not be pleased to be brought into such a deal only after it had been made, and it was up to D Branch to know that.

D Branch primarily existed to counter ongoing threats, such as the piracy operation that was still a going concern when Deke Sharp had first gotten involved. The piracy operation was now defunct, due largely to Sharp's involvement. This current operation was about justice, not an ongoing threat, and the Justice Department needed to be involved.

Pasha logged back into virtual terminal and placed a meeting request with Claude Allard.

Allard and Pasha sat on a bench along the walking path around the lake on the corporate campus of D Branch. Just two men in their sixties stopping for a rest during their walk.

Pasha had had the area thoroughly swept for eavesdropping devices within the last hour.

"You know I dislike all this cloak and dagger stuff, Otto."

"Yes, Claude, I know, but I think you'll agree with me it is necessary in this case once I tell you what is going on."

Pasha brought his superior up to speed on what the D Branch team had found on Elizabeth, and what the proposed resolution of it all was.

"That's quite a story, Otto. And you trust this team?"

"Yes, sir. Deke Sharp is my best man, and he's assembled quite a pick-up team for this investigation. A financial whiz-kid, a senior financial corruption investigator with the Humphreys planetary DoJ, and a high-priced cyber security consultant."

Allard nodded.

"Quite a team. And all working with Sharp?"

"Yes, sir. Recruited by him, working directly under his supervision."

Allard sighed.

"Very well. I will discuss all of this with Mort Dearborn."

"And timeliness?"

"I will call him immediately once I'm back in the office, Otto. Christine is a couple hours behind us right now, so I can catch him in the office, I think. But I don't have any control of the timing of his response."

"Of course, Claude. I understand."

It was late morning when Morton Dearborn got a call request from Claude Allard, the Director of D Branch.

Justice had nothing going on at the moment with D Branch, but Dearborn and Allard had interacted quite a bit a year ago, when the Justice Department had to evaluate the actions D Branch operatives had taken with regard to the piracy operations they had shut down with extreme prejudice.

Dearborn was not a fan of extrajudicial proceedings. Judicial proceedings is what the Justice Department did, after all. The relationship with Allard had therefore started out a bit testy.

But Allard and D Branch had been on solid legal ground. What's more, they had provided all the evidence and analysis they had accumulated to the Justice Department. Analysis within Justice had confirmed all of their findings. D Branch had not overstepped at all, which was usually a problem with operations-oriented groups.

And, of course, they had wiped out the pirates' operations and their supporters in the government and private sector. No mean feat.

That had all been most of a year ago, though. Dearborn had no idea what this current call request was about.

Perhaps some follow-up on those operations.

Curious, Dearborn accepted the call request immediately.

"That's quite a story, Claude."

"That was my reaction, Mort, when it was brought to me. At the same time, it's a great team we have working on it. Deke Sharp, who you'll remember from the pirate operations last year. One of our top people. Plus a top financial analyst, a cyber security guy, both from the private sector, and, get this, a senior financial corruption investigator on loan from the Humphreys DoJ."

Dearborn nodded. The Federation Justice Department worked with all the planetary organizations. The Humphreys Department of Justice was pretty good, especially in the financial crimes area. A *senior* financial corruption investigator in Humphreys DoJ would be top-notch.

"A solid team, Claude. And I think they have the correct sense of it. We would be unlikely to secure convictions of people who unknowingly provided funds to support or initiate the piracy operation. We would probably not even indict in those circumstances. A deal that would provide restitution of that magnitude to the victims would be welcome, and something very difficult to acquire by legal arm-twisting.

"At the same time, people who knowingly financed piracy are subject to the same legal jeopardy as those who Mr. Sharp and your other people dealt with so effectively last year. You were on solid legal ground then, and are now."

"We have your approval for the plan, then, Mort?"

"I hesitate to go on record with an open-ended approval, Claude. But if your people carry out this plan with the same clarity and precision with which they carried out the initial actions against the pirates and their supporters, Justice is unlikely to have any problems with it."

"And the asset seizures and calculation of penalties, Mort?"

"We can handle that, Claude. I'll send you the contact information for the correct people on Elizabeth. I'll also warn them something big is coming down, and that it will come from D Branch people on Elizabeth."

"Excellent. Thanks, Mort. I appreciate it."

"No problem, Claude. Thanks for the heads up."

The kids were in bed, and the four adults were out on the lanai of one of the bungalows having an evening drink after supper, when Deke Sharp got a notification.

"Huh. My Project Notes file just got updated. Let me look and see what we have. Some questions about the plan, probably."

Sharp got the distracted look of virtual terminal use, then came back to the here and now.

"OK, I think we just set a record. 'Plan approved in all respects.' What's it been? Eight hours? Nine?"

"No shit," Camden said.

"Now the fun begins," Fuller said.

The Flood

It was early enough that Dominic Trask might still be up, so Deke Sharp put in a call request. He left it at low priority so as not to wake Trask if he had already retired.

Trask took the call immediately.

"Good evening, Deke."

"Good evening, Dominic. I hope this isn't too late."

"No, not at all. I was just enjoying a last cigar of the evening on the terrace."

"Excellent."

"But it seems we met just yesterday, Deke. What's come up? Some questions, perhaps?"

"No, Dominic. I've just heard back from my superiors. The plan we discussed last night has been approved. 'In all respects,' they said."

"That was fast. I had not expected anything so quickly."

"Yes, it surprised me, too. But we have a deal."

"Wonderful. I was hopeful, and we started collecting materials today. The things I promised to send you. We should have a first transmission late tomorrow, with supplemental productions later. Is this a good address to use?"

"Yes, Dominic. This is the best address for me."

"All right, Deke. Thanks for letting me know. I look forward to working together on this."

"No problem, Dominic. We'll be in touch."

Hours later, Sharp lay awake, staring at the ceiling. Fuller was curled up to his side, snoring softly.

He had told the others of Trask's promise of a data

download tomorrow, and they all looked forward to it. As Fuller had observed, the real fun was about to start. The uncovering of the real perpetrators, and Sharp's necessary tasks dealing with them.

That could get very dicey, indeed. These people were all billionaires, and had resources with which to fight back. Especially after Sharp hit the first one. The second and third could be big problems. Would likely come after Sharp if they could, even as he maneuvered against them.

Sharp had spent last night in the city, after the meeting with Trask. He had taken a gun, of course, and wore his special right arm prosthetic, the one with the popup camera in the wrist. That camera allowed him to get the sight picture on his weapon at any angle, without lifting the gun to use the cameras set into his face to aim.

They had not been sure how the meeting would go, after all. They'd had their surmises, and doubted Trask wanted to give D Branch cause célèbre to go after him, but they hadn't been sure. Hadn't known if Sharp would survive the encounter.

Now they were going to get the data that would allow them to go after the true troublemakers. The people with resources who also had a very loose relationship with the rules. It promised to be dangerous as hell.

Then why had he and Fuller fallen on each other like otters in springtime once they were in bed?

Adrenaline junkies. Both of them. The D Branch senior field operative and the Humphreys DoJ senior financial corruption investigator. They lived for the chase, the danger, the high of taking such risks. Of, ultimately, prevailing.

When the hunt was on – when the danger was close – was when they were most alive.

And risks there were. Sharp was proof that it didn't always

work out. Oh, sure, he had survived the destruction of *Circe*, but not by much, and not without some serious effort. Even now, much of him was artificial and prosthetic. And still he persisted, in taking after the pirates. Persisted now in going after their funding sources.

Sharp shook his head at his own irrationality. The movement caused Fuller to stir. She mewed and cuddled closer.

He logged into his internal processor, adjusted his hormone levels, and dropped off to sleep.

The room service waiter set up breakfast on the lanai of Camden and Thompsen's bungalow and left. Everyone was up, and they all sat down to eat together.

"Well, there's no sense working today," Thompsen said. "Not with a major data dump coming in later."

"We can spend all day on the beach," Camden said.

"We could rent a boat," Sharp said. "Have the resort pack us a lunch and cruise up and down the coast a bit."

"Oh, can we, Uncle Deke?" Mike asked.

"Yeah. Boats are cool," Matt said.

"Let me check availability," Sharp said.

He closed his eyes and dropped into virtual terminal mode, then opened them and was back.

"Yep. Cabin cruiser. Four adults and three children. Six hours of gas. Lunch. Not a problem."

"But I want to swim," Sarah said.

"We can swim off the boat, Sarah," Fuller said. "We stop and we swim right off the boat."

"Oh. OK. That sounds fun."

"How much will this cost, Deke?" Camden asked.

"Don't know. Don't care. Not my problem."

"It's nice to be D Branch," Fuller said.

"Oh, yes," Sharp said.

"Well, then. Let's do it," Thompsen said.

"Done," Sharp said.

At this resort, one didn't go looking for the marina or whatever to find the boat. No, a staffer drove the boat up to the dock the bungalows shared, tied it up, and gave the keys to Sharp. He then got a lift back from another staffer who showed up in an electric cart.

Half an hour after ordering it, they had a boat, with their lunch in the refrigerator and the oven in the galley, with the oven set to keep it warm.

As one would expect, it was a very nice boat.

"Do I have to wear this dumb life pezerber?" Sarah asked.

"Yes, Sarah. The water here is so deep, the whole Gotham Astoria hotel wouldn't even poke above the water."

"Gosh."

"But Uncle Deke isn't wearing one," Matt said.

Sharp was already in the water off the swim platform that extended off the aft of the boat.

"But I am wearing one, Matt. My arms and legs float. See?"

Sharp removed his left arm and let it set on the water, where it floated high.

"Oh. OK, I guess."

For the first part of the swim, Camden stayed on the boat. For the second part of the swim, Sharp took his place. But there was always one person on the boat.

And everyone in the water wore life preservers, if one considered Sharp's floating prosthetics to be a life preserver.

"Well, that was fun," Fuller said.

They were sitting around the table on the lanai, just having finished dinner. The boat was gone, picked up by the resort staff and moved back to the marina for cleaning and servicing before its next renter tomorrow.

"You can swim a lot longer with a life pezerber," Sarah said. "I'm not even tired."

She said that last while stifling a yawn, and the adults all laughed. The boys, too, were looking pretty worn out after all day out of doors, then a good dinner.

"Well, you can all nap for now on the couches there," Thompsen said. "You don't need to go to bed yet."

The kids happily went over and stretched out on the couches, and were soon asleep.

"We're going to have to carry them in when it is bedtime," Camden said.

"That's OK," Thompsen said. "We'll manage. They were good kids. All day, really."

"Well, tomorrow we'll have our work cut out for us," Sharp said.

"Really?" Fuller asked.

"Oh, yes. I've got data coming in from Dominic Trask. It's been running for a while now, and it's on part seventeen of twenty-five."

"Oh, my," Camden said. "Across the interplanetary link from Elizabeth to Ariel? Isn't that a high-speed link?"

"Yes. And he's running at the interpersonal maximum rate."

"Well, it won't be long before I go to bed, then," Thompsen said. "The kids will likely be up early, and I want to get started on that download first thing tomorrow."

Sharp woke with a start to a hand on his shoulder.

"Wha'?"

"We should probably go in to bed, dear," Fuller said.

"The kids?"

"We moved Sarah and the boys inside, and Paul and Lydia both just went in."

"OK. Sounds good."

Sharp half-walked, half stumbled in to the bedroom in half-sleep.

"You should take everything off after the salt water today, Deke. I'll help you in the morning."

"Awright."

Fuller helped Sharp get the last prosthetic arm off, then they crawled into bed and were soon fast asleep.

Sharp woke up in the morning in bed alone, with none of his prosthetics on. Since he needed one arm to mount any of the others, he got out of bed and went to the bathroom. All of his prosthetics lay in a pile next to the bed.

He walked on his knees to the bathroom and peed into the walk-in shower. He turned the shower on with the stump of his right arm. It remembered its last set temperature.

When the temperature had stabilized, he got into the shower and sat on the low chair there and simply enjoyed the spray.

Fuller stuck her head in.

"Oh, you're up. Let me get you your prosthetics."

Fuller went back into the bedroom and brought him his arms. Sharp held up his right stump, and Fuller, after a couple seconds to pick the correct one, made the connection. She set the left arm down next to him.

"Be right back."

She brought his leg prosthetics in one at a time, and set them down next to him as well.

"You have the soap and your salve handy, D.K?"

"Yeah, I'm good. I just need a fresh towel."

Fuller pulled a fresh towel from the shelf and set it on the towel bar.

"OK, D.K. See you at breakfast."

Sharp washed each of his three remaining connections in turn. He then carefully washed each prosthetic. Long-term exposure to salt – such as that in salt water – was not good for stainless steel, and some of the connection hardware was stainless.

He mounted the left arm, then took off the right. He cleaned the connection on his right arm, and then washed the prosthetic.

Sharp mounted his right arm and his legs, then stood and took a normal shower. When finished, he shut off the shower and dried off with the towel. The towel and the salve he took into the bedroom.

Sitting on the bed, Sharp removed each prosthetic in turn, dried and then salved his skin at the connection, and remounted the prosthetic. Once all four connections were salved, he took the towel and salve back into the bathroom.

In the bathroom, he applied makeup to the portions of his scalp and face that did not tan quite the same as the rest of his skin, making his appearance less blotchy and patchwork.

Just another morning if you were Deke Sharp.

Sharp got dressed in beach clothes and went out on the lanai, where everyone else was digging into breakfast.

"Morning, everybody."

"Morning, Uncle Deke," Sarah said.

Sharp ran his plate down the small buffet they had delivered every morning and joined the adults at the big table. Eggs Benedict, some bacon, a croissant with orange marmalade all looked good this morning.

"Have you taken a look at that download, Deke?" Camden

asked.

"No. I just moved it to the workspace and sent you guys pointers to it. What's it look like?"

"I don't think Trask's holding back. He sent us everything but the kitchen sink."

"Actually, I think I saw the kitchen sink in there," Fuller said.

Camden chuckled.

"We'll get started on it right after breakfast, Deke. We thought we were drinking from a fire hydrant before, but this is a flood."

"You gonna be able to make heads or tails of it all, Paul?"

"Oh, sure. The data visualization engine will make short work of it, I think. On the big issues, we know what we're looking for."

Sharp nodded. Who knew, and when?

"All right. Let me know if you need any help."

With Camden, Thompsen, and Fuller working on the analysis of Trask's data dump, Sharp watched the kids on the beach today. All four of the adults were stretched out on the big blankets on the beach, but only Sharp was keeping an eye on the kids.

Which was fine with Sharp. He liked children generally, and they were good kids. They knew not to go into the water without an adult nearby, and there were no issues.

He even helped the boys with their sand castle. Without the sand being wet, it couldn't be molded. Sharp fetched a couple of buckets of water from the slight surf to fill the hole they had dug so they could mold using wet sand.

While they did that, Sarah walked the beach looking for shells and interesting stones, but she kept out of the water.

At lunch, Sharp asked how the analysis was going.

"It's going well, Deke," Camden said. "I think we'll have things pretty well nailed down this afternoon."

Thompsen and Fuller nodded.

"How's it going with the kids, D.K?" Thompsen asked.

"Good, Lydia. They're good kids, and there haven't been any problems."

"Good. Let us know if you need help there, D.K."

"Sure. So far, though, no issues."

Fuller looked thoughtful. Throughout this whole adventure, Deke Sharp had been great with the kids.

And Suzie Fuller was getting to that age.

After dinner that evening, with the kids on the couches coloring – though Matthew had already fallen asleep – Camden took Sharp on a tour of the data map in D Branch's data visualization engine.

Thompsen had been concerned about the expense of the boat yesterday, and all of them had asked about the expense of the resort and the Gotham Astoria before that. Sharp knew, however, that it was their extensive use of the data visualization engine – and the high-speed data links from Elizabeth to Ariel required to use it properly – that had been the really expensive part of this mission.

Which is why he had shrugged off the day-to-day expenses of their mission. They just weren't either important or material.

"Well, Deke, here's the combined dataset."

"Geez! What a rat's nest. Now I know what you meant when you said a flood."

There were over a hundred correspondents shown, all of them interconnected with communications. As they went forward into the center of the three-dimensional display, they came up to a core of highly-interconnected individuals.

"And here is Trask's investment group. They didn't all take part in all investments, and the membership changed over time, but this knot at the center is his investment partners."

"There's a lot more here than we had. So Trask did send you all those communications."

"Oh, yes. This is what's interesting, though."

Camden raised his voice and spoke to the display in front of him.

"DV. Set filter: pirate or piracy. Set date: minus twenty-five years. Retain correspondents as displayed."

None of the correspondent descriptors moved, but all the communications disappeared, except one.

"That one you see there is from someone who replied 'Arrrgh' to bad news, and his correspondent mailed back, 'You sound like a pirate.' Otherwise, there's nothing."

"OK. So it hasn't come up yet."

"No. Now watch this. DV. Advance date one year."

A solid stream of communications appeared between two correspondents.

"Elton Thomas and Paul Thurl. There's our idea men, right there."

"You're sure, Paul?"

"Yes. We've read all those communications. They worked out the scheme. DV. Advance one year."

A third correspondent was added to the growing net.

"They recruited this fellow, Mark Anderson, into their scheme, because he had connections into the Navy. They needed those connections to get warships diverted from the breakers."

"And that's the core bunch, Paul? The ones who knew, before the investments were made, what it was really all about?"

"Yes, Deke. Watch this. DV. Advance date five years."

The map didn't change. The only people with communications containing pirate or piracy were still Thomas, Thurl, and Anderson.

"The piracy operation is in full swing by this point, Deke, and the other investors don't know anything about it."

"Have you seen their presentation for this investment, Paul?"

"Yes. No mention of piracy. There is a large sum set aside for 'marketing and lobbying', though. Now watch this. DV. Advance date seven years."

A thick knot of communications popped into place, including Dominic Trask and the other investment partners. The focus was on Thomas, Thurl, and Anderson.

"By this point, Trask has found out?" Sharp asked.

"Yes, Deke. And we've looked at these communications as well. Trask is pretty hot in some of them. He evidently did some research on why their investments in the insurance companies and military contractors were going so well, and didn't like what he saw."

"He turned up where the marketing and lobbying funds went."

"Yes, and he was hot about it. Thomas, Thurl, and Anderson also threatened the other investors with exposure if they ratted."

"You've seen that, Paul?"

"Yes. Mostly it was Thomas, but Thurl and Anderson backed him on it."

"Have you got pull-outs for me? Specific example communications, with dates and all? The presentation? All of that backing material, including Trask's finding out?"

"Yes, Deke. We just pulled that together before dinner."

"Excellent."

Octavius Pasha looked through the new file in Sharp's top-level directory, Project Findings.

Well, there it was, in black and white. The original concept, worked out between Thomas and Thurl. The implementation, using Anderson's Navy contacts. The provision of funds from the capital re-investment fund. Trask's finding out what was going on, and the anger of him and the other investors. The threats of disclosure.

Pasha opened the Project Notes file and made a new entry at the bottom.

'Next steps: Move against Thomas, Thurl, and Anderson.'

Pasha thought about it, then added a second line to that entry.

'Use extreme prejudice.'

Preparation

They were at breakfast on the lanai. Sharp had already checked his notification of a change in the Project Notes file, and told the others what it said. The kids were playing nearby, but out of casual earshot.

"What does 'use extreme prejudice' mean, D.K?" Thompsen asked. "Does it mean what I think it means?"

"Yes. Kill them. Then turn FDoJ loose on their assets."

"Does this mean we're all moving back into Gotham?" Camden asked.

"No. It means I am moving back into Gotham."

"And I as well," Fuller said.

"Suzie—" Sharp began.

"D.K., you need me. Alone, you're a dangerous looking man. Somebody to keep an eye on. With me, you're a businessman with his pretty, younger wife. Those are a dime a dozen in Gotham.

"And how many people can hide an 8mm HP in their brassiere?"

Her hand came up above the table holding a very nice compact semi-auto pistol. A Ross Arms Platinum, no less.

Ross Arms made some of the finest firearms available. They were intended for people who made a living with arms, who relied on them every day for survival. The 8mm High-Power was a caliber intended for social work, as Sharp liked to say. Platinum bullets and high chamber pressure made for a heavy round and maximum impact in a small package.

The Ross Arms Platinum 8mm HP had a platinum slide as well, to absorb the recoil of those fast, heavy rounds.

Unthinkably expensive before space travel, platinum was almost a waste product of asteroid mining. With twice the density of lead, its mass, malleability, and conductivity made it useful for certain things, however, and firearms was one of them.

Fuller was right in another thing, though. Her body, a veritable garden of Earthly delights, offered plenty of opportunities to hide a small, powerful package like the Ross Arms Platinum 8mm HP. Sharp had been watching for it, and had not seen her packing.

"I'll have backup from D Branch in Gotham, Suzie."

"Do you really want to call in other people yet, D.K? They seem to have penetrated the police on at least two planets. Why not D Branch?"

OK, that was fair. Sharp wanted to lone-wolf this for a while yet. And having competent backup from someone already in the know would help.

He held up his hands in surrender.

"All right, Suzie. Fair enough."

"When do we leave?"

"After lunch."

"I'll go pack."

Sharp and Fuller did not check out of the bungalow at the beach, but stayed booked in, just as they had all stayed booked into the Gotham Astoria. Checking out would generate financial entries that documented their movement and current location.

It also allowed them not to have to move all their luggage on the planet every time they changed location. They had only taken vacation-style clothes to the beach.

The beach resort's limo took them to a hotel in a suburb

nearer to downtown Gotham than the beach. From there, the limo from Gotham Astoria took them downtown to the big luxury hotel.

When they got to their room, there were two big trunks just inside the door. Shipping labels indicated they had come from off-planet.

"What's all this, D.K?"

"More parts for the dog suit. I got notification from the Gotham Astoria that they had arrived day before yesterday."

"What kind of parts?"

"My flight gear."

"Flight gear? Really?"

"Yeah. Balloon and paraglider."

"For the dog suit?"

"Yeah."

"Nice."

The next day was Saturday, and Sharp was less interested in surveillance on a Saturday or Sunday. He preferred to hit targets on weekdays. They moved around more, and usually did so without their families along.

If some security personnel died during a hit, no one blinked an eye, but family members dying during a hit were usually considered unacceptable collateral damage.

Sharp liked clean hits.

Instead of doing surveillance, they had the Gotham Astoria car deliver them and the trunks to *Hecate's* shuttle at the Elizabeth Navy Shuttleport. They used the bigger shuttle bus rather than the limo, due to the size of the trunks.

In addition to complete instructions, Dr. Weatherly's people had included a small toolkit with the flight rig, which was handy if unnecessary. The common tools required were part of the shuttle's cargo complement. One thing they didn't include was a battery drill, which Sharp selected rather than the ratchet driver they provided.

Sharp was pleased to find Fuller was competent with tools, and he could tell her what he needed as he worked.

"I'm going to need a five-sixteenths nut driver next, Suzie."

"Got it."

Fuller selected the five-sixteenths socket, looked at what Sharp was doing, then mounted it on a five-inch extension and secured it in the battery drill.

Sharp reached for it and she handed it to him.

"Perfect."

There were some parts – body parts, mostly – on the dog suit that had to be changed out to accommodate the flight rig. Those parts could be left in place whether the flight rig was used or not. That was what the permanent fasteners were for.

The actual flight rig then connected to the dog suit at hard anchor points on the modified body. Those connections were a clip-on setup. It looked like those hard anchor points had been selected to balance Sharp and the dog suit so that he didn't hang at some weird angle.

Nice job.

Sharp stood up next to the dog suit. He picked up one of the balloon modules – they had sent him three – and clipped it onto the dog suit in front of the compartment where he would lie.

"You gonna mount them now, D.K?"

"Yeah. If I use the dog suit in Gotham, I need a way out of there. I can't just walk the streets in this thing."

"How you gonna get into town?"

"That's where you'll come in, Suzie."

She nodded and handed him one of the paraglider modules – also one of three – and he mounted it to the dog suit behind his position. He also made the handle connections to the new cable units on either side of the body.

"OK. That should do it."

"You gonna test it first, D.K?"

"Nah. The suspense is part of the fun."

She rolled her eyes and he laughed.

"Besides, I've been paragliding before."

"But not in the dog suit."

Sharp shrugged.

"Same-same."

They called the hotel limo, then stowed the trunks with the extra modules in one of the cabinets, and stowed the dog suit back in its niche.

The limo showed up and took them back to the hotel.

Sunday was a lazy day, though they were both really wound up over the action that would start tomorrow.

Sharp put on a hotel robe to meet the room service waiter with breakfast. He and Fuller both ate breakfast in the big terry cloth robes with the hotel logo on them.

After breakfast, they went into the bedroom to get dressed for the day. Sharp thought about it, then just threw the robe on a chair and went back out to the living room naked.

Fuller shrugged and did the same.

They hung around the suite all day, lounging around in the nude. It became something of a game. Anytime Sharp hit the switch in his body controls, he would get a rock-hard erection, and Fuller would come over and screw him wherever he was.

They explored lots of different ways to accomplish the goal, on various pieces of furniture, the floor, the bar, whatever.

At one point, Sharp was lying out on the balcony in the warm sunshine, and he heard Fuller come out onto the balcony. He hit the switch, and they did the dirty right there on the chaise, in full view of the city. Fuller's cries of pleasure wafted away on the breeze, lost in the commotion of the city around them.

By bed time, they had both worked off all the tension and were ready to meet the first week of real action for this mission.

That is, the first real action they initiated.

Their response to the earlier police attacks against them had been purely reactive and didn't count.

Target Research

That Sunday – in between couplings – they also planned their surveillance strategy for the coming weeks.

"What's your plan for surveilling the targets?" Fuller asked.

"I'll spend three or four days on each, getting a baseline. I expect the other two will change their habits when I hit the first one."

"So two, three weeks?"

"Or a month. Yeah, something like that."

"Long time, D.K."

"You gotta have patience in this business."

Fuller nodded. Same thing with DoJ investigations. This she was used to. Still…

"You know, D.K., we could cut that time in half if we split the surveillance."

Sharp opened his mouth, then closed it. His knee-jerk reaction was to say No. He was a lone wolf, always had been. Then again, on this mission, he had relied heavily on the experience and expertise of Fuller, Camden, and Thompsen. He would not be this far along without them. Would, in fact, probably still be waiting on the analysis section.

It wasn't like she didn't know how to do this. Senior investigator for the DoJ on any planet was not purely a desk job. Anything but.

Fuller spoke into his hesitation.

"It also reduces the odds you get made."

"And if you get made? No offense, but you sort of stand out. Particularly to men."

"It's happened before. I'll manage."

Sharp nodded. That had to have happened before. They were going to be doing surveillance in crowded public spaces as well, so there was a limit on the methods that could be used against her.

"All right. Sounds good. Let's go over who and when and what information I need."

With Gotham's subtropical location and the resulting pleasant climate, there were a lot of sidewalk cafés in Elizabeth's capital city. In particular, there was one across the street and a bit down the block from the building in which Elton Thomas lived.

Thomas was the richest of the three targets, and the most dangerous. The piracy operation had been his idea, and he had made out very well from it. Then in his mid-thirties and now approaching sixty, he was wealthy, powerful, and ruthless.

Sharp was inclined to execute Thomas first, because he had the greatest capability to go after Sharp. Take him out first, though, and he was neutralized before he knew what was going on. Were Sharp to hit one of the others first, Thomas would be off the leash in going after Sharp.

Sharp noticed something the first day watching Thomas' residence. A weakness. A crack in his defenses. Rather than watch his work location in subsequent days, Sharp watched his residence every morning. He changed tables each day, until he had the location he wanted.

It would be perfect.

Fuller had started watching Thurl, both in the mornings and the afternoons. Then Sharp took the afternoons on Thurl, after Thomas in the morning, and she spent the afternoons on Anderson.

Now done with Thomas, on the fourth day Sharp took Thurl both morning and afternoon, and Fuller concentrated on Anderson.

On Friday, her second day watching for Anderson in the morning, two men approached Fuller in the coffee shop seating in the lobby of the building where he lived. They wore suits, but both men were what one would classify as muscle, and Fuller could see from the cut of their suits that both were armed with pistols in shoulder holsters.

"Come with us, miss."

Fuller stood.

"Come now, officers. Badges first, like they taught at the Academy."

"Come with us, I said."

The leader started to move towards her.

"No badges, eh? Pity."

Fuller then let out a terrifying scream. It reached down into the primal subconscious brain of those hearing it. In most women, it inspired the fight or flight response, while in most men it inspired the 'run toward the guns' response of their instinctive defense of women.

The two men, alarmed, looked around the lobby as a hundred people stopped and turned toward them. When they turned back to Fuller, they were facing the muzzle of a Ross Arms Platinum 8mm HP semi-automatic pistol.

"Unlike you gentlemen, I do have a badge, and kidnapping a law enforcement officer is a capital crime on every planet of the Federation, for which I now have a hundred witnesses."

The second man, who had held back, started to sidle behind the first. Fuller moved to her left.

"Oh, no, you don't. You stay out where I can see you or I'll kill you both right now."

The second man froze.

"Better. Now, we have three choices. I can kill you both in self-defense, I can arrest you both on capital charges, or you can back away slowly, keeping your hands where I can see them, and then walk away. I lean toward killing you both, but I'll let you decide."

The leader nodded, then held his hands out from his sides. The second man followed suit. They both backed away from her under the watchful muzzle of her pistol.

When they were thirty feet away, she nodded.

"OK. Now, go away."

The two men turned and walked away toward the elevators.

Fuller held her gun at the ready in her open purse as she left the building, only then reholstering it under her jacket.

"I got made today," Fuller told Sharp that night at dinner.

"At Anderson's?"

"Yes. Two armed men accosted me in the lobby coffee shop and told me to follow them. I demurred."

"They didn't get physical?"

"They were going to, then decided it was not in their best interest to charge an 8mm HP pistol, and the person who could produce it that fast, in front of a hundred witnesses."

Sharp chuckled.

"Good. OK, today's Friday. We'll switch on Monday. I'll take Anderson, you take Thurl."

"Not Thomas?"

"No. I already have what I need on him."

Fuller raised an eyebrow.

"I just need a clean shot, Suzie. One clean shot."

"OK. Got it. You know, I never did see Anderson. Thurl, sure, but not Anderson. He never went out or came back while

I was watching."

"Maybe he's not in Gotham at the moment."

"But his security people are there. D.K. Maybe he's just a homebody. Is he retired?"

"We'll have to check. We have to nail him down."

They switched transportation multiple times again on the way to the beach that evening, getting in late. They traveled light, since they had left their vacation clothes in their bungalow at the resort.

The next morning at breakfast, Camden and Thompsen were curious.

"How did things go last week, Deke?" Camden asked.

"Good. Really good."

"When will the action start?" Thompsen asked.

"Likely this week."

"Really?"

"Oh, yes."

"Wow."

Other than that, they didn't really talk business that weekend. Camden and Thompsen didn't need to know what was going on in town, and Sharp and Fuller had been doing nothing but surveillance and comparing notes all week.

Sharp and Fuller enjoyed a relaxing weekend on the beach, then headed back into Gotham Sunday night.

Monday night, after a quiet day of surveillance, Sharp and Fuller compared notes.

"OK, so we have a pattern established on the other two guys. I think it's time to move on with Thomas."

"How are you going to proceed, D.K?"

"I know what my window is with him. I'll sit and wait for

the shot. Maybe tomorrow, maybe Wednesday, maybe Thursday."

Sharp shrugged.

"What I won't do is screw up my chance by rushing a shot that won't work. If he goes way underground, it will be much harder to get at him."

Fuller nodded.

"Weapon?"

"Let me show you."

Sharp went to his luggage in the bedroom and came back with a prosthetic left arm.

"Looks like the one you have on, D.K."

"Yes, but it's got some additional features."

Sharp pulled the left hand off at the wrist, exposing the muzzles of a fifty-caliber magnum rifle and a forty-millimeter grenade launcher.

"Oh, my. Which one?"

"For the gap I saw, the fifty. One frangible round. Subsonic. Suppressed. Head shot."

"Suppressed?"

"Yes. I have a longer barrel for it, but at that distance I'll use the short barrel with the suppressor."

"Is that going to be accurate enough?"

"Oh, sure. With the longer barrel, I can take out a shuttle coming in for landing from a mile away. For something like this – maybe thirty yards – the short barrel is plenty."

"It's gonna be messy."

"Yes. Assuming I hit him, they're gonna have to clean up the car. A lot. No doubt about it."

Elton Thomas

Tuesday morning found Deke Sharp sitting in his favorite spot at his favorite table, reading the news while he drank his coffee.

Rather, that was what he appeared to be doing.

Sharp was actually keeping his attention on the view from the sighting camera in the left elbow of his weapon prosthetic, which he had routed into the feed from his left eye camera.

Today his prosthetic mounted the fifty-caliber magnum rifle in the single-shot, short-barrel, suppressed version. The one shot he needed had been loaded back at the hotel. That arm lay on the table top as a bench rest, his right hand on top of the left wrist. It would look to anyone walking by like his right hand was over his left fist.

The weapon itself was almost more pistol than rifle. The barrel, from the chamber to the muzzle, was just six inches long. Even so, with the barrel, the four-inch-long chamber, the firing mechanism, and the suppressor, the unit was fourteen inches long, extending into the palm of the left hand.

That detached left hand was currently in his left jacket pocket, while the left sleeve of his jacket and his right hand covered the end of the suppressor and obscured the stump of his left forearm. A sighting tube along the top of the suppressor kept his jacket clear of the line of sight of the camera in his left elbow.

He was waiting for Elton Thomas. Waiting to see if the weakness he had seen in Thomas' security would open up again.

Waiting to take the shot.

TOO SHARP TO HOLD

Thomas' limousine pulled up at the normal time. The shotgun remained seated on the passenger side of the front seat. The driver got out and walked around the car to the rear passenger-side door and opened it.

There were security people who preferred this arrangement. The idea was that the shotgun was unencumbered by any duty other than keeping his eyes and surveillance cameras on anything possibly threatening. He was also not remote from any of the methods he might use to respond to the threat.

Foolish here, though, Sharp thought. Here, the passenger side of the limousine was toward the building close by, while the driver side of the car was toward the street.

When the driver opened his door, from his vantage point Sharp had a clean shot into the back of the car between the windshield and the door's window frame. It wasn't a big gap, but it didn't have to be.

As long as it lined up.

Elton Thomas exited the front door of the building and walked the short distance to the car. He got in and the driver closed the door.

The driver walked around the car and opened the driver's door to get in.

There! Now!

Nope. Thomas was off-line. Not a lot, but enough to make the shot difficult through the narrow gap. Too close to the door's window frame. A little off and it would hit the window frame instead of Thomas.

Sharp needed to be a little further left. In the next chair at his own table should work, actually.

The moment passed.

Good enough. Tomorrow would come.

Sharp put his left wrist into his jacket pocket and reconnected it to the hand concealed there, covering up the weapons.

The limousine pulled away, but Sharp paid it no attention.

Wednesday morning found Sharp at the same table, though he sat on the left chair on this side of the table, not the right one. That might not be the right chair today, though. Minor variations in the sidewalk café's table locations, in the spot where the limousine stopped, in exactly where on the seat Thomas sat, could all mess up the shot.

He would have to see. If it wasn't perfect, he wouldn't take the shot.

Thomas got into the car, the driver walked around the limo. Here it comes.

Sharp didn't have to worry about jerking the trigger or anything like that. He just had to push the Fire button in his internal controls and the mechanism would take care of the rest.

With his right eye, Sharp saw a panel van come down the street and past the limo, blocking his shot.

When the van was gone, the moment had passed.

Thursday morning. Another morning, another cup of coffee, another chance at Elton Thomas.

The limousine pulled up. The driver got out and walked around. He opened the rear passenger door. Thomas walked out of the building and got in the car. The driver closed the door and walked around the limo.

The driver opened the driver's door, and—

Now!

The fifty-caliber frangible platinum round was a bit low and to the right. Rather than hit Thomas in the center of the forehead, it hit him in his left eye.

The plastic point collapsed back into the hollow center of the round on impact, forcing its frangible wings wide. The bullet bloomed as it passed through Thomas' brain.

Under the hydrostatic shock of that ballooning, heavy, platinum round, Thomas' head exploded, showering brains, blood, bone, skin, and hair all over the rear passenger compartment. The bulk of it, though, hit the rear window where the shards of the bullet embedded in the inner plastic layer of the bulletproof glass.

Though the subsonic round was suppressed, that didn't mean a rifle shooting a five-hundred-grain, fifty-caliber bullet at a thousand feet per second didn't make any noise.

Sharp turned to his left with the recoil in his left forearm, and looked behind him, as if the sound of the shot had been from behind. Other people looking for the location of the shooter took the cue from him and also looked behind him.

As he turned, Sharp put his left wrist into his jacket pocket and reconnected it to the hand concealed there, hiding the weapons in his forearm.

He turned back toward the limo across the street. Thomas' security people, both the shotgun from the car and the security people on the building door, were looking around with guns drawn, but didn't know what to do. They could see no shooter, and the person who had hired them to protect him was pretty obviously beyond their help anyway.

In the distance, Sharp could hear police sirens approaching. He took his cue from the other café patrons. He got up and left the area at a brisk walk, before any other shots were fired.

A clean kill. He nodded in satisfaction. Nice.

Sharp also sent a message to the Federation Department of Justice contact name he had been given. He sent it from his actual D Branch account.

Seize the assets of the late Elton Thomas pending adjudication of the compensation rights of his victims. Do it quietly.

"Hey, Mark. Look at this," Dick Laramie said.

His coworker in the Elizabeth offices of the Federation Department of Justice came over to look at his display.

"The late Elton Thomas?" Mark Benson asked. "Did I miss something on the news this morning?"

Laramie opened a news panel on his display. Did a search. Nothing about Elton Thomas.

"I don't know. I don't see anything."

Then it came. A news flash. 'Billionaire Investor Elton Thomas Killed By Assassin's Bullet On Gotham Street.'

"Says here the shooting was at eight-seventeen," Benson said. "What time was that mail sent, Dick?"

"Eight-seventeen."

"So it's the shooter, or one of his team, anyway. Now what do we do?"

"We got orders last week, right, Mark? We get any D Branch communication to seize assets of individuals on Elizabeth, we do it," Laramie said.

"And that mail is from D Branch?"

"Got it in one."

"OK, then. Let's get going on it."

Benson thought about it.

"Damn, that's fast, though."

"Well, like you say, Mark, let's get going on it. Because I doubt it's the last one."

"Really?"

"Did our orders say only one individual?"

"No. It says 'seize assets of individuals on Elizabeth' per D Branch."

"Right. So likely more than one. Let's get going and get this one done before the next one comes in."

That news flash came across the open news feed of Dominic Trask, already at work in his office this morning. He searched on the story, which he read with satisfaction.

Elton Thomas had been a truly evil man. Good riddance.

Trask searched his resources more broadly, on images, and found the actual police photos of the crime scene.

"Good heavens."

No question that Thomas was actually dead, then.

Whatever else you could say about Deke Sharp, he apparently didn't believe in half measures.

They were on the same side, for the moment at least, and Trask couldn't be happier.

That news flash also came across the open news feed of Paul Thurl. He read the news story with growing concern.

When he found the same police crime-scene photos Trask had found, his concern turned to abject terror.

Not knowing what else to do, he put in a call request to Dominic Trask.

He would know what was going on.

"Good morning, Paul. How can I help you this morning?"

"Dominic, did you see what happened to Elton?"

Trask considered how to play this. He certainly didn't want to do anything that would make Mr. Sharp's job harder. Particularly in the case of Paul Thurl, Thomas' side man in the piracy investment. He had backed up Thomas' threats, which had not left him on Trask's good side.

Trask had always maintained friendly relations with Thurl, however, at least on the surface.

"Yes," Trask said with the slightest hesitation. "Clearly, our erstwhile partner angered one person too many, and they decided to act on it."

"Do you think we're in any danger, Dominic?"

"I do not consider myself in any danger from this circumstance whatsoever."

"You won't be changing your security measures?"

"No, Paul. As I say, I don't think I am in any danger from Elton's assassin. He clearly angered someone who decided to do something about it."

"He angered you, Dominic. Several times over the years. So did I, for that matter."

"That's true, Paul, but let me hasten to say that I did not order Elton's assassination. No one in my employ or under my control had anything to do with it. My preferred method of retribution in our circle is to make more money than the other fellow. To make him say, 'Damn! How did he do that?' with some financial coup of mine."

Thurl chuckled.

"You've done that to me once or twice, Dominic."

"Indeed I have, Paul. With a great deal of satisfaction, I might add. But I will not be changing my behavior one bit. Whatever Elton did to bring this down on himself, I do not expect it to extend to me. It's been a number of years since I did any business with Elton, and this seems more recent than that."

Thurl nodded.

"That's comforting, Dominic. It's been a few years for me as well."

Thurl took a deep breath and sighed.

"All right, Dominic. Thank you for taking my call this morning."

"No problem at all, Paul. You take care."

Trask severed the connection and sat back in his office chair with satisfaction.

"Well, there you go, Mr. Sharp," Trask said to his empty office. "Good hunting to you."

Sharp was back at the hotel room in the Gotham Astoria by mid-morning.

"I told you it was gonna be messy," Fuller said.

"I never doubted it."

Sharp spread a fresh hotel towel at the dining area table, then changed out his left prosthetic for the non-weapon version. He went into the bedroom and came back with a firearm cleaning kit.

He disassembled the fifty-caliber from the arm and cleaned it thoroughly, lubed it, and reinstalled it in the left weapon prosthetic. He then took it into the bedroom and repacked it in his luggage.

Sharp came out into the living room where Fuller was sitting, and sat down across from her.

"Clean hit. Nice job," she said.

Sharp nodded.

"The big thing is to be patient. Wait for your opportunity. Not rush things. It can be frustrating, but you have to maintain your detachment."

Fuller nodded.

"So now what, D.K?"

"Thurl next, I think, but I need to decompress first. We'll see what changes he makes to his security, if any. That can wait until tomorrow. Or Monday."

"Sounds good."

"In the meantime, how about a little romp, Suzie? Help me burn off some adrenaline."

"Ooo. Right here, right now."

She was already peeling out of her clothes.

Paul Thurl

Deke Sharp was back on surveillance the next morning, Friday, now at the condo building Paul Thurl called home.

Thurl never committed the same error as Elton Thomas. No door in the limo opened on the street side. In fact, no other door opened at all, just Thurl's. The driver and shotgun remained in the car.

It was the building's doorman who opened the car door for Thurl to get in.

Looking at that doorman, Sharp had an idea.

He headed back to the Gotham Astoria.

Fuller had been running a discreet body camera during all of her surveillance, while Sharp could record anything his artificial camera eyes saw.

Sharp ran back through the recordings of the Thurl surveillance, looking specifically at the doorman. It was the same doorman Wednesday through Sunday, but a different man on each of Monday and Tuesday.

What's more, it wasn't the same different man every time. It looked like it was someone from a security service, and would be whoever was available.

And Thurl never tipped the doorman.

Perfect.

On Sunday, Sharp went back to Thurl's condo building. He went in through a side door to the lobby, then walked out the front door.

Sharp looked at the doorman and raised an eyebrow.

"Yes, sir," the doorman said.

"Taxi, please."

"Of course, sir."

The doorman raised a whistle to his lips and blew a shrill note. A taxi down the street – first at the cab stand – pulled down the block to the front door of Thurl's condo.

When the cab was on the way, Sharp spoke to the doorman.

"You work every day, don't you?"

"No, sir. Wednesday through Sunday. Monday and Tuesday are my days off."

He looked around conspiratorially, then continued.

"Gratuities are considerably better on the weekend, sir."

"Ah. Makes sense."

The doorman opened the cab door for Sharp, and Sharp put a five-credit coin into the doorman's left hand as he entered.

"Thank you, sir. Have a good day."

The doorman closed the cab door and the cab pulled away from the curb.

It was a self-driver, of course, but the self-drive cab that couldn't recognize a doorman's whistle had never been programmed.

Sharp gave it an address two blocks away from the Gotham Astoria, and sat back for the ride while he thought this through.

"So what are you doing again?"

Sharp continued to tinker with a forty-millimeter grenade round. It was over one-and-a-half inches in diameter and over three inches long. It looked like an oversized display model of a pistol round.

There were screw adjustments in the side of the ballistic cap on the front of the grenade body, with which Sharp tinkered.

Sharp glanced up at Fuller.

"Setting this round for delay. Two seconds after firing ought to do it."

"Two seconds? Isn't that cutting it kind of close, D.K?"

"Nah. Two seconds is a long time when things are happening. I don't want him to be able to react."

"Just so you keep your ass out of the way."

"Oh, I'll be good. Do you have that data on the limo for me?"

"Yeah. Piece of cake. They do limo work for the government officials here, so it was all part of the bid."

"The door latch and hinges?"

"Replaced with a latch and hinges that won't blow open."

"And the bulkhead between the passenger compartment and the driver compartment?"

"Is also armored."

"Excellent."

"Just be sure you get that door latched within two seconds."

Monday morning at six thirty found Sharp in the basement service spaces of Thurl's condo building. He was dressed in a zip-up coverall and work shoes, and carried a tool bag.

The nice thing about a coverall, work shoes, and a tool bag was that they got you into almost any place. In addition, they made you effectively invisible. You were immediately classified, sorted, and dismissed. No one took the time to note your appearance.

He also wore a wig and a cap. It was a less well-fitting wig than some of them, and the cap obscured that. Both would be discarded.

At quarter to seven, a man walked by him wearing the black slacks and red jacket and cap of a doorman. Sharp stood up from where he was pretending to work on a steam valve and shot him in the back of the neck with a small dart gun.

"Ow!"

He reached toward the back of his neck but did not complete the gesture. He sagged and went down like a puppet whose strings had been cut.

Sharp dragged him into the open janitor closet across the hall and closed the door. The coverall and work shoes, wig and cap all went into the tool bag. Dress shoes and a better-fitting wig in a different color came out.

It took just a couple of minutes and Sharp was properly dressed for the day as the doorman of Thurl's condo building.

Sharp exited the janitor closet, closing the door behind him, and set off for the lobby. He dropped the tool bag in the large basement garbage bin as he walked past.

The doorman job wasn't particularly difficult. Push the 'open door' button for people entering the building. Whistle for a cab for the occasional person leaving the building. Open and hold the door for people entering or exiting cabs and limos.

There were a lot of 'Good morning, sir' and 'Good morning, ma'am.'

At ten of eight, a limousine pulled up. Sharp walked up to the car and opened and held the door. He also reached up under his jacket and detached his left hand into the right breast pocket of his shirt.

Paul Thurl came out of the building and got into the limousine.

"Good morning, sir."

Thurl seated himself and nodded to the doorman.

Sharp bent his left arm across his body and hit the mental 'Fire' button on the forty-millimeter grenade launcher.

FOONT!

The grenade hit the padded bulkhead to the right of the small communicating window to the driver's compartment – which was closed – and stuck there.

Immediately upon firing, Sharp closed the door of the limousine firmly, so the latch was sure to catch. The car started to pull away from the curb…

BOOM!

The car shook with the force of the explosion but the armor held. The bulletproof windows were starred but intact, the view of the interior occluded by smoke and blood.

The anti-personnel round was designed for a kill radius of fifteen feet, while the rear passenger compartment of the limousine was seven feet long, seven feet wide, and merely four feet high. The shrapnel of the grenade shredded the passenger compartment and its occupant.

The car came to a stop and the driver and shotgun staggered out and collapsed on the ground. There would have been some overpressure in the driver's compartment due to the shared ventilation system.

Sharp grabbed at his chest, as if having a heart attack, as he staggered back to the building. In fact, he was reattaching his left hand over the muzzles of his forearm weapons.

He held himself up with his right arm against the building as he reattached the hand, then turned around to lean back against it. All attention of the people on the sidewalk was on the limousine.

Sharp shrugged out of the jacket, swept the cap and wig off his head, then walked around the corner of the building and down the block. Clean kill. Nice.

The doorman had effectively disappeared.

Dick Laramie, of the Federation Department of Justice office on Elizabeth, received a new mail message that morning.

Seize the assets of the late Paul Thurl pending adjudication of the compensation rights of his victims. Do it quietly.

Fuller was reading the news when Sharp got back to the Gotham Astoria.

"I didn't think you could do it, but that one was even messier," she said. "They may have trouble identifying the body."

"I'm sure they'll do fine."

Sharp got a fresh hotel towel and spread it on the dining room table, then went into the bedroom to get his normal left prosthetic and the gun-cleaning kit.

As he cleaned the forty-millimeter grenade launcher from his left weapons prosthetic, Fuller kept him apprised of the news as it developed.

"They say now, based on his identification, that it was Paul Thurl, billionaire investment wizard, and they noted that he was the second billionaire assassinated within four days."

Minutes passed while Sharp cleaned and lubricated the grenade launcher, then mounted it back in his weapons forearm.

"They say now that the doorman is missing. They just found his uniform jacket and cap, and a wig. The driver and shotgun have been taken to the hospital for observation, but they'll likely be OK."

Sharp took the weapons forearm and cleaning kit back into the bedroom and stowed them in his luggage. He returned to the living room to stand opposite Fuller.

She was already peeling out of her clothes, and Sharp followed her lead.

"Oh, and the actual doorman was discovered in a janitor's closet in the basement of the building. He'd been drugged. Shot with a tranquilizer dart from behind by a service worker."

"Enough talk."

The news flashes came to Dominic Trask via his open news feed. It had only been four days since the murder of Elton Thomas.

"My word."

He read all of the releases. A grenade? Well, once again, there was no doubt that Paul Thurl was completely and thoroughly dead. The police crime scene photos were most explicit.

Another closed-casket funeral, to be sure.

Once again, Trask was happy that he had thought to make his peace with D Branch when he detected them closing in on him. He had been more relaxed and at peace the last couple of weeks than he had been for over a decade. Since he had found out what Thomas, Thurl, and Anderson had done.

This Sharp fellow was certainly effective. A very dangerous man. Trask wondered if he would consider commercial employment once he qualified for retirement from his government job.

Unlikely, he supposed. That sort of fellow normally died with their boots on.

Cold-blooded murder wasn't an approved private-sector activity anyway.

Still nude, they were relaxing on the lounges out on the

balcony.

"What now, D.K?"

"Mark Anderson. Maybe Cam Flannery."

"And then?"

"And then I'm probably done here, Suzie. Any other cleanup can be done by someone else. These are the tough ones."

"Then what, D.K?"

He looked over at her. He caught mental glimpses of the probable future. Back up to *Medea* on the shuttle. The trip back to Humphreys. Saying goodbye to Camden and Thompsen and the kids.

Saying goodbye to Fuller.

That would be hard.

"I don't know, Suzie."

Recluse

That afternoon, Monday, Sharp and Fuller headed back to the beach. They had stayed in Gotham over the weekend prepping for the Thurl execution, and could use the break.

After dinner that night, they sat with Camden and Thompsen while the kids colored on the couches on the lanai.

"Thurl was pretty messy, Deke," Camden said.

"The system needs to send the message to people with money and power that certain behaviors will not be tolerated, Paul," Sharp said. "He couldn't just die in a car accident or something."

"For all that, it was quick," Thompsen said. "More than he deserved, actually."

"Yeah, quick but terrifying.," Camden said.

Fuller glanced over at the kids. They were absorbed in what they were doing and not listening.

"He was gone before he even had time to feel any pain," she said.

"Yeah, but most people want to end up being more than a stain on someone's upholstery, Suzie," Camden said. "That was horrific."

Sharp shrugged.

"Mission accomplished," he said. "What about Anderson?"

"He's gonna be difficult, D.K.," Thompsen said.

"Why?"

"We don't know where he is."

Sharp looked to Camden, who was nodding.

"He's got four or five places. He basically retired about ten years ago, and he rotates around among them. We never know where he's going to be. We don't even know which one he's at right now."

"He's retired?" Sharp asked.

"Yeah," Thompsen said. "Thomas and Thurl were in their mid-thirties when the piracy thing started. They were just approaching sixty when you took them down. Anderson was in his mid-fifties when the piracy plan came up. Thomas and Thurl needed him for his Navy contacts. He was buddies with Janos Stepic. That's how they got the ships diverted."

Sharp nodded. Janos Stepic had ultimately been the High Commissioner of the Federation, but he had been Defense Commissioner when the piracy plan started.

"He's pushing eighty now, and his health is failing," Camden said.

"That's a bit early," Sharp said.

Camden nodded. With medical advancements, most people now lived past a hundred.

"Yeah, but his family history is supportive of that," Camden said. "Short-lived bunch. That's why he retired early."

"And we don't know where he is now?" Sharp asked.

Thompsen shook her head.

"Nope. We can sometimes tell when he's been somewhere, but not where he is when he's there. He seems to have pulled back from society and lives in seclusion."

"Some people do that, D.K.," Fuller said. "Make their billions and then withdraw from society."

"What do they do with their time?" Sharp asked.

Camden shrugged.

"Read books? Watch movies? Don't know. But he's basically a recluse."

"Hmm. Maybe I can use my status as a Navy captain to access observation satellites."

"Observation satellites?" Thompsen asked.

"Sure," Sharp said. "Have to know what the weather is going to be like to make shuttle landings. No sense coming down in a hurricane or something. But those observations are recorded."

"We should be able to see his people show up to prep his next location, anyway, Deke," Thompsen said. "That would be a big help."

"Let me look into it. If I can get to it, I'll send you the pointer to the data."

Mark Anderson sighed.

The assassination – you could call it nothing else – of Elton Thomas had been curious. The assassination of Paul Thurl made it a pattern.

That pattern fit in with the assassination of his friend Janos Stepic last year.

The link, of course, between Janos Stepic on the one hand and Elton Thomas and Paul Thurl on the other was Mark Anderson. It was he who had been the go-between in setting up the piracy operation.

And now all three of them were dead.

He mentally kicked himself yet again for allowing himself to be cornered into it. But Thomas and Thurl had the goods on him. Evidence of past indiscretions that would be extremely damaging if they were released.

So Anderson had arranged the acquisition of warships for the piracy operation through Stepic. Stepic had gone on to use the pirates as evidencing a need for much greater military spending on the Navy, suited to going after the pirates, which had gotten the military contractors heavily on his side for his eventual rise to High Commissioner of the Federation.

Not that Anderson could complain. He had made money – a great deal of money – on the investments their group had made in the insurance and defense industries.

It had left him feeling dirty, though, and every atrocity the pirates committed reinforced that view. He had begun to expect that, sooner or later, it would all blow up on them. He had retired from his business a decade ago rather than continue to be associated with them.

And, last year, it had blown up, rather spectacularly. Janos Stepic assassinated. Several insurance industry and defense contractors. A couple of Navy admirals. The piracy operation destroyed, even to the space stations they had arranged.

He had expected then to be targeted as well. But it had all blown over and he was still alive.

His poking around with his Navy contacts indicated it was all over. And, while the Navy had taken credit, his Navy contacts had told him something else. It hadn't been the Navy behind it after all.

It had been D Branch.

The Navy was one thing. D Branch was something else altogether.

Now it looked like D Branch was cleaning up loose ends. They had twigged to the financing behind the whole thing and were now cleaning that up as well.

Anderson considered hiding from the inevitable, but hiding from D Branch was likely impossible, especially at his age and in his health.

Unlikely as it had once seemed, he had survived the rest of his life, or nearly so, without paying the price for his part, coerced as it was, in Thomas' scheme.

That was likely about to come to an end.

At lunch on Tuesday, Camden had progress to report.

"The satellite data helped a lot, Deke. We can tell now when Anderson changes locations. His own movements are small, but significant staff heads out to his new location in advance, and that we can see."

"There's another thing, D.K.," Thompsen said. "One of his locations is here on the coast."

"Really? Where?"

"About twenty miles down the coast."

"No kidding. Sounds like we may need to take the boat out again. Is he there now?"

"No," Thompsen said. "We're keeping an eye on it, though. It would be the best approach, though, if he comes out here. With scuba and an underwater scooter, you could get right up to his beach without being seen."

"I can do better than that. I'd better go out to the shuttle and fetch my underwater kit. I have a set of prosthetics for underwater work."

"That sounds fun," Fuller said.

"Oh, it is. What's more, it's effective. I just walk up on the beach, do the job, and leave the same way. No heavy extra equipment to take off and put back on. Nothing lying around to be tampered with or removed while I'm away from it. It's all with me the whole time."

"That would be perfect," Camden said. "Assuming, of course, he visits the beach any time soon."

"Keep an eye on him. I'll get my water kit this afternoon."

On Wednesday after breakfast, Sharp performed periodic maintenance on everything, then swapped out his prosthetics for his water kit. These prosthetics included longer, webbed fingers and toes for swimming, air tanks built into the arms and legs, the ability to adjust his flotation, and water-jet propulsion in his calves.

Sharp's air supply with his water kit was good for ten minutes. He could make ten miles an hour with his water-jet propulsion, and the batteries gave him a ten-mile range.

Once swapped over, he showed the setup to Fuller. He spread his fingers and toes to show the webbing, and pointed out the inlets for the water-jet in his calves. The water-jets outlets were in his heels.

"Wow. That's pretty slick, D.K. One question. Where did your, um, manhood go?"

"It retracts. Gives me less drag in the water. I got this women's bikini bottom to wear for modesty, because it was the only swimsuit that didn't have extra space for something that didn't stick out in this mode."

"Oh. OK. From the waist down, you look like a girl. Which isn't a bad thing, mind you, but if that was permanent, I would miss it."

Sharp chuckled.

"No, not permanent. But good in the water. I get a bit more speed, and it extends my battery life."

"But everything's still there?"

"Everything's still there, Suzie."

"OK. Good. Just checking."

That morning, Sharp put the water kit through its paces, made sure his mental battery and oxygen indicators were working properly, did some timed runs. Everything checked out.

Back on shore, Sharp removed his spent air bottles and called the resort to have staff pick them up and refill them. They were standard units, and they didn't have any trouble with them, returning them late that afternoon.

Sharp remounted the air bottles in his prosthetics and did periodic maintenance on the system again.

By dinnertime, he was ready for the mission he would perform if Anderson showed up at his beach estate.

Mark Anderson

Mark Anderson looked out at the mountain vista and sighed. He loved the mountains, but lately they had gotten him depressed. Stark in their beauty, yes, but there was just something about them.

Between his terminal illness and his expectation of a rather nasty end at the hands of D Branch, his mood was too fragile for their majesty.

Perhaps some time at the beach would be better. The weather there was excellent right now, and the smell of the ocean was full of life and vitality.

That was always good for his mood.

It had been two weeks of waiting, then Camden had news.

"He's moving, Deke."

"Where? Do we know?"

"Not yet. But his advance staff just left his mountain lodge for somewhere."

Hours later, there was an update.

"He's coming here, Deke. To the beach. The advance staff just showed up here."

"Excellent. What's the weather going to be like the next three days or so?"

"Rough seas for a couple days, but then great weather for a week."

"I'll reserve the boat."

They were a mile out to sea and three miles down the coast from Anderson's estate when Sharp stopped the boat.

"This should be good. Far enough away not to be threatening, but within my range for the round trip."

"When you come back, if you can't make it all the way, let us know where you are, Deke," Camden said. "We'll be watching for a call request."

Sharp nodded.

"Sounds good."

Sharp tucked his Ross Arms 8mm HP semiautomatic pistol into the holster in front of his women's bikini bottom.

"And you have the plans of the estate ready?" Thompsen asked.

"Yeah. I'm good."

"Hey, get this," Fuller said. "I'm watching in satellite view, and he's sitting out on the beach in a lounger."

"Does he have staff with him?" Sharp asked.

"No. He's alone."

"Couldn't be better," Sharp said. "Time to go."

He dropped off the swim platform into the water, rolled onto his back, and was soon motoring away from the boat with the water-jet propulsion.

"Why is he on his back?" Thompsen asked. "Isn't he going to go underwater?"

"He only has ten minutes of air," Fuller said. "He'll go underwater for the last mile."

"Oh. I see. Well, good luck, D.K."

Twenty-five minutes later, Deke Sharp peered up at the beach in front of him. Mark Anderson sat in an Adirondack chair on the beach, looking out to sea.

Deke got his feet under him on the bottom and walked out of the ocean up onto the beach.

"Good afternoon, Mr. Sharp. It is Deke Sharp, isn't it?"

"At your service. You were expecting me, Mr. Anderson?"

"Yes, Mr. Sharp. Not necessarily today, but at some point. Your dismissal of Mr. Thomas and Mr. Thurl from this earthly veil did not escape my attention. I expected to be on your list."

"And yet you sit out here on the beach, alone?"

Sharp glanced up at the house, two hundred yards distant.

"No one is coming from the house, Mr. Sharp. I have not called security."

Sharp raised an eyebrow, and Anderson continued.

"I am nearly eighty years old, Mr. Sharp, and from a short-lived family. I have a terminal illness, and the doctors say I have perhaps a year or a year and a half left, the end of which will be long and painful. Just deserts, I suppose, for what I have done.

"Elton Thomas and Paul Thurl coerced me into supporting their piracy plan over two decades ago. They needed my contacts with the Navy to procure the ships, so they blackmailed me into assisting their plan. I should have said no, but, fearful of their disclosures, I went along. I have regretted it ever since, especially when reports of pirate atrocities came in, but I had no way to stop it at that point.

"And now, facing a long and agonizing illness, I instead have the opportunity to die more quickly. You could, I suppose, walk away and leave me to that illness as a more fitting punishment, Mr. Sharp, but you need the example, don't you? That one should not offend in such a way, lest the system strike you down in retribution."

"That's correct, Mr. Anderson."

"As I suspected. So instead you offer me welcome escape from my oncoming troubles. A question, if I might, Mr. Sharp."

"Of course, Mr. Anderson."

"What of my assets, much of which were illicitly gained?"

"They will be seized by the Department of Justice for adjudication as to the compensation rights of the victims of the pirates."

"Oh, good. And the remainder, if any?"

"To your heirs."

"Very well. I realize you owe me nothing, Mr. Sharp, but I would ask one final favor."

"Yes, Mr. Anderson?"

"Make it quick."

"Very well. Goodbye, Mr. Anderson."

Anderson laid his head back in the chair and closed his eyes. Sharp raised the Ross Arms 8mm HP pistol and shot him once, low in the center of the forehead, just above the bridge of his nose.

That done, Sharp turned around and walked back into the sea from which he had come.

Dick Laramie, of the Federation Department of Justice office on Elizabeth, received a new mail message.

Seize the assets of the late Mark Anderson pending adjudication of the compensation rights of his victims. Do it quietly.

Sharp did the first mile or so of the trip back to the boat underwater, in case Anderson's security people got feisty. When the air ran out, he surfaced and rolled onto his back to keep his face out of the water. The range on his water-jet thrusters was more than enough for the entire trip, so he didn't end up swimming any of the way.

When he got to the boat, the kids were in the water with

Camden and Thompsen. Fuller helped him up onto the swim deck.

"We should get everybody out of the water and move the boat further away, in case Anderson's security tries to come after me."

"Do you expect it?" Fuller asked.

"No, but I don't like to take chances I don't need to take."

Camden had heard him, and he and Thompsen were already getting the children organized and headed toward the swim deck.

Sharp went below deck and Fuller followed him inside.

"Well, that was disturbing," Sharp said.

"In what way, D.K?"

"He was expecting me."

"He was?"

"Yes. He actually appreciated me giving him early release from some terminal illness he had. He basically asked me to shoot him."

"Wow."

"Yeah."

Sharp got in the shower and started removing his prosthetics one at a time. He washed them, and the connections on his stubs, then dried them off. One at a time he handed the swim-kit prosthetics to Fuller, and she handed him back the normal replacement. He salved the connection and mounted the prosthetic, then on to the next one.

Fuller stowed each of the cleaned swim-kit prosthetics in their case.

When Sharp was completely changed over, he took off the women's bikini bottom and took a regular shower. Fuller was relieved to see his genitals reappear when he un-retracted them.

Sharp got out of the shower and dressed. He stowed the pistol for now in the swim-kit case, which he locked, intending to clean it later, once ashore.

"How about a drink, D.K?"

"That sounds like a great idea."

Sharp and Fuller went up on the main deck. Camden was above, on the bridge, piloting the boat along the coast away from Anderson's estate and toward the resort. He was taking it easy, but keeping an eye behind for pursuit.

"Anybody following us?" Sharp called up.

"Nope. Nobody."

"Good."

They thought to give the kids more time in the water once they got closer to the resort, but, as they neared the resort, they saw that the kids were already sacked out on the couches on the main deck.

Camden maneuvered the boat in to the bungalows' dock and Thompsen tied it up. They all decamped the boat and headed to the bungalows, each of the adults carrying one of the kids but Sharp, who carried the case with his swim-kit.

Sharp called the resort for staff to come and collect the boat.

The kids were asleep on the couches for the afternoon nap after the boat ride. Thompsen and Camden were out on the lanai with them, watching the news feeds for any news of Anderson.

Sharp was inside, cleaning the pistol on a resort towel spread over the inside dining table. Fuller watched. Sharp rambled absently while he worked.

"It was really strange, Suzie. He welcomed me when I walked up out of the water. By name. I had a nervous eye on the house, but he said he would not call security. When I showed surprise, he explained that he had a terminal illness. A year, year and a half, after a long painful decline, and he would be gone.

"Thomas and Thurl blackmailed him into helping them. He didn't want to, but he feared disclosure more. But every time a report came in of a pirate atrocity, he regretted it. He said that leaving him to die such a painful death would be no more than he deserved, but he understood I needed the kill. As a warning to others.

"Then he asked me to make it quick."

"Geez. How weird."

"Yeah. All the people I've killed – all fighting me, all denying any guilt – and this is the one that bothers me. Go figure."

"So did you? Make it quick, I mean?"

"Yeah. One shot."

Sharp touched his right forefinger to the spot where the round had hit Anderson.

"Suzie, I didn't even break his sunglasses."

"Well, I can understand why that bothers you, D.K. Not what you trained for. Not what you expected. Not what you had yourself worked up to. Just boop, OK, job done. He's just as dead, though."

"Oh, yes. As you say, job done."

"So what now, D.K? Is that it?"

"I'm not sure, Suzie. I want to see what else you three get out of Trask's data. Maybe. Maybe not. There could be one more in there, I think."

"One of the attorneys? Like this Flannery guy?"

"Yeah. Easier job. Maybe I'll leave that one to someone else. My call. I just have to see what you guys come up with."

"So no frenetic adrenaline screw this afternoon?"

"No. No, I don't think so. Sorry, Suzie."

"That's OK, D.K. How about a nice, slow, tender screwing tonight instead?"

"That sounds nice, actually. Better fits my mood."

"Excellent. It's a date."

It was late that evening, after the kids were in bed.

"You need us to make another pass over Trask's data, Deke?" Camden asked.

"Yes. Is there anyone else we need to take care of before we leave? Or should we just head back to Humphreys."

"That'll be weird, won't it?" Thompsen asked. "To be home after so long?"

"It's only been a few months, Lydia," Fuller said.

"Yes, but it feels longer."

"What are the criteria, Deke?" Camden asked.

"Anyone who knew what Thomas and Thurl were up to — that it was a piracy operation — and took an active part to assist them anyway."

"So if someone helped out somehow in their scheme, but didn't know what their method was, they're out, and if someone knew their method, but didn't assist other than keeping quiet, they're out as well?"

"That's right. Incontrovertible proof they knew about the piracy and they assisted. Other than that, we can't prove 'aided and abetted piracy.'"

"OK. Got it. We'll see what we come up with, Deke."

Later still, Sharp lay on his back while Fuller did the work. Her ample breasts against his chest, her moans in his ear, she writhed atop him, impaled.

They delayed the denouement as long as they could. It was something of a metaphor for their time together, with the end of the mission looming in front of them.

Neither of them wanted it to end.

Final Research

Camden, Thompsen, and Fuller dove into the data once more while Sharp decompressed and watched the kids. They spent over a week at it before they were ready to report to Sharp on what they had found.

That afternoon, just after lunch, Camden and Thompsen briefed Sharp on their findings while Fuller watched the kids.

"First off, Deke, we didn't find evidence that any of the other investors in the group knew what Thomas and Thurl were up to. Only Anderson was brought into their plan, which they called the Balfours-Navy Play."

"Balfours after the spaceship insurance company, Balfours of Juliet?"

"Correct. They made other investments in the shipping insurance industry, but that's what they called it."

"And when the piracy started, they had no clue?"

"No, D.K.," Thompsen said. "They thought it was just good luck. Some investments work out, even though your reasons for making the investment aren't sound. They thought they just happened to have their money in the right place at the right time, and lucked out."

"Interesting."

"Cam Flannery is innocent, too. He was basically Dominic Trask's attorney. He learned about their involvement with the piracy the same time Trask did. In fact, Flannery was the guy Trask had hire the private investigator who turned up the cash flow from the investment fund to the piracy operation."

"So Flannery's off the hook as well."

"Right. Thomas' attorney, a guy named J. Philip Maxwell,

however, is not. When Thomas started asking him pointed questions, he always answered, 'In the hypothetical case in which....' That sort of thing. Maintaining deniability. That went away over time, and some things he wrote to Thomas indicated he knew."

"And he continued to work on Thomas' dealings with this particular investment?"

"Oh, yes. Aiding and abetting is not a problem with this guy. He was in it up to his neck."

"And, of course, he made a lot of money camping on the group's investments."

"A ton of money, Deke."

"But so did Cam Flannery, D.K.," Thompsen said. "The attorneys for the various members of the investment group often piggybacked on their client's investments. That doesn't mean they knew what was going on. Mostly they didn't, for any of the investments the group made."

"But Maxwell did?" Sharp asked. "He knew explicitly about the piracy and Thomas' role in it?"

"Oh, yes. No question, Deke."

"All right. Looks like one more, then we go home. So where is Maxwell now?"

"Retired, but living the good life in Gotham."

"And you have all the particulars for me?"

"Oh, yes. Also, a write-up on everybody else. What we found – and didn't find – for the members of the investment group and their attorneys."

"Does that include Thomas, Thurl, and Anderson?"

"Yes, Deke."

"Excellent. All of that is going to have to go to D Branch's analysis section when we finish here."

"And Suzie has some criminal referrals for Humphreys and

Ariel DoJ as well, D.K.," Thompsen said.

"The guys who manipulated police records to get us arrested?"

"Yes."

"Good."

"But Trask skates, Deke?" Camden asked.

"No, he pays twenty to thirty billion credits in reparations and prevails on his partners to pony up as well."

"He buys himself out of criminal prosecution, then?"

Sharp shrugged.

"The world is imperfect. We wouldn't have all this data without his cooperation. And I predict he will keep his nose very, very clean going forward. That's a much better outcome than a big trial where he gets off on a technicality on appeal and pays nothing to the victims."

"Yeah, that's basically what Suzie said."

"And she's right."

"It just doesn't seem right somehow that the big-money guy gets off."

"The big-money guy usually gets off. But don't forget, Paul. Trask got unwittingly snookered into an illegal operation by his partners. These other people were guilty of official corruption while on the taxpayers' dime."

"At Trask's request, though, Deke. He bribed them."

"Ah, but Trask isn't the guy who swore oath to uphold the law in return for a cushy job and a nice pension, now is he? They are. Big difference."

"OK. I can see that."

Then it was Sharp's turn to do research. Where did Maxwell live? What were his habits? What security did he have? What were the holes in his security? How might Sharp take advantage of those?

Sharp settled in to learn as much as he could about J. Philip Maxwell.

He didn't get much.

"Maxwell is turning out to be hard to research," Sharp said to the group two days later.

"Not finding anything, Deke?" Camden asked.

"Not finding anything useful. A man of temperate habits. Doesn't go out much since he retired. Lives at home with his wife of forty years. Three kids, all out of the house. Wealthy from his investments, though maybe one percent of Trask's wealth. Which is still a lot of money. Has published four novels – murder mysteries – which have sold well. Has a contract for three more."

"Wait," Fuller said. "He's a writer?"

"Apparently so. Why?"

"Well, that's why he doesn't go out much. I dated a writer at one point. Great guy, if you could ever pry him away from the book he was currently writing. I gave up."

"So you're saying...."

"Find out where he writes, D.K. You'll find him there ninety percent of the time. Or more. Are there any interviews with him?"

"A couple, I think."

"See if they ask him about his writing habits. Common question for an author interview. Plan around catching him writing and doing the job then. You could probably walk right up to him and club him over the head. He won't even see you coming if he's writing."

"You're kidding."

"Not at all. I once walked in on my boyfriend when he was

writing. Completely naked, just to get his attention. He didn't notice I was naked. 'Hi, hon. Not right now. This is getting good.'"

Sharp had thought the man who could ignore Suzie Fuller being completely naked didn't exist. Couldn't possibly exist.

"Wow."

"Yeah. Catch him writing, D.K. Make the job easy."

That night, in the wee hours, Sharp logged into the dog suit via the comm link from *Medea* to the shuttle. He had the dog suit get an extra balloon and paraglider out of the equipment cabinet and put them into the passenger compartment. The dog suit then left the shuttle and set out from the Elizabeth Navy Shuttleport on foot.

Running cross-country, the dog suit passed out from under the shuttleport controlled airspace. Once clear, Sharp deployed the balloon he had mounted previously, and the dog suit rode it to five thousand feet. At that point, Sharp cut the balloon loose, letting it pull the paraglider free of the deployment bag as it went.

Almost at the coast, Sharp kept the dog suit over land, where the updraft of the warmer land would give him longer range. He directed the dog suit to fly toward the resort.

A mile down the coast, Sharp steered the paraglider for the coast, landing on the beach. The dog suit hit at a run, cutting the paraglider loose when it hit. It ran along the beach in the pitch darkness of the late night.

Half an hour after it left the shuttle, the dog suit walked up onto the lanai of Sharp and Fuller's bungalow.

"Cute trick, D.K."

"Getting it into the city will be harder."

"Nah. I got it."

Fuller told him the plan while Sharp plugged the dog suit in to recharge and mounted the other balloon and paraglider.

The next day, Camden was concerned with the plan.

"You're sure this is OK, Deke? I mean, we've sort of been in hiding since we've been here. Doesn't this give us away?"

Sharp shrugged.

"All the people who would want us dead are dead themselves, Paul."

"Still, D.K." Lydia said. "I would feel better about the whole thing if we decamped our hotels and were waiting for you in the shuttle. You don't take chances, you said."

Sharp looked at her for a moment, then nodded.

"That's probably fair."

He looked around the bungalow.

"I guess it's time to pack."

After lunch, the resort's van delivered them and all their vacation gear to *Medea*'s shuttle at the Elizabeth Navy Shuttleport. They loaded everything aboard the shuttle.

Everybody except Sharp then took a rental car to the Gotham Astoria in town, while Sharp stretched out on the shuttle's command chair and took a nap. He needed to be awake late tonight.

At the Gotham Astoria, Fuller packed her and Sharp's things while Camden and Thompsen packed up their suite. They ordered dinner into the suites for one last time.

After dinner, the Gotham Astoria's van delivered Camden, Thompsen, the kids, and all the luggage to *Medea*'s shuttle at the Elizabeth Navy Shuttleport.

Fuller, though, took the rental car back to the resort. They had not checked out yet, and left the dog suit in Sharp and

Fuller's bungalow. Fuller told the self-drive rental to back up to the bungalow door and open the trunk.

Sharp, now awake in the shuttle, logged into the dog suit when Fuller called to say she was ready. Under Sharp's control, the dog suit walked out to the car and climbed into the trunk.

Fuller headed back out to the shuttleport in the rental car.

"Sorry about that, D.K. I guess you didn't have to run the dog suit into the resort last night, if we were going to all be out here anyway."

"That's OK, Lydia. I wanted to do a test run on all that stuff anyway. Now I know it all works, I'm much happier."

"OK. Good. So when you're done, you'll come back here?"

"Right. And then we'll lift off for *Medea*."

It was dark when Fuller got to the shuttle after the detour to the resort. Sharp had taken some dinner with him – an extra meal ordered with lunch – to the shuttle when they left the resort.

"You ready, D.K?"

"Yeah. All fed and rested."

"Well, let's go."

Sharp walked out to the rental car. Fuller opened the trunk and Sharp got into the dog suit, first removing his regular prosthetics and then connecting his knees into the shoulders of the dog suit. He lay back in the passenger compartment and nodded to Sharp.

"OK, Suzie."

"I won't see you at the other end. Good luck, D.K."

Sharp nodded.

"See you back at the shuttle. You'll know everything's all right when the shuttle starts its engines for warm-up."

"Got it."

Fuller closed the trunk and got into the rental car. She ordered it to head into Gotham, and gave it the address of an alley next to Maxwell's condominium building.

J. Philip Maxwell

The rental car spoke to Fuller as it maneuvered in downtown Gotham.

"We are approaching the alley that corresponds to the address you provided."

"Back into the alley and park ten feet past the sidewalk."

"Understood."

Fuller switched to her virtual terminal and sent a message to Sharp.

"Almost there, D.K."

"All right, Suzie."

It was a bit after midnight now, and this was a residential quarter of the downtown. The sidewalks were quiet, most residents using cabs to get home from whatever night life they had attended.

The cab pulled past the alley, then engaged its reverse gear and backed around the corner, across the sidewalk, and into the alley. It cleared the sidewalk by ten feet, then stopped.

"Open the trunk," Fuller said.

The trunk opened, and Fuller saw Sharp get out. He rapped the fender twice.

"Close the trunk," Fuller said.

The trunk closed and latched.

"Return to the Elizabeth Navy Shuttleport, pad number one eighteen."

"Understood."

Using the camera-eyes on the dog suit's head, Sharp watched the rental car pull out of the alley and depart. Then he looked at the side of the building he stood next to. Based on the external finishes, it was the correct building. He counted windows across on the third floor above him. Check.

OK, the sixth window across of the lower floors corresponded to the window he wanted on the thirty-third floor. Not a penthouse, but an upper floor, with great views. Even a balcony.

The window he wanted, though, was the office window. Straight up from right there. Just to one side, then.

Sharp deployed the sticky pads of the dog suit's feet and started to climb. He let the dog suit do the climbing in automatic mode. He didn't feel good interfering with it. He was more likely to misstep than the onboard processor was.

Sharp stayed in the armored passenger compartment and watched as the machine climbed.

The one bit of discomfort was that he was hanging from his knees, upside-down in the passenger compartment, as the dog suit climbed.

Well, based on progress so far, it wouldn't be long.

When Sharp got to the thirty-third floor, there was a design feature on the building that allowed the dog suit to hang on with the sticky pads, making him more secure. He ordered the unit to rotate to one side, so he was horizontal on his right side within the passenger compartment.

Sharp was perched to one side of what should be Maxwell's office window, which, unlike most of them on the way up, still had a light on.

Sharp extended the dog suit's head to the edge of the window and peered around the corner. The occupant was working at a terminal, facing to one side, his profile to the window. Sharp waited until the occupant looked to one side, at some map on his desk, so he could get a full-face view.

Yup. J. Philip Maxwell.

Good. Now do the job and get out of here.

The windows on this building were, per code, a double thickness of tempered glass.

Not a problem for the fifty-caliber.

Sharp deployed the balloon, letting it rise above him as it filled. He did not fill it completely, but just enough to hold him steady at this altitude.

He released the grip of three of the feet, hanging onto the window frame feature with the left front hand of the dog suit, his weight being held up by the balloon.

Sharp took aim with the fifty-caliber rifle, sighting it with the camera-eye on the breech end of the barrel. He lined up the head shot.

He was prepared to fire more than once if required to clear the glass, or if the bullet was deflected. But the tungsten-penetrator-point round he had selected for this mission had no problem bulling through the glass.

The five-hundred-grain platinum round shattered both window panes and kept going, hitting Maxwell in the right temple. It continued through his head and embedded itself in the concrete wall behind him, in the center of a lurid splash of blood and brains.

Maxwell's head hit the keyboard, then he fell off the chair to one side. Toward Sharp, with the huge exit wound on the left side of his face showing.

Yeah, that there fellow is dead.

Sharp turned on the gas to the balloon and released his grip on the window frame.

The dog suit shot up into the air.

Dick Laramie, of the Federation Department of Justice office on Elizabeth, received a new mail message, though he wouldn't actually see it until morning.

Seize the assets of the late J. Philip Maxwell pending adjudication of the compensation rights of his victims. Do it quietly.

Once that is complete, you may announce that the Navy's actions against the funding sources for the piracy operation that was terminated last year have completed. You may also announce FDoJ's role in seizing the assets of criminals Thomas, Thurl, Anderson, and Maxwell for compensation to the victims of piracy.

Sharp blind-copied the FDoJ mail to Otto Pasha back on Ariel. It was currently morning in New Destin, so Pasha saw it right away. He made a call to Admiral Kurt Jurgens, Chief of Naval Operations for the Federation Navy on Meredith.

"Good afternoon, Otto," Jurgens said, it being afternoon in the capital of Meredith.

"Good morning, Kurt."

"I imagine you're calling about that cross-jurisdictional request to hold Deke Sharp at any navy facility for transfer to New Destin police department."

"Actually, I wasn't, Kurt. Has there been any result on that?"

"Yes. JAG denied the request. The Navy will not hold Deke Sharp or anyone on his ship or under his command for transfer to local authorities, as it might interfere with Navy operations."

"That's pretty strong."

"It's happened before," Jurgens said drily.

"Interesting. I think New Destin P.D. has also rethought its approach to D Branch since that request was filed, Kurt."

"I wouldn't be surprised, Otto. But this gives me a precedent. No need to run things through JAG in the future. I already know what they will say."

"Excellent. Good news. Actually, Kurt, I was calling about something else. You're about to get the credit for rolling up the funding sources that set up that piracy operation in the first place."

"This the brouhaha I saw about what the media is calling 'The Billionaire Hunter' on Elizabeth, Otto?"

"That's the one, Kurt. It was an investment play. We buy up stock in shipping insurance companies and defense contractors, then we use a piracy operation to drive up the stock prices."

"How many people were involved, Otto?"

"Four."

"Four? That's it? The pirates killed how many thousands of people over the years, so four people could make more money?"

"The whole investment group was a dozen people, but only four people knew about the piracy part of the investment. They called it marketing and lobbying in their plans."

"And the status of those four now, Otto?"

"I have just been advised that, as of this morning in Gotham, all four have passed, Kurt."

"Good. Miserable bastards."

"Oh, and FDoJ is seizing all their assets for compensation to the victims. They'll be announcing that this morning. They're also going to announce that the *Navy's* operation against the pirates' original funding source has concluded."

"You giving us credit again, Otto?"

"Yes, Kurt."

"Well, thanks for that. Send me some details, if you would.

We may even issue a press release on this one."

"Will do. Take care, Kurt."

The mails sent to FDoJ and Pasha, Sharp logged into *Medea* and sent the warm-up message from *Medea* to the shuttle. He also requested takeoff clearance from Elizabeth Navy Shuttleport for an hour hence.

Back on the shuttle, Fuller was a bundle of nerves until the shuttle shuddered as the turbines started up. They wound higher as they warmed up, but Fuller paid no attention.

She was celebrating.

Deke Sharp was OK. The mission was over.

They were outta here.

Of course, Sharp still had to make it to the shuttleport without making a hole in the ground.

He cut the balloon loose at seven thousand feet. It pulled the paraglider from its deployment bag as before. After a brief, disconcerting fall, the paraglider unfolded and bit at the air.

Sharp turned the paraglider toward the shuttleport twenty miles distant, and checked his map for rising heat sources to fly over in extending his range. The infrared vision of the dog suit's camera eyes helped.

Sharp was approaching controlled airspace when he finally ran out of altitude. The dog suit hit the ground running, cutting the paraglider loose as soon as it hit the ground.

Sharp ran the final few miles to the shuttleport. As he ran up to pad one-eighteen, he cycled the shuttle door. He didn't bother with the ramp. He just jumped inside.

"Deke!" Fuller cried, but there was no one to hug, just the metal dog suit.

Then Sharp opened the cover of the passenger compartment and levered himself up into a centaur-like position.

"You're OK!"

"Of course, I'm OK."

"Mission completed?" Camden asked.

"Mission completed. So, weightlessness pills everybody. Sarah in the command chair, the boys in the jump seats, and adults on the floor. The adults need to tether to the pull-up handholds, and you all need a cushion for your heads."

They all stood and stared at him.

"Well, come on, everybody. Let's get out of here. Those engines are about ready."

At that, everyone moved at once.

Five minutes later, Sharp gave the command to *Medea* in orbit.

"*Medea*, shuttle returning to ship. Operate shuttle in normal occupied mode."

"Aye, Sir. Shuttle returning to the ship in normal occupied mode."

The shuttle's engines spooled up from idle to a high-pitched whine over the next minute, and then they were away.

On the way to *Medea*, Sharp called Otto Pasha. They had communicated through Sharp's Project Notes file to protect the team and their location from discovery, but that was no longer necessary.

"Hi, Otto."

"Hi, Deke. Mission accomplished, I take it?"

"Yes."

"Ah. Given that you were calling in, I figured you and your team were out of danger."

"Yes, we're on the way up to *Medea*."

"And the resolution, Deke?"

"Four executed. All clean kills."

"You're the best, Deke. And the evidence?"

"Incontrovertible."

"You have those packages for me?"

"Of course, Otto."

"Good. FDoJ and the Navy are both going to want those."

"We also have a large data map from which that evidence was drawn, but that should stay internal to D Branch."

"That's Trask's data?"

"Yes. Lots of confidential stuff in there. He didn't hold back."

"OK, Deke. We can do that."

"There are some other things hanging, though, now that the mission is over. What's my status with the Navy, Otto?"

"Neither you nor anyone on your ship or under your command will be held by Navy authorities on local warrants. That's directly from JAG, and it's iron-clad."

"Nice. What about Ariel and Humphreys jurisdictions? New Destin P.D. was pretty annoyed with me there for a while."

"Not a problem on Ariel, Deke. The Department of Justice here told the police that, once they had violated your civil rights, they were operating outside the law. That made your resistance justified. And there were to be no police reprisals against you. Any slow learners would be indicted for further civil rights violations against you."

"Wow."

"Yes. My understanding is that the chairman of the Senate Judiciary Committee leaned all over the DoJ to crack down on police overreach. He was most insistent."

"That's surprising."

"My understanding is that he is a personal friend of Daphne

Duplay, and was not amused at their treatment of her."

"Ah. That explains a lot."

"Indeed. So you are now on the way to Humphreys?"

"We will be soon. Do you know what the status of Fuller, Camden, and Thompsen are on Humphreys?"

"No, I'll have to inquire. You, too, right, Deke?"

"Yes, but I won't go down to the planet. Not this time at least. Probably best to have it resolved, though."

"I will make inquiries."

"All right, Otto. That's it, I guess."

"OK, Deke. Nice job on Elizabeth. We finally got that all cleaned up."

"I think so, Otto. Unless analysis section finds something else in Trask's data, but we went through it pretty thoroughly."

"All right, Deke. Excellent. Good spacing."

Leaving Elizabeth

When the thrust dropped to one gravity, Deke Sharp released his grip on the floor handholds and walked over to the cabinet where the dog suit was kept. Fuller got up off the floor and joined him.

Sharp disconnected his knees from the dog suit's shoulders and sat in the passenger compartment while Fuller handed him his normal prosthetics, which she had retrieved from the rental car's trunk and stowed earlier when she got back to the shuttle after dropping him off at Maxwell's condo in Gotham.

He connected his normal prosthetics and climbed out of the passenger compartment, then logged into the dog suit. He walked it into the storage cabinet, then closed and latched the door.

"The dog suit is nice for some activities, Suzie, but it's always nice to be back on two legs."

Fuller nodded.

"Still, it's an amazing contraption, D.K."

"Oh, yes."

The shuttle docked with *Medea* at Elizabeth Station without any issues, and they were soon back in the ship.

Of course, it was at zero gravity.

The kids let out a cheer and floated for the other shuttle, their normal home aboard *Medea*. They had not been able to take all their toys to the surface on Elizabeth, and now they had them all back.

"I talked to Otto when we were on the way up. The Navy has decided anyone with me on *Medea* is immune to Navy detention in the name of any local warrant, so you can all walk around the station. Even go to the spinning portion for normal gravity if you want."

"I would just as soon have normal gravity on the way home, D.K.," Thompsen said. "Did Otto say anything about our legal status on Humphreys."

"He said he would look into it, Lydia."

"I can look into it as well, D.K., if we're out from under communications silence," Fuller said. "Humphreys DoJ will know, and I can check in. With one of my alias accounts, if it comes to that."

"That's probably a good idea, Suzie. Regardless of what they tell Otto, you're likely to get the straight scoop from internal documents."

"I'll check on it."

"What's the ship's status, Deke?" Camden asked.

"She should be completely stocked and ready to go, Paul. I just need to do inventory and make sure that's true. That something didn't get omitted."

Camden nodded.

"Always check yourself."

"When dealing with space? Oh, yes."

"Did Otto say anything about Elizabeth, D.K?" Fuller asked.

"Yes. He said 'Nice job.'"

"That's it?"

"In D Branch, Suzie, that's as good as it gets."

Helen Maxwell woke up at four o'clock that morning. Phil still hadn't come to bed. She sighed and got out of bed. Time to go pry him away from his latest novel.

Honestly, he was obsessive about his writing.

She knocked on his office door, then entered. The completely glassless window, the thousands of pebbles of shattered tempered glass on the floor, and Maxwell down on the floor, the gaping exit wound on top, all hit her at once.

She shrieked and slammed the door as she ran down the hall to the living room.

"Police?" she said shakily. "My husband's been murdered."

When Dick Laramie of the Federation Department of Justice office on Elizabeth got into the office that morning, he checked his mail first thing.

"Oh, shit."

"What's the matter?" Mark Benson asked. "Another execution?"

"Yeah. They hit J. P. Maxwell."

Laramie was hitting the news feeds now. The first police photos were available to him.

"The mystery writer? That's the guy you like, right?"

"Yeah. He writes the best stuff. Well, not any more. Popped him right in his office at home. Looks like a head shot with a fifty-cal."

"Damn. That had to be messy."

"Yeah. It is. The mail says it's the last one. We need to seize his assets, then we can announce the Navy's operation is concluded."

"Navy's operation? I thought it was D Branch."

"Yeah. I guess D Branch is letting the Navy take the credit."

"The Navy got the credit last year as well. You think that was D Branch, too?"

"Probably. The Navy could never get the pirates before, but they sure did get them last year. Somebody did, anyway."

"Wow. Just doesn't pay to mess with some people."

Laramie stared at his screen for several seconds.

"I wonder if they'll publish whatever he was working on."

"But if it's not finished...."

"It would still be worth reading."

Dominic Trask checked the news feeds the first thing when he arrived in the office that morning.

Phil Maxwell? Good. That slimy bastard deserved it. He was in on the whole thing from the get-go, and he had lied to Cam Flannery about it.

Some lawyers deserved the reputation most people applied to the entire profession. Trask wasn't one of those people. He had known and worked with some excellent, honest attorneys.

Maxwell wasn't one of them.

Trask accessed the police crime scene photos. Yuck. Messy. At least it was quick.

Probably better than Maxwell deserved.

It took a few hours before *Medea* was ready to go. Sharp adjusted the supplies a bit, mostly adding some things as a just-in-case move. Camden and Thompsen took the kids to pick out some new coloring books for the two-week trip to Humphreys, and to get out of zero gravity for a while.

Fuller was burning up the interplanetary connection to Humphreys. Sharp didn't know what that was all about, but he figured she'd tell him when she had something to report.

Finally, they had it all together, and Sharp requested departure clearance. They got a slot only thirty minutes away.

When the slot opened, *Medea*, still transponding as FNS *Hecate*, dropped away from Elizabeth Station and headed out of the system.

The envelope was a day away.

Sharp called Pasha to let him know they had departed Elizabeth, and to inquire about the situation on Humphreys.

"Everything's OK on Humphreys, Deke. They got all that cleared up. Nothing outstanding on any of you."

"You sure, Otto?"

"Got it from the assistant state's attorney in Humphreys DoJ New Denver office, Deke. I would think that's pretty good."

"What's his name, Otto?"

"Eugene Simmons."

"Got it. OK. Thanks, Otto."

When Fuller dropped out of virtual terminal for supper, Sharp relayed the news to her.

"Otto says there's no problem with Humphreys, Suzie. He talked to an assistant state's attorney in the New Denver office of Humphreys DoJ, and he told Otto all that had been cleaned up."

"Which assistant SA, D.K? Or wait. Better yet. Let me guess. Gene Simmons."

"Got it in one. What's going on?"

"There's an arrest order for us. 'Armed and extremely dangerous. Use overwhelming force.' And it's signed by…?"

"Eugene Simmons, if I had to guess."

"Yep. Now what do we do, D.K? It's extremely hard to arrest an assistant state's attorney without him finding out what's going on."

"Not for the Federation, it's not."

"But is it a Federation matter, D.K? Yeah, he's corrupt, but isn't that a planetary matter?"

"Is he the guy that did the original arrest order for Trask?"

"Yeah."

"And we have the evidence in Trask's mails?"

"Oh, yeah. Plenty of evidence."

"And then Trask wired him the money, right?"

"Right! So it is a Federation matter, because the bribe money was interplanetary."

"Correct. And now, as a result of that bribe, he's lied to D Branch on an official inquiry. Also a Federation matter."

"So now what, D.K? You know the Federation boys better than I do."

"Make me up an evidence packet on this guy. I'll add the conversation with Otto. Then I'll send it all back to Elizabeth FDoJ before we hit the envelope."

"You think they'll act on it?"

"Oh, yes. I suspect they will."

It was late in the day that J. P. Maxwell had been killed that Dick Laramie received another communication from the same alias address as the execution notices. This one, though was a video message.

A man – his avatar, really – in Navy captain's uniform addressed him from the screen.

"Mr. Laramie.

"Please find attached an evidence packet on one Eugene Simmons. He is an assistant state's attorney in the New Denver offices of the Humphreys Department of Justice.

"Mr. Simmons is corrupt, and has accepted interstellar payments to manipulate police records on Humphreys violating the civil rights of Federation citizens Paul Camden, Lydia Thompsen, Suzanne Fuller, and Deke Sharp. This is a violation of the Federation criminal code.

"Mr. Simmons, when questioned about the current legal status of Camden, Thompsen, Fuller, and Sharp by D Branch in an official communication, lied about the current status. This is also a violation of Federation criminal code.

"I would appreciate it if you would forward this video and the attached materials to the appropriate Federation Department of Justice personnel on Humphreys for action against Mr. Simmons.

"I am heading now to Humphreys.

"Thank you, Mr. Laramie.

"Captain Deke Sharp.

"FNS *Medea.*"

Laramie muttered under his breath, then raised his voice.

"Mark! You have to see this."

Mark Benson watched the video, then turned to Laramie.

"This came from the same address as the seizure notices?"

"Yes."

"So this is the guy who offed Maxwell and the others? A Navy guy, like they said?"

"You missed something. Look again."

Laramie pulled up the first frame of the video as a still photograph.

"Notice anything?"

"No. What am I missing?"

"Something that isn't there," Laramie said.

Benson stared for a few more seconds, then snapped his fingers.

"No decorations. Dick, you don't make Navy captain without decorations."

"And what's the one outfit that doesn't give out commendations, Mark?"

"D Branch."

"Yup. Commendation for what? Nothing happened. We weren't involved."

"So Sharp is a—"

"D Branch wet-work guy. Field operative or something like that. Yeah."

"What are you going to do, Dick?"

"I'm going to send this all on to FDoJ on Humphreys with a recommendation they act on this guy before 'Captain' Deke Sharp gets there and shoots him."

Laramie shook his head.

"Mark, why do some people seem to think it's ever a good idea to fuck around with D Branch?"

An hour after he sent the message to Dick Laramie at FDoJ Elizabeth, Sharp got a video answer back.

"Captain Sharp:

"Thank you for the evidence package and other information on Eugene Simmons of Humphreys DoJ.

"I have sent this information on to Federation DoJ on Humphreys with a recommendation they take action against Simmons before your arrival at Humphreys.

"Thank you, Captain Sharp.

"Dick Laramie.

"Federation DoJ, Elizabeth."

"Eugene Simmons may not be a problem by the time we get to Humphreys, Suzie."

"Why not, D.K?"

"I sent your evidence package to FDoJ on Elizabeth with a request they send it on to FDoJ Humphreys, and noting I was on my way to Humphreys. I just got a message back saying they sent it on with a recommendation that Humphreys FDoJ act against Simmons before I get there."

"Why would they do that, D.K?"

"Because I sent it from the same mail alias I used to tell them to seize the assets of the four dead piracy funders on Elizabeth, often within minutes of the execution."

"Oh, ho! So they know you're D Branch."

"Or can make a pretty good guess."

"Well, that makes sense, then."

A day out of Elizabeth, *Medea* hit the envelope and disappeared from normal spacetime. Sharp brought her on course for Humphreys and brought her up to ten gravities.

Then they all settled in for the two-week trip to Humphreys.

Arrival At Humphreys

Deke Sharp was taking a turn watching the kids when Sarah came up to him.

"Are we going home now, Uncle Deke? To our real house?"

"Yes, Sarah. This trip is coming to an end, and all of you will be going back to your regular home."

Sarah nodded.

"Are you and Aunt Suzie going home, too?"

"Yes, Sarah. Aunt Suzie and I are both going home, too."

"Will we see you again, Uncle Deke?"

"Oh, I'm sure you will, Sarah, but it could be a long time. I live on another planet, and it takes a long time and a lot of money to change planets."

"Are you going to miss us, Uncle Deke?"

"I'm going to miss you a great deal, Sarah."

"What about Aunt Suzie? Is she going to another planet, too?"

"No, Aunt Suzie lives on the same planet as you do."

"Are you going to miss Aunt Suzie, Uncle Deke?"

That hit Sharp hard. Oh, yes. He would miss Suzie.

"Yes, Sarah. I'm going to miss Suzie, too."

"Maybe you should stay on our planet then, Uncle Deke."

"I can't do that, Sarah. My work is on another planet."

"That's too bad. That would be more fun."

Sarah gave Sharp a hug and then went back to her coloring book, leaving Sharp to consider the future.

On his last visit to Humphreys – the trip that ended with the shootout with police and fleeing in *Medea*'s two shuttles –

Sharp had set *Medea* to transpond the ship ID of FNS *Hera*. He didn't want to do that this time, in case things weren't settled yet.

While decelerating toward Humphreys, he changed the transponder from *Hecate*, which he had used on Elizabeth, back to *Medea*.

Decelerating while in the envelope was always very fast, so it was near the end of the trip that Sharp steered *Medea* around a sharp u-turn to align its thrusters against their current velocity. The thrusters remained firing, so they had gravity for the entire turn.

Medea was also aimed to one side of Humphreys. Especially on long trips, one didn't aim directly at the planet of one's destination. A navigational miscalculation could result in disaster, both for the ship and the planet.

Medea dropped out of the envelope just short of and to one side of Humphreys. At frigate speeds, which Sharp was careful to maintain when in normal spacetime, they were just over a day from the Navy's orbital Humphreys Station.

As soon as they were out of the envelope, they were back in touch with the communications network. Fuller immediately logged in to one of her supplemental accounts at Humphreys DoJ. She was not happy when she logged off.

"Those fuckers," she said.

"What's going on, Suzie?" Sharp asked.

"They have me down as having quit the agency. And they stopped paying me, from the time we left."

"Ouch."

"Did that screw up your bills, Suzie?" Thompsen asked. "Your rent and utilities and all are auto-pay, right? Did those get screwed up?"

"No, because someone else has been making payments to my account. Big payments. From some outfit called D. B. Analytics."

Sharp and Thompsen both laughed. Fuller looked back and forth between them.

"What?" she asked.

"D. B. Analytics is an alias of D Branch," Sharp said.

"Really. But those are big payments, D.K. Three times my normal salary."

"Yeah, that's about right. Double for consulting rate, then half again for hazard pay. You were basically in a hot zone."

Camden had gone into virtual terminal and now came back to the here and now.

"Us, too, Deke. Both of us. D Branch paying us?"

"Yeah.

"Nice."

"Oh, one other thing, D.K.," Fuller said.

"Yes?"

"Eugene Simmons has been arrested by the Federation Police on Federation charges, and is being held without bond as a flight risk."

"Excellent. So what about your job, Suzie?"

"What I am going to do is use one of my supplemental accounts to re-activate my actual user account – which the IT morons have suspended – and then call the Humphreys AG and give him a piece of my mind."

"Oh, my," Thompsen said.

Sharp just nodded. He actually felt sorry for the AG.

Suzie Fuller with a bagful of attitude was a force of nature.

Frederick Gammon III, the planetary attorney general of Humphreys, sat at his desk and contemplated the events of the last four months. It was not a pretty picture.

First, an arrest order had been issued for one of his senior investigators, one who worked financial corruption cases. Common enough to have anti-corruption people involved in corruption themselves, but certainly not a good look for his organization.

Second, when police moved in to arrest that investigator, it had ended up in a wild shootout in a public place – a seaside resort – in which three police officers were killed, two injured, and the investigator escaped, along with, presumably, her cronies.

Now the Federation Police had arrested an assistant state's attorney from his office – right here in this building – on Federation charges of official corruption and civil rights violations. They were refusing to plea deal, and were going to throw the book at him.

None of this was good public relations for the department, or for himself, for that matter.

His display announced an incoming call. When he looked at the caller identification, his eyebrows shot up.

Suzanne Fuller. The senior investigator who had fled justice four months ago. And it was a Humphreys local call.

Gammon accepted the call and the display showed an attractive woman in her early thirties.

"Ms. Fuller."

"Hi, Fred. How ya doin'?"

Gammon raised an eyebrow at her and she laughed.

"Hey, Fred, you guys fired me, so I owe you no more respect than a passerby in the street. Rather less, I would think."

"You were listed as having resigned when you fled justice four months ago, Ms. Fuller."

"Fled justice? Oh, that's a good one, Fred. I had a bunch of thugs break into my resort bungalow guns a-blazing. And if you've done the ballistics, you know some of those trigger-happy assholes shot each other."

"They were acting on an arrest warrant, Ms. Fuller."

"Were they, Fred? Did you know that no arrest warrant was issued? No court considered the matter? Did you know that? Or did Mr. Simmons keep that from you?

"No, there was no warrant. They broke into a rented domicile – my seaside bungalow – without a warrant. They were outside the law. Criminals, Fred. They got treated like criminals.

"Actually, they got treated better than criminals, because D Branch didn't kill them all, despite them being in the commission of a felony and putting innocent lives at risk. D Branch only killed the guys with the mortar. Those assholes brought a fucking mortar on a home invasion.

"Including children, Fred. They were shooting at *children*."

Gammon shuddered.

"D Branch?"

"Yes, Fred. D Branch operatives on the scene neutralized them and extracted me and my friends."

"I— I don't understand, Ms. Fuller."

"Where do you think I've been the last four months, Fred? A Senior Investigator with a sterling record? I was on loan to D Branch. I've spent the last four months on Elizabeth in a major corruption investigation."

"They never told us, Ms. Fuller."

"D Branch, Fred? *D Branch??* Of course, they didn't tell you. They never tell anybody anything. But I will tell you this. It was I who uncovered the evidence of Federation crimes committed by Eugene Simmons, and I sent the criminal referral against him directly to the Federation DoJ on Elizabeth."

"*You* did? But I have no indication that your story is what actually happened, Ms. Fuller."

"Other than the word of a senior investigator – by the age of thirty, I might add – in your own office. One with a spotless record, by the way. I suppose I could have the director of D Branch call you to verify my story, Fred. If you want that kind of attention."

"Uh, no. No, Ms. Fuller. That won't be necessary."

"Good. So I want my employment with Humphreys DoJ reinstated. Without a gap, mind you. I want the arrest record against me and my friends, signed by the indicted Federation criminal Eugene Simmons, stricken from the record. And I want the police told that no reprisals against us will be tolerated. They'll be messing with D Branch.

"Now, if you think about it, Fred. This solves two big problems for you."

"It does, Ms. Fuller?"

"Of course. Instead of having a senior investigator going crazy and killing police officers in a wild escape, and having an assistant state's attorney arrested by the Federation Police for official corruption – all of which looks really bad for the Humphreys DoJ, Fred – you actually have a senior investigator looking into official corruption fleeing a violent false arrest attempt – without a warrant – and getting the evidence against a corrupt assistant state's attorney in your department.

"Instead of two incidents it's one, and instead of an outside organization finding corruption in your department, it was an *internal* investigation that turned up one bad apple. Oh, and the investigation is continuing against the police who attempted an illegal arrest against the corruption investigator who was closing in on them."

Fuller was right, Gammon realized. That was a much better

scenario, both for him and the department. He almost visibly shifted gears as he changed course.

"I see, Ms. Fuller. Well, I have to say, after receiving this preliminary report from you, I am pleased that your investigation has gone so well. The entry in your records to indicate that you had resigned was, of course, intended to ensure your cover during the investigation, and it will be reversed immediately now that the investigation has concluded."

"And back pay."

"Of course, Ms. Fuller. Again, a subterfuge to protect your cover."

"Excellent."

"One more thing, Ms. Fuller. This is a local call? You are back in the Humphreys system?"

"Yes, but let me be clear about something. I am currently under the protection of both the Federation Navy and D Branch. Any attempt at reprisals or other actions against me or my friends will be met with deadly force by the two most competent death-dealing organizations in the Federation. Make sure people understand that."

"Of course, Ms. Fuller. I understand. I was thinking more in terms of when I could schedule a press conference at which you would speak and handle any questions the press may have about your investigation."

"I think I need a week to decompress from what has been a very busy four months. The second Monday coming or sometime after that would probably be best."

"Excellent, Ms. Fuller. I will see to it."

"In that case, I have taken more than my share of your time today, Attorney General Gammon. Thank you for your attention, sir."

"My pleasure, Senior Investigator Fuller."

Suzie was in a much better mood when she dropped out of virtual terminal mode.

"Things OK, now?" Sharp asked.

"Oh, yes. Everything's all taken care of."

"We can go down to the planet now?" Thompsen asked.

"Oh, I would give it until tomorrow for the paperwork to clear, but yes, we can go down soon."

For the last night on Humphreys Station, before heading down to the planet the next day, Sharp insisted on them taking rooms in the spinning portion of the station. Gravity here was just half of one gravity, but that was a lot compared to zero gravity.

Nobody argued with him, even though it was much more expensive than, say, the Gotham Astoria.

They had supper in the restaurant that evening, and breakfast in the restaurant the next morning. The furnishings themselves were spartan by planetside standards, both in the restaurant and in the rooms, but they were pure luxury compared to the seven of them camping out in zero gravity on *Medea* and its two shuttles, and eating their dinner and breakfast from toothpaste tubes.

After breakfast, Fuller logged into her Humphreys DoJ account and checked on their status.

"Everything looks good," she said to Sharp. "All the paperwork is cleared up, I'm a DoJ employee again, and they've paid me back pay. So I think we're good."

"All right, then. How about heading for the planet? After two weeks aboard ship, it sounds good to me."

"We're going home!" Sarah said.

"Yay!" the boys cheered.

"I think you have a consensus here, D.K.," Thompsen said.

They had to take two shuttles to the surface. First, there were seven of them and only three seats per shuttle. Sharp would ride down on the floor of one of the shuttles, piloting them both in virtual terminal.

Second, there were all their clothing purchases during the trip. The kids had all the coloring books and crayons, plus the toys they had manufactured using *Medea*'s 3D printer. The kids, their parents, and Fuller had fled the bungalow at the Humphreys beach resort with just the clothes they were wearing.

All now had wardrobes aboard *Medea*, both of city clothes and beach clothes, that they had purchased on Humphreys Station and in Gotham on Elizabeth. No sense leaving them on board, as Sharp couldn't use them.

Camden and Thompsen packed all their and the kids' stuff in the two big shipping trunks Sharp's paraglider/balloon equipment had come in. They were taking up a big chunk of the floor space in one shuttle, tied down to the pop-up handholds.

Fuller had more clothing items than anyone else, as she had been doing surveillance and had tried to vary her appearance enough not to get made. It hadn't worked in the case of Anderson's security, but it had for Thurl's. She had her things packed in a dozen shopping bags jammed into some of the other shuttle's storage cabinets.

Sharp, too, had bought significant clothing, having fled the police attack on his Ariel condo unit nude, but most of his things were staying on *Medea*. He had packed clothes for a lengthy planet stay on Humphreys, though, as Fuller had eleven days before she had to report back to work.

Sharp would normally take time between assignments anyway, no sense not taking it on Humphreys with Fuller.

They all floated aboard the two shuttles and strapped in, the twins with Camden in one shuttle and Sarah with Thompsen and Fuller in the other. Sharp locked his prosthetic hands to a pair of the pop-up handholds in the floor, face up, and his head on a cushion.

When their departure clearance from Humphreys Station came up, Sharp cut both shuttles free from *Medea* and fired the engines against their orbital direction. The shuttles began dropping toward the surface.

On Humphreys

The shuttles touched down nearly simultaneously, on adjacent pads of the Humphreys Navy Shuttleport outside the capital city of New Denver.

A self-drive passenger van, ordered by Sharp on the way down, showed up just minutes later. Camden and Sharp wrestled the big shipping trunks to the rear cargo compartment of the van while Fuller, Thompsen, and the kids ferried all her shopping bags.

Sharp went back and got his Navy-issue planet duffel off one of the shuttles and added it to the growing pile in the back of the van.

Sharp locked up the shuttles, then all seven of them got into the passenger compartment. Once they were all seated and belted in, the van set out for Camden and Thompsen's suburb.

"Oh, D.K.," Thompsen said. "I'm going to add the local grocery as an en-route destination. Everything in the fridge at home is going out the moment we hit the kitchen. After four months it isn't worth sorting it. So we need milk right away."

"Yeah," Camden said. "That and ketchup."

Thompsen nodded as she added the destination.

"You guys are staying for supper, right?" Camden asked.

"But if the contents of the fridge are history...?" Fuller asked.

"The deep freezer will be fine."

Fuller looked to Sharp, who gave a slight nod.

"Sure, Paul," she said. "Why not?"

The van pulled up in the driveway of a trim suburban house much like the houses Sharp and Thompsen had grown up in, if quite a bit larger. More modern, of course, now almost forty years later. Thompsen had moved to the capital from their hometown, but she hadn't moved away from the lifestyle they had grown up with.

There was a car parked out in front of the house that just screamed 'Cop' to Sharp.

"Everybody stay in the van for right now."

Sharp got out and walked over to the plainclothes car, keeping his eyes on the occupant's hands. He walked up to the driver's door, the window of which was open.

"Is there a problem, Officer?"

"No, Mr. Sharp. I'm from the Humphreys Department of Justice. I'm here to make sure no one who didn't get the message shows up and starts anything. We would rather you not be put in a position that would require you to respond."

"Ah. Yes. The police were pretty annoying the last time I was on Humphreys."

From anyone else, the DoJ officer would have laughed, but not from Deke Sharp. Last time Sharp was on Humphreys, he and his party were attacked by a police tactical team of a dozen members, all with body armor and military weapons. He had neutralized them by himself while the other members of his party ran for his shuttles.

The DoJ officer had doubted the story, but not anymore. The man in front of him radiated a scary level of confidence and competence. His doubts were gone.

"As you say, Mr. Sharp. There will be no repeat of that behavior. Attorney General Gammon is most insistent in this regard."

"Very well. Thank you, Officer."

"Of course, Mr. Sharp."

Sharp walked back over to the van.

"OK. Everybody out."

"Home!" Sarah yelled, as she and the boys jumped down and ran for the front door.

Sharp decided to let the van wait on the meter rather than ferry all of Fuller's clothes into the house and back out when they left. He locked up the van and they all walked to the front door.

"Looks like the service has kept up on the lawn," Camden said.

"That's good," Thompsen said. "Imagine what it would look like in four months if they hadn't."

She opened the front door and walked into the house, the kids rushing past her into the living room.

"Oof. Let's air out the house a bit while we tackle the fridge," Thompsen said when they got inside.

She hadn't been kidding about tossing the contents of the fridge. Just about everything in the refrigerator and freezer section went in garbage bags and out to the cans. A hot kitchen towel mopped all the shelves in both, and only then did she empty the two shopping bags of new groceries into the fridge.

While she did that, Camden set the oven to preheat. Then he took the garbage bags out to the cans.

"Mommy, what's for dinner," Sarah asked.

"Pizza."

"Yay!" the boys cheered.

Thompsen turned to Sharp.

"There's a pizza place near here that's a lot like Jimmy's was back home. We buy their pizzas prepped and frozen, and then bake them here. Even better than delivery, they're hot from the oven. We have a bunch of them in the deep freezer."

"That's OK with me," Sharp said. "Jimmy's was great."

There were some survivors of Thompsen's pillage of the refrigerator, including a twelve-pack of beer. Beer and pizza went great together. Together with milk for the kids, they were all set.

The pizza was every bit as good as Sharp's memory of Jimmy's, maybe even a bit better. The meal was relaxed and happy, back on their home planet, the police issues resolved, the mission over.

The kids soon were off to bed, but not before Sarah came up to Sharp for a goodnight hug.

"G'night, Uncle Deke."

"Good night, Sarah."

"Will we see you again, Uncle Deke?"

"I will not leave the planet without coming back to say goodbye, Sarah."

"Promise?"

"I promise."

That satisfied her, and she followed her brothers and their mother off to the bedrooms.

"You're awfully good with children for a man whose job it is to kill people, Deke," Camden said.

"Not incompatible at all, Paul. I kill the people who would harm them."

Fuller looked on, but said nothing.

Thompsen came back into the living room.

"Straight to sleep. Makes a big difference being back home, I guess."

"Speaking of which, we need to be leaving, Lydia," Fuller

said. "I still have my own refrigerator to deal with."

"Buy supplies on the way, Suzie. You don't want to have nothing for breakfast tomorrow."

Fuller nodded.

"Will do. You ready, D.K?"

"Yeah, I'm good."

There were lots of hugs all around, and a firm handshake with Camden. Mission over, the team was breaking up.

"Thanks again for all the help," Sharp said. "It went really well having my own analysis section along."

"Make sure you guys stop by before you leave Humphreys, Deke," Camden said. "Maybe we can have a barbecue that last Sunday before Suzie goes back to work."

"Sounds good, Paul."

"All right, guys. See you later," Fuller said.

They did stop at the same grocery store before they left the neighborhood. Fuller stocked up for a week, plus staples that would have expired over the last four months. Sharp insisted on paying.

"I'm still on expense report, and I'll probably eat more of this than you will."

"I suppose, but I made so much money on this caper it seems silly to have you pay."

"Yes, Suzie, and you almost got shot, by your own police."

"Yeah, there's that. What a ride it was."

Fuller lived in a stand-alone house that was nevertheless legally a condominium. The houses in her large block were all built around a commons, a park behind all the houses, which all faced the street.

When the van pulled up in the driveway, there was a

plainclothes car parked in front of the house. Sharp got out and waved to the officer, and he saluted back.

They carried the groceries in, and Fuller opened up windows on the warm evening, airing out the house after four months of being closed up. They then went back out to the van and ferried all her things inside.

That done, Sharp dismissed the van, and it backed out of the driveway and drove off.

Back in the house, Fuller went after the refrigerator with the same lack of discrimination as Thompsen had, then wiped down the shelves. She stored all the groceries requiring refrigeration, then took the garbage bag out to the can in the garage.

"I still have beer that's cold, D.K."

"Sounds good."

They each took a beer and Fuller led him out the back door into a walled garden. All the houses in the little community around the central park were single story, and the garden was very private.

"Nice little garden, Suzie. And private. You could sunbathe naked out here."

"You see any tan lines on me, D.K?"

Come to think of it, he hadn't. Then again, Daphne Duplay didn't have any tan lines, either, so it had been a long time since he had even seen tan lines, and Sharp hadn't noticed the lack on Fuller.

He sat back in the comfortable chair and sighed.

Life was good.

"Hmph. Wha'?"

"Wake up, sleepyhead. Time to go to bed, and you're too heavy to carry."

Sharp let himself be led inside to Fuller's bedroom. He removed both prosthetic arms to let the skin around his connections breathe overnight.

He wouldn't normally remove both arms at night, but with Fuller there to help both disconnecting and connecting, he could.

They walked around the central park of the small subdivision the next morning after breakfast. The park was criss-crossed by walking paths and lushly planted, with trees, flowering shrubs, and ground covers.

"This is really pretty, Suzie. A little island of beauty near the heart of the city."

"Yeah. I bought it ten years ago when I got out of college. It was just being built, and none of the gardens were in yet. It's turned out to be a great investment. The HOA fee is a little high, but it's been well spent."

"I'll say. This is stupendous."

"I took a chance and it worked out. I've considered selling it to get my money out before somebody screws it up, but I just can't bring myself to move."

"I can see that. What an oasis."

Mid-morning, they were sitting with coffee in the private walled garden behind Fuller's house.

"So what do we do for the next week and change?" Sharp asked.

Fuller perked up with a big smile.

"Besides that," Sharp added.

"Ah. Well, George might want to come and visit this weekend. He sometimes comes into the capital and he stays here. You guys can talk about old times."

"That would be fun."

Fuller nodded.

"There's a zoo, and some sights downtown. The ocean is nearby, if you haven't had your fill of seaside living for a while. That's what keeps the climate here so nice. The proximity of the ocean."

Sharp nodded. Given the choice of where to build on colony planets, subtropical zones near an ocean were the common choice for the capital.

"We could go back to the old hometown and visit, if you have any nostalgia for that," Fuller said.

"Not really, Suzie. I have my memories, and I think I'd rather leave them as they are."

"That's fair. Of course, we can just laze around here. I don't know about you, D.K., but for me it's just nice to be outside after the last two weeks crammed into your ship with six other people and no chance to sun or walk."

"That actually sounds good to me, Suzie."

In the end, they spent the ten days hanging out at the house. There were a lot of walks in the central park, sunning nude in the walled garden, and making love, whether in the bed or in the garden.

Fuller's brother George did come for the first weekend, and Sharp and George Fuller drank beer in the walled garden and talked about old times.

The second Sunday finally came, and they went over to Camden and Thompsen's house for the promised barbecue.

"Uncle Deke!" Sarah shouted as Sharp and Fuller came out into the back yard.

Sharp picked her up as she ran up to him.

"I told you I'd be back, Sarah."

Sarah nodded vigorously.

"You *promised*."

"Indeed I did."

Sharp kissed her cheek and set her back down, at which point she took his hand and led him over to the picnic table like he was her prized possession. Some well loved pet.

Sharp chuckled and sat at the picnic table. Camden was cooking on the grill, and Thompsen was ferrying things out to the picnic table from the kitchen. Fuller went off with her to help. Sarah and the twins colored at the picnic table, waiting for supper.

"So what now, Deke?" Camden asked after dinner.

"Back to Ariel. Suzie's dropping me at the shuttleport on her way home."

"Not one last night before leaving?" Thompsen asked.

Fuller glanced at the kids.

"We made sure to have a party last night."

And indeed they had. Out in the private walled garden.

"Ah."

"Suzie needs to be at work tomorrow," Sharp said. "I would just be in the way. And I have to get back to work as well, for that matter."

Having been together four months, the goodbyes were a bit emotional. The kids were very sad Uncle Deke would be leaving for a long time, with no idea when they would see him again.

Camden and Sharp shook hands firmly.

"Thanks for rescuing us, Deke."

"Well, you were only in trouble because of me, Paul, but it

worked out."

Camden nodded.

"You take care."

Thompsen hugged Sharp, and kissed him on the cheek.

"You take care of yourself, D.K. Try to stay out of trouble."

"I always try to stay out of trouble."

Thompsen rolled her eyes at him, and Sharp laughed.

One more hug for a weeping Sarah, and then they were gone.

At the shuttleport, both shuttles were already warming up when the rental car pulled up to the landing pads.

"Gonna make a fast getaway, huh?" Fuller asked.

"It's probably easiest."

Fuller nodded, then hugged him. They stood there for a couple of minutes, then pulled away from each other.

"Well, get going before I lose it," she said.

He nodded, gave her a quick kiss, then boarded the shuttle with the dog suit on it. Best to always stay together with his most capable weaponry. He would pilot both shuttles, the second one in remote.

Fuller sat in the rental car and watched as the shuttles spooled up, then lifted off and headed for Humphreys Station and *Medea*.

They were out of sight before she told the rental car to take her home.

Camden and Thompsen were standing in their yard watching the twin artificial stars head for space.

"I wonder when we'll see him again," Camden said.

"With D.K., there's no telling."

246

Back Home

Deke Sharp arrived back at *Medea*, both shuttles docking with their mother ship. The ship had been serviced and her stores topped off while he had been down on the planet, and she was ready to go.

He saw no sense in hanging around. When his departure clearance came up, *Medea* thrust away from Humphreys Station and headed for the envelope, accelerating at frigate speed.

It was uncanny how quiet the ship was, even with the engines accelerating for the envelope.

Sharp had become used to the crowded conditions, and being alone on the ship now seemed alien.

A day out from Humphreys Station, *Medea* hit the envelope and disappeared from normal space.

Once in the envelope, Sharp made the turn for Ariel and let *Medea* have her head. She sped for her home station.

Fuller got back home from the shuttleport about the same time as Sharp got to the ship.

The house was so quiet, it was unnerving.

She usually listened to music in virtual terminal, where, without being degraded by speakers or room acoustics, the fidelity was perfect.

But Fuller called up some music on the house system now, just to have some noise.

She slept fitfully that night, no longer used to sleeping alone.

Fuller finally put the bolster from the living room couch in the bed, lengthwise, and cuddled up to it to get some sleep.

It was ten days to Ariel, even given *Medea's* speed. When *Medea* dropped out of the envelope in the Ariel system, Sharp called in to report his location to Octavius Pasha.

"Hi, Otto."

"Hi, Deke. You back in Ariel?"

"Yes. I just dropped out of the envelope."

"Great. Give me a call when you start down in the shuttle. I'll pick you up at the shuttleport."

Sharp raised an eyebrow.

"I have something to show you, Deke."

"All right, Otto. Figure— about twenty-two hours from now."

"Got it. See you then, Deke."

Sharp also logged into the news feeds, searching on Humphreys DoJ over the last ten days. Here it was.

Oh, it was delicious.

Humphreys Attorney General Frederick Gammon III started the press conference with a short statement.

"Good morning, ladies and gentlemen.

"There has been a lot of speculation in the press about the arrest and indictment of former Assistant State's Attorney Eugene Simmons and former New Denver Police records clerk Dorothy Pratt.

"The Humphreys Department of Justice is holding this press conference to clear up some of the confusion on these issues. Due to the pending charges and other considerations, we won't be able to be completely forthcoming, but we can clear up some issues.

"Senior Investigator Suzanne Fuller will have a statement for you and then answer some questions.

"Ms. Fuller?"

Gammon moved away from the podium and Fuller stepped into his place. She was dressed in a business suit of the sort she had worn in Gotham during surveillance. In fact, it was one of the suits she had bought on Gotham.

Damn, she looks good, Sharp thought.

"Thank you, Attorney General Gammon.

"This statement will be about the extent of what I can say about this matter. I will probably have to leave most of your questions unanswered, but we'll see.

"For the last four months, I have been on loan from the Humphreys Department of Justice to a Federation entity I will not name. I assisted in the investigation of official corruption and other illegal acts on another planet of the Federation. While this is somewhat unusual, that investigation had ties to Humphreys, hence my involvement.

"During that investigation, evidence was discovered that indicated that Mr. Simmons and Ms. Pratt were receiving bribery payments in return for illegal acts committed in their official positions here on Humphreys. That evidence was provided to the Federation Department of Justice in a criminal referral, resulting in the indictments you have reported on.

"That's about what I can say, ladies and gentlemen. I will entertain questions."

"Ms. Fuller, was the other planet on which you conducted this investigation Elizabeth?"

"I'm sorry. I cannot divulge that information at the present time."

"Were you on loan to the Federation DoJ, Ms. Fuller?"

At the mention of Elizabeth, another jumped in.

"Were you on loan to the Federation Navy, Ms. Fuller?"

"As I stated, I will not divulge the Federation organization to which I was on loan."

"Ms. Fuller, were you involved in the investigation into the funding of piracy operations that resulted in the execution of four businessmen on Elizabeth?"

"I will neither confirm nor deny participation in that investigation."

"Ms. Fuller, were you *the shooter* in those executions?"

"As I said, I will neither confirm nor deny participation in that activity."

"Ms. Fuller, it was widely reported four months ago that you were a fugitive from justice and had resigned the Humphreys Department of Justice. Is all that not true, then?"

"I will say this about that. The investigation of which I was a part was a covert investigation. It was necessary for me to disappear for months in order to assist Federation personnel in successfully carrying it out. Attorney General Gammon was instrumental in assuring that my cover for this covert operation was secure."

Gammon stepped toward the microphone.

"I think that's all that we have for you today. Thanks for coming, everyone."

Gammon waved goodbye to the press, and he and Fuller walked off the stage and out of the press room.

"Nicely done, Ms. Fuller."

"Thank you, sir."

Of course, 'neither confirm nor deny' was a phrase the press took to mean 'yes.' Usually it was OK to say no, it was only the yes answer that people wanted to avoid. So the press would take her 'neither confirm nor deny' answers to mean yes, she was involved in the investigation into the piracy operation's funding, and yes, she was the shooter.

Sharp chuckled. He predicted Fuller would have no problems with her personal security on Humphreys for quite a while.

Broadening his search of the news feeds to include Elizabeth and Meredith, he saw the Federation Department of Justice press release from the Meredith office about the investigation of the piracy funding and the seizure of assets. They also noted that the Navy's operation was concluded. He had seen this press release when he was on Humphreys.

What was new was the Navy's press release from Meredith in which the Navy acknowledged the operation and its conclusion. Upcoming would be the release of further information proving the participation of the four executed businessmen.

Also new was the filing of a motion for injunctive relief by the families. The Federation had seized all of the assets of the piracy funders. The families noted in their motion that there had been a lot of assets that had nothing to do with the piracy operation. Their motion also pointed out that the assets seized were much larger than any likely wrongful death payout, even assuming triple damages for willful and malicious behavior.

As the seizure stood, however, the families were likely to be thrown out into the streets, penniless and without any means of support.

The motion asked for injunctive relief in the form of the release of ten percent of the seized assets, including each family's primary residence, to maintain the families while the adjudication of damages was underway.

That all actually sounded reasonable to Sharp. He wondered what the FDoJ on Elizabeth would do. If they would fight the motion for injunctive relief or acquiesce to it.

Sharp also went through his pending communications on his D Branch account. He had been in transit for ten days, after all.

And there it was. A call request from his contact in the FDoJ on Elizabeth. He recognized the address. He put through an acceptance – it was morning in Gotham right now – and used his avatar in a Navy captain's uniform, as he had with Laramie before when he forwarded the evidence against Eugene Simmons.

"Dick Laramie."

"Good morning, Mr. Laramie. Captain Sharp here."

"Yes, Captain Sharp. Thank you so much for calling. Have you seen the motion for injunctive relief of the families of Messrs. Thomas, Thurl, Anderson, and Maxwell?"

"Yes, I just read it."

"We wondered if you had a recommendation, Captain. We're still working through the masses of evidence you discovered, and which were forwarded on to us last week. We thought you might have the most informed opinion about this."

Sharp nodded.

"My own view is that the families were likely uninvolved and unaware of the activities of those gentlemen, Mr. Laramie. It is not the sort of thing one regales one's family about, after all. I would be inclined to acquiesce to the motion. The sums involved are quite large, I imagine."

"Oh, yes, Captain. We have to date seized some two hundred and seventy billion credits in various assets, and are holding them in kind pending adjudication."

Sharp nodded. Trask had been the ultimate big wheel out of that investment group. If Sharp recalled correctly, he had been worth more like a hundred and fifty or sixty billion credits by himself. Thomas, Thurl, and Anderson were each worth less than Trask, and Maxwell much less, being an attorney who merely piggybacked on their much larger investments.

"Then I think the motion is correct, Mr. Laramie. The adjudication is unlikely to award anything anywhere near that large. As the point of the seizure is to make sure the funds required for just compensation are not squirreled away, you lose nothing of your ability to seek justice for the victims."

It was Laramie's turn to nod.

"That's what we had been thinking here, Captain. I just wanted to make sure we weren't missing anything in our analysis."

"No, I think you're right, Mr. Laramie. At least, that's my impression."

"Very well, Captain. Thank you for accepting the call."

Laramie made a little wave with one hand and cut the channel.

Medea arrived at the Navy's orbital Ariel Station and docked as directed. Sharp was all packed and ready to go, so he put in for departure clearance with the shuttle that had the dog suit and the swim kit aboard.

He had already replenished his ammo stocks in that shuttle from *Medea*'s supplies. The ship's supplies would be topped off by the maintenance crew once they came aboard.

As his departure clearance approached, Sharp called Pasha.

"Hi, Deke."

"Hi, Otto."

"You on the way down?"

"Got a couple more minutes to wait on my departure clearance, and then I'm on my way."

"Good. I'll meet you at the pad."

"And you're sure I'm good to land on Ariel, Otto? No cops

waiting for me or anything like that?"

"No, no, Deke. That's all taken care of. Claude and Senator Jeffries were most direct with the police and the DoJ here. You won't have the problems you had on Humphreys."

"OK, good. Just checking."

"Of course. See you in a bit."

When Sharp walked down the ramp from the shuttle at the New Destin Navy Shuttleport, Pasha was waiting in a rental car. Sharp put his Navy planet duffel in the back seat and got in the front.

"Deke! It's good to see you."

"You, too, Otto. Lotta water under the bridge since last time."

"Indeed, indeed."

Pasha pushed the proceed button on the dash and the rental car started off in self-drive. Sharp had no idea where they were going.

"I'm not sure what you heard about what went on with me, Deke."

"I think I'm pretty caught up, Otto. I was reading the field ops message boards. Looks like they had quite a bit of fun with the police while you were in custody."

Otto chuckled.

"Oh, yes. The police have learned not to mess with D Branch. Lots of things go wrong, sometimes spectacularly so."

"I thought surging the sewer was particularly good."

"Yes, though Chief Mulcahy was less than amused, especially because it kept happening when he was in the bathroom."

"Yeah, that was fun to read about."

"And you've been through the wringer a bit yourself, Deke."

"Just a bit, Otto. Never injured on this job."

"But Lydia Thompsen was. I wasn't pleased about that. The police on Humphreys were out of control."

"Yes, Otto, but Attorney General Gammon put a stop to that. The guy who ordered it is in jail pending trial, and the guys who went along with it got five years of desk jobs. No guns at all. Not even badges while they think about it."

"Good. They should have shut that down, orders or no orders. Imagine if they had killed one of the children."

"Then they would have all died, Otto."

Otto Pasha knew better than to underestimate Deke Sharp, either his capabilities or his temper. If the police on Humphreys had been so out of control as to kill any of the children, yes, they all would have died. Pasha had no doubt about that at all.

"Thanks for sending me your final report on the way in, Deke. Nice job all around. Sounds like Mark Anderson was a little disturbing, though."

"Yeah, he basically asked me to kill him. Regretted the whole thing, and had a terminal illness to boot. His only request was that I make it quick. Which I did. Seemed only fair. The others were all quick. Never even had time to feel pain. Just bang, gone."

Pasha nodded.

"Well, it's not our job to punish, Deke. It's our job to keep things from happening. Sometimes the easiest way to do that is to send a message."

The rental car slowed and pulled under a porte cochere.

"Ah, here we are," Pasha said.

Deke hadn't been paying attention on the way into the city. He looked around now at a very familiar scene – the front door of his condo building.

What the hell?

"Otto—"

"Come along, Deke. I told you I wanted to show you something. Bring your duffel."

Pasha buzzed them into the building. They went to the elevators and he pushed for the top floor. They walked down the hall to Sharp's unit, and Pasha opened the door and waved him past.

"Welcome home, Deke."

Sharp couldn't believe it. It was his condo as it had been before his security system had taken out the police tactical team with a couple of claymores placed in the walls.

The furnishings, the artwork, the glass doors out onto the balcony. Everything, just as he had left it.

He looked around in wonder.

"Nice, huh, Deke?"

"I can't believe it. Otto, how did you do this?"

"Well, we couldn't exactly leave it the way it was. You would have become most unpopular with your fellow residents. We hired an outfit to put it back. Everything was pretty shredded, but not so much they couldn't figure out what it was before."

Sharp walked over to the bathroom. Even his toiletries were where he had left them.

"We didn't have to do much with the bathroom. There were two police standing between the bedroom device and the bathroom door. They didn't fare as well."

Sharp walked over to the painting on the hallway wall, lifted it away from the wall at one corner. There was a claymore, set back into the wall, as it had been before.

"OK, Otto. How did you manage *that*?"

"Yes, that one was a bit dicey. Claude called me in on it. 'Is this truly necessary, Otto?' I told him, 'Well, it was necessary this time, sir.' He gave me a hard look and then signed off on it."

"No shit."

Pasha shrugged.

"This is all really unexpected, Otto. I expected to sleep in a hotel tonight."

"Welcome home, Deke. This mission was a tremendous success. You've earned it. We owed it to you to set it right."

Sharp woke in the middle of the night disoriented. He wasn't sleeping in the command chair of the shuttle, his normal position when aboard *Medea* alone. He wasn't sleeping with Fuller, his normal position for the four months prior to the voyage home to Ariel.

"Lights on."

The lights came up and he was at home, as it had been five months ago, before he had fled his own home. Memory flooded back, of his life before the last mission, and of Pasha's bringing him home to his remarkably reconstructed condo last night.

"Lights off."

Sharp struggled to get back to sleep. Without Fuller, it was hard. He hugged one of his pillows and finally drifted off.

The next morning, after washing and salving his prosthetic connections, Sharp made an espresso and took it out on the balcony, where he lay down nude on the chaise and let the rising sun warm him.

He kept waiting for the alarm, like the one over four months ago that had precipitated his flight from Ariel.

Sharp finally relaxed, finally felt the tension subside, at least a little, and basked in the warm sunshine.

Daphne Duplay

It was Friday night when Deke Sharp arrived back in New Destin. He went in to the office the next Thursday morning. For an operative between assignments – indeed, just back from an assignment – this was neither unusual nor unexpected. Office attendance was optional.

Pasha knew Sharp was in the office, though, and called him about eleven o'clock.

"Hi, Deke."

"Hi, Otto."

"What are you doing for lunch?"

"No plans. I was just going to grab something in the cafeteria."

"Let's go to Maxine's. My treat."

Sharp raised an eyebrow. Maxine's was the finest restaurant on Ariel. Such an offer was not to be passed on.

"OK, Otto. That's always good with me."

There was no lunch menu at Maxine's. The 'Mid-Day Menu' had both a lunch section and a dinner section, depending on which meal would be one's largest of the day. As a married man, Pasha selected from the lunch section, while Sharp selected from the dinner section.

They sat back with cognac – the superb Dufort *Esprit* – in the captain's chairs of one of Maxine's private booths. As Maxine's booths were scanned for electronic surveillance devices to D Branch's standards after every use, they could talk business.

"So how's it going, Deke? Settling back in OK?"

"Is that the excuse for Maxine's, Otto? Checking up on me?"

"Of course. It's a wonderful excuse to do something I want to do anyway."

"Do you take every operative out to Maxine's every time they come in from the field?"

"No, Deke, not every operative. You're a special case. First, you've recovered from the most severe set of injuries I've ever had with an operative. Second, this recent outing was a follow-up to the case that gave you those injuries. Third, you're the best field operative I've ever had. And fourth, you're getting to the age where field people start to think about hanging up their spurs. Retiring from field work. So I worry about you more than about others, and I just wondered how you're doing."

Sharp nodded.

"Fair enough, Otto. It's always a bit disorienting being back, especially after a long mission. This one's no different in that respect. Some sleep issues. Some tension issues. Normal stuff."

"I see."

Their food arrived. Pasha had ordered his favorite, a steak and avocado salad, with a creamy balsamic vinaigrette and a small brioche on the side. Sharp varied his selections more, and this time chose the prime rib of Caroline beef, medium rare, with Maxine's famous Bordelaise sauce, plus sides of fried new potatoes basil and fresh greens.

The planet Caroline was famous for its beef, and rightly so. Unlike most interstellar products that could spoil, it was never frozen. As freshly slaughtered beef should hang in a cold room for at least two weeks anyway, they shipped it interstellar refrigerated while it was hanging in specially equipped ships, and its price on the other planets of the Federation reflected that expense.

The conversation stopped during the meal. Neither gourmet would fail to do justice to a meal at Maxine's, ignoring it to pursue anything as mundane as conversation. After the meal, as they nursed the remains of a particularly good cabernet – the '37 Chateau Bescond Private Reserve – they picked up where they had left off.

"So nothing special about the wind-down from this mission, Deke?"

"Not really, Otto."

"I see. And how is Ms. Fuller doing? Have you spoken to her since you arrived back on Ariel?"

Sharp realized he couldn't hide anything from Pasha. They had worked too closely together, been friends too long. Pasha could read between the lines of his reports and know much more about what had gone on than Sharp perhaps had intended to reveal.

He also realized with a start that he had not called Fuller since his return, and he wondered why that was. Sharp was not big on introspection, and he let it drop.

"No, I haven't."

"Surprising."

"It feels like— I don't know, Otto. It feels like picking at a scab, somehow."

"A wound to the heart?"

Sharp hesitated, then replied.

"Perhaps."

"Maybe you should talk about it with Ms. Duplay, Deke. See what advice she might have to offer."

"Now there's a thought."

The conversation turned to lighter topics over a dessert of chocolate dainties, finished off with a remarkable Amaretto.

Maxine's was, as always, remarkable, start to finish.

When Sharp got back to the office, he put a call request in to

Daphne Duplay. Surprisingly, he got a call acceptance almost immediately.

"D.K! How are you?"

"I'm fine, Daphne. How are you?"

"I'm good, but I worried about you."

"Worried about me?"

"Sure. There were these lurid stories of an explosion at your condo building. And then a shootout on Humphreys that involved your old high school girlfriend Lydia, right? Then there were those executions for funding piracy on Elizabeth. Two weeks ago, there was a press conference on Humphreys about the shootout being faked somehow. And a corruption investigation there. It just went on and on, and every time something weird happened, I thought you must be involved. Was I wrong?"

"No, Daphne. You weren't wrong. Much of that was about me. Or caused by me, I guess."

"I want to hear the story, D.K."

"What about you, Daphne? You got arrested."

"Yeah, but it was nothing. They held me for a couple hours, then George showed up and bailed me out."

"George?"

"George Jeffries."

Sharp raised an eyebrow. Senator George Jeffries? The chair of the Senate Judiciary Committee? Oh, that must have been delicious. One should never, ever, mess with Daphne Duplay. She had friends.

Duplay continued.

"I mean, I would never mention him, except this has so much to do with you, and the fact he bailed me out is public knowledge anyway."

"Yes, Daphne, I think we should definitely get together and

261

compare notes. When's a good time?"

"Tonight work for you, D.K?"

Sharp was surprised again. One normally didn't see Duplay without two weeks' notice. She would have to cancel whatever she had scheduled for tonight, he knew.

"Tonight works for me, Daphne."

"The usual place then."

Sharp nodded, and Duplay cut the connection.

Daphne Duplay wasn't conventionally beautiful. She was attractive, however, and made the most of what she had. Her clothes, hair, and makeup were always perfect, and perfect for the occasion.

More to the point, Duplay was a professional companion. She spoke all the common languages of the Federation. She was well read in history, science, politics, and current events. She was fit, and a capable companion in many sports, including scuba, water skiing, snow skiing, horseback riding, shooting, and archery.

Duplay was also a willing and enthusiastic sex partner, if that was the companionship one of her male friends wanted.

There was no charge for her services. No quid pro quo. She did, however, accept gifts from her male friends, particularly gifts of cash. If the gifts were not large enough, she would stop returning your calls.

Sharp was waiting outside Piatti's, the little Italian restaurant around the corner from his condominium building, when Duplay arrived in a self-drive cab. She was dressed in a one-piece bodysuit with a big zipper up the front.

"D.K!"

She ran up to him and gave him a big hug, and he escorted

her into the building.

Once seated and dinner ordered – lighter than usual for Sharp, since he had eaten at Maxine's at lunch – Duplay turned to him with a question.

"OK, D.K. Who is she?"

"Who is who, Daphne?"

"The woman who stole your heart. The reason you hugged me like your sister and not your lover. Is it Suzanne Fuller? That woman from the press conference on Humphreys?"

Whatever else you could say about her, Duplay wasn't stupid.

"Yes. Well, maybe. Mostly, I think. Really, I just don't know, Daphne."

"Well, start at the beginning, D.K. The police tried to arrest you. And they blew up your condo?"

"No, I blew up my condo."

"You blew up your condo, D.K? Why?"

"The police tactical team sent to arrest me broke into my condo. I was up on the roof. Once they were all inside my condo, then I blew it up. Or rather, set off a couple of anti-personnel bombs. Claymores."

"I know what a claymore is, D.K. Nasty. And then you escaped?"

"Yes, I called the shuttle of my ship to come pick me up off the roof, and got out of there before the police sent up another team. When I heard that you and my boss had both been arrested, I decided whoever it was had targeted me and my familiars, and I went to Humphreys."

"To rescue other friends there?"

"Yes. My old high school girlfriend Lydia, her husband, their kids, and Suzie Fuller, the younger sister of a friend of mine in high school."

"Then what happened?"

"We tried to figure out who bought off the cops, and we found the source of the money. We went to Elizabeth and found four people who had been instrumental in funding the piracy operations we put an end to last year."

"And then you killed them. The four billionaires, the press called them."

"Yes. Although it was really three multi-billionaires and their attorney. I killed them, and then I took everybody back to Humphreys and came home."

"What about your poor condo?"

"D Branch rebuilt it while I was gone."

"And all your lovely furnishings?"

"Replaced like for like."

"Wow. So tell me about Suzanne Fuller, D.K. How long were you together on the mission?"

"Four months."

"What does she do? Is she really a Senior Investigator for Humphreys DoJ?"

"Oh, yes. That's real."

"And the shootout on Humphreys, did that really happen or not?"

"Oh, no. That really happened. Police and DoJ officials there were bought off to get my friends arrested, same as with me and you and my boss here."

"And they escaped while you fought the cops."

"Yes. We all escaped after I more or less pinned the cops down."

"So what's she like, D.K? She looked very pretty at the press conference."

"Suzie? She's beautiful, Daphne. She's also competent and extremely dangerous."

"That's how I would have described you, D.K. What about your prosthetics? They don't turn her off?"

"No. Not at all. She helped me with them. Cleaning them and servicing them. Helping me switch the normal ones out to special versions that were mission-oriented. You know, with built-in guns and such."

"So how does she feel about you, D.K? Is she sitting home pining away after you?"

"I don't think so, Daphne. She's beautiful, powerful, has her own money. She can have any man she wants."

"But not you?"

Sharp shrugged.

"She sounds like a good fit as a partner, D.K."

"Oh, she was, Daphne. She was an excellent partner on the investigation. She did some of the surveillance, a lot of the documents searches, putting the facts together. She was terrific."

"I meant as a life partner, D.K."

"I don't see how that can be, Daphne. She has her career there, a really nice house there. I have my career here, and a really nice condo here."

"A hundred light-years away."

"And change. Yeah."

"Hmm."

Dinner came and they ate in silence. After dessert, Daphne looked over to Sharp.

"So no play time tonight, D.K? Or can we indulge ourselves one last time? For old time's sake, if nothing else."

"Sure, Daphne. I don't know what, if anything, is ever going to happen between me and Suzie, anyway, so it's not like I'm off the market."

"Yeah. Right. I won't bet on that. But for right now, take me home and make love to me, D.K. I won't even be hurt if you think of her when you fuck me."

When they got to his condo, Duplay looked around.

"They did a nice job, D.K. Everything looks the same as before."

"Yes, they found everything and bought like for like, as much as they could."

"Kitchen appliances are all new, too. And the cabinets."

"Yeah, the cabinets were shredded, or so I was told. The appliances were all dented."

Duplay went on into the bedroom. She glanced into the bathroom.

"Not much change here."

"They were shielded from damage by a couple cops standing in such a way as to block the doorway."

"Closet doors are new. Looks like all your clothes survived, though."

"Yeah. The closet doors were out of the direct blast, but they got damaged, even while protecting the clothes behind them."

"And you were undamaged as well?"

"Yes," Sharp said, gesturing up. "I was on the roof."

"Well, I am going to have to inspect most carefully to make sure."

The next morning when Sharp woke up, Duplay, as usual, was long gone. He looked over to the dresser, to where he always left a wallet with a cash gift to Duplay. The wallet was still there, the money still in it. Alongside it was a note.

"Thank you, love, but that one was for old times. DD."

Daphne Duplay put the call request through to the private

number. It was accepted immediately.

"Jeffries."

"Hello, George. It's Daphne Duplay."

"Hello, Daphne. What's going on?"

"George, dear. I was wondering if I could ask you to do me a favor...."

Of course, when you're the attorney general of a planet, and the chairman of the judiciary committee of the planetary senate calls you, you take the call.

"Yes, Mr. Chairman," Attorney General Hank Branson said.

"Good morning, Attorney General Branson."

The formalities taken care of, Branson switched to the familiar.

"What can I do for you today, George?"

"Hank, I'm worried about the corruption issue. To have our citizens arrested on bogus charges bought and paid for by some off-planet billionaire pisses me off. And to use a police tactical team to do it? That's just frosting on the cake."

"I agree, George. I agree. I'm at a little bit of a loss on how to proceed there, however. We do have an anti-corruption office, but this all got past them."

"We need a senior corruption investigator, Hank. Somebody good at it. Maybe somebody from outside. I think people may be a little too palsy-walsy with all their friends down the hall in the DoJ to get the job done internally."

Branson nodded.

"Any leads for me there, George?"

"Maybe. What about that Fuller gal over on Humphreys?"

"Suzanne Fuller? The one in the press conference a couple weeks back?"

"Yeah, that's the one."

"I don't think we can pull her away from Humphreys, George. She's a senior investigator over there already, and has the eye and ear of the Humphreys AG now. She's set over there."

"I have it on good authority that if we made her an offer as principal investigator here on Ariel – you know, some rank higher than senior investigator – we could get her, Hank."

"We don't have an investigator title higher than senior investigator, George."

"You put a proposal through the committee, Hank. Let me take care of that part of it. But with that and bridging her retirement credits, I'm told we can probably get her."

"All right, George. That would be great if we can swing it. Let me work on it."

"OK, Hank. Get me that position proposal as soon as you can."

Suzanne Fuller

That first week after Deke Sharp left Humphreys, Suzie Fuller was busy wall to wall. She had turned over to the Federation DoJ the evidence against Eugene Simmons and Dorothy Pratt that she had discovered on Elizabeth. Now she needed to track down the evidence here on Humphreys.

Mail records, bank records, New Denver Police arrest records, and Humphreys DoJ criminal indictment and warrant records – all of it came under the scrutiny of her forensic analysis.

For what had they been paid? What all had they done? For whom? To what nefarious ends?

Fuller prepared and presented briefings to Federation DoJ investigators on Humphreys, documenting the money flows, the records alterations, the civil rights violations, going back years.

She also prepared her statement for the press conference and participated in the press conference. It was a short statement and a short press conference, but the stress and anxiety over her performance left her drained.

Every night Fuller staggered back into her cute little house on the park and collapsed from exhaustion. Sometimes she got undressed and ready for bed first, and sometimes not, simply passing out on the sofa in the living room.

The first weekend without Sharp was a different matter.

Fuller caught up on her sleep that weekend, often laying out nude on the chaise lounge in the walled garden. She drifted in and out of sleep most of the day.

Was it Sharp, actually, or was it the situation? The strange locales, the looming danger, the excitement of the mission? All of it excited the hell out of her. How much of it was Deke Sharp?

Then again, Sharp had been there throughout, even when there was no danger. No strange locale, just the cramped confines of the ship and its shuttles, for weeks on end. Or on the way back, with no excitement, the mission complete. Throughout it all, Sharp had been there.

He had been so good with her. Had been so good with the children, for that matter. Sarah, when her Uncle Deke left, looked like Fuller felt, crushed by the loss of him. The loss of his company.

Once when she woke, Fuller's face was wet with tears. Crying in her sleep? Oh, that's not a good sign.

But what was she to do? Her home was here. Her career was here. And asking him to move – to leave D Branch – wasn't fair to him, either.

The weekend ended and the next week began without any answer presenting itself.

Another crazy week was a respite from her introspection, then it was the weekend again. Two days of inactivity. Two days of wondering what to do.

Sharp should have gotten home last night, if her calculations were right. A day to the envelope, ten days in the envelope, then a day to Ariel. Twelve days from that emotional Sunday leavetaking was Friday evening.

Had he made it home?

Would he call her?

In fact, he didn't call her. Then again, fair's fair: she didn't call him, either.

Why not? Because they both knew it couldn't work?

This week would be worse. Fuller was running out of things to do with regard to transferring the case to the local office of the Federation DoJ. She wouldn't be as busy. Wouldn't be as exhausted when she got home.

Would have more time to think.

By Thursday, Fuller was climbing the walls. In addition to missing Sharp, her biology was giving her problems. A girl had needs, dammit. And she had no current paramour on Humphreys.

Of course, Fuller had friends. Male friends. Friends with benefits, as the old saying went. Thursday was a great night for it. One could zero one's clock going into the weekend. Head into the weekend hunt with a take it or leave it attitude that many people found attractive.

Not scare them off by seeming desperate.

OK, Suzie, she thought. *You know it can never work out with D.K. Now get back up on that horse and ride, as Lydia always said.*

But who?

Hmm. Gary. Yeah. A couple years younger. Cute. A cute little house like hers, right across the garden. Not husband material, though. That was OK, that's not what she wanted right now.

"Hi, Gary."

"Hi, Suzie. Hey, I saw you on the news. You looked great. All dressed up in your work clothes and all."

"How'd you like to peel me out of them tonight, honey?"

"Sure! Dinner first? I'll cook for you."

"Then bring it over. I have work in the morning and I don't want to walk the garden in the middle of the night."

"All right. See you then. Sevenish?"

"Works for me."

Actually, she was much more dangerous to a potential attacker than Gary was. But she was also much more likely to be targeted by an attacker, and shooting him would entail all kinds of other problems.

Whereas Deke Sharp would kill an attacker like that without even hesitating. Quietly and with no fuss or foo-foo. Someone would find the body in the morning. Good enough.

Now why had Deke Sharp popped into her head all of a sudden?

As was their custom on Thursday evenings, Gary let himself out between two and three in the morning, and Fuller woke up alone. It was good to get her biology taken care of. Being so damned horny made it hard to think rationally about her situation.

It had been fun. Gary was cute and attentive. He was a sweet boy.

Wait. Just two years younger than her, why did she think of him as a boy? He was in his thirties, if just. But she didn't think of him as a man.

Not like she thought of Deke Sharp.

Well, she wouldn't resolve anything now. Time to go to work.

She didn't know it, but, a hundred and more light-years away, Deke Sharp also woke alone that Friday morning after spending the evening with Daphne Duplay.

On Saturday morning, Fuller faced another empty weekend. Around noon, however, she got a call request. It was an interstellar call, from Ariel, but it wasn't from Deke Sharp. His mail address she would have recognized.

Fuller accepted the call, and her virtual terminal displayed the avatar of an attractive young woman -- perhaps Fuller's age, more or less – with perfect hair and makeup.

"Suzanne Fuller."

"Good morning, Suzanne. My name is Daphne Duplay. I'm a, er, friend of Deke Sharp."

"Oh, I remember. D.K. mentioned you. You were one of the people they arrested five months ago in that corruption scam."

"That is correct. I don't know how much D.K. told you about me, Suzanne, but I have good friends in various high places on Ariel. It has come to my attention that they are about to create the position of principal investigator in the Justice Department here. The chairman of the Ariel Senate judiciary committee has lost his patience with the level of corruption that incident has exposed. He wants it cleaned up."

"What does that have to do with me, Daphne?"

"The chairman thinks one of the problems in cleaning up the corruption is that there isn't a senior enough person assigned to it. The other thing is that he thinks it will probably take someone from off-planet – someone who isn't all buddy-buddy with the DoJ staff – to do the heavy lifting. Someone like you, Suzanne."

Realization flashed through Fuller. *Principal* Investigator? On *Ariel*? That's where Sharp was!

She gaped at the display as Duplay continued.

"Of course, there would be issues with things like bridging retirement benefits, paying for the interstellar relocation, a sign-on bonus, enough independence to ensure effectiveness. All that sort of thing. It is my understanding that all of those issues can be resolved."

"How would I submit myself for consideration, Daphne?"

"Oh, they already have their eyes on you, Suzanne. You

made an interstellar splash with that press conference on your recent activities. The chairman mentioned to the attorney general here that you were just the sort of person they should hire. The AG expressed doubt they could attract you away from Humphreys, but the chairman had already been briefed on your situation, and he encouraged the AG to make a play for you."

"Why do I detect a little creative involvement on your part here, Daphne?"

"As I said, Suzanne, I am a friend of Deke Sharp. A very good friend. And that man has got a serious case for you. When I asked D.K. about you, he described you without any hesitation as beautiful, competent, and extremely dangerous. I can't think of any higher praise from a man like Deke Sharp."

Fuller couldn't either. Her heart soared.

"It sounds too good to be true, Daphne. Thank you."

Duplay nodded.

"I just wanted to get in touch with you first so it didn't hit you cold. But sometime in the next couple weeks, you are probably going to get feelers from Ariel DoJ about making a career move to a more senior and self-directed position. I suggest you give it serious thought."

"Oh, I will, Daphne. Thanks again."

Duplay nodded and cut the connection.

Later that weekend, doing household chores, Fuller caught herself humming as she worked.

It was almost two weeks later, on a Thursday evening, when Fuller heard from the Ariel DoJ. The interstellar call request came in when she was relaxing after a routine day at the office. Things had quieted down considerably from the first two or three hectic weeks after her return.

"Suzanne Fuller."

"Good evening, Ms. Fuller. My name is Arne Gunderson. I am the head of personnel at the Ariel Department of Justice."

Fuller's heart skipped a beat at that last. Was this what Daphne had told her about, finally?

"Yes, Mr. Gunderson."

"The Ariel Department of Justice has requested, and the Ariel Senate Judiciary Committee has approved, the creation of a position within the Ariel DoJ of Principal Investigator for Official Corruption. We were wondering if you would be interested in exploring that opportunity."

"Yes, Mr. Gunderson. I'd like to talk about it, at least, and learn more about the position."

"Very well, Ms. Fuller. That is gratifying to hear. Your accomplishments on Humphreys have come to our notice here, and we were hoping you would be open to discussing it.

"The key features of this position are that it is a level above Senior Investigator. It would report directly to the Attorney General, Hank Branson, rather than through the investigations division. It is a self-directing position specifically targeting official corruption within the Ariel government and beyond."

"And beyond, Mr. Gunderson?"

"Yes. It is anticipated that an investigation into official corruption that begins on Ariel might lead to interstellar crimes. Some investigations may thus require coordination with Federation officials, a role you have already performed in your activities on Humphreys."

"This all sounds very interesting, Mr. Gunderson. Of course, I am going to want to speak with Mr. Branson about this position before making any decision."

"Of course, Ms. Fuller. As he would be your immediate superior, I would expect nothing less. My role here is to gauge your interest and to present you with the more nuts and bolts aspects of the position."

He turned to one side and made some key entries, then turned back to Fuller.

"You should have received an offer letter now, Ms. Fuller."

Fuller looked to one side and called up the offer letter. There was a bunch of government rigmarole that ran on for several pages, but the salient facts were up front.

The salary was rather breathtaking – more than half again what she was making now – with a generous sign-on bonus, a relocation package, bridging of retirement benefits, and a hazard-pay multiplier. Direct superior was the Attorney General. Title was Principal Investigator.

"Yes, Mr. Gunderson. I have it. Everything looks satisfactory."

"Excellent, Ms. Fuller. And when would be a good time for Mr. Branson to call you?"

Fuller left work at noon on Friday so she could take the call at home. It would be by virtual terminal, but, even so, she would feel more comfortable at home.

Hank Branson called her at the appointed time.

"Suzanne Fuller."

"Yes, Ms. Fuller. This is Hank Branson."

"Hello, Mr. Branson. Thank you for taking the time to speak with me."

"Of course, Ms. Fuller. Mr. Gunderson said you have some questions for me."

"Actually just one big one, Mr. Branson. This position is described as self-directing. What exactly does that mean to you?"

"You will perform your own research, Ms. Fuller. Other

people may forward leads to you about suspect activities. You will decide what you work on, and what that work entails. The goal is to put an end to official corruption on Ariel, whether that is through criminal referrals to prosecution or simply putting the fear of prosecution into everyone's head so they cut it out. Our legislative oversight has had enough of the situation as it is, and wants it stopped. That, put simply, will be your job."

"And my reporting to you, sir?"

"Will be status reports only, Ms. Fuller. I will not give you assignments, or take you off one assignment to put you on another. I expect you to be sensitive to the department's inputs, particularly statements made by our legislative oversight, but the decisions will be yours. That's the only thing that can work anyway, as I have enough on my plate already."

"One more question, sir. What access to resources will I have?"

"The same as the senior investigators within the department, Ms. Fuller, but with priority over them."

"And if an investigation leads to the rich or powerful, sir?"

"You will follow corruption wherever it leads, Ms. Fuller. I hope that you will give me a heads-up if it looks like you're steaming into troubled waters, but corruption will find no shield here anymore. Those are my marching orders from my oversight."

"Excellent. Then, Mr. Branson, I am pleased to accept your offer of employment."

"Wonderful. Mr. Gunderson will be in contact with you about all the details, Ms. Fuller. I'm looking forward to seeing you on Ariel soon."

Getting Together

Deke Sharp noted that the Ariel DoJ had requested a new position be created and the judiciary committee had consented. Principal Investigator for Official Corruption.

Good. About time, actually. He hoped they hired somebody who knew what he was doing.

Somebody – whether male or female, young or old – as good as Suzie Fuller.

Not knowing what else to do about the problem, Fuller put in a call request to Daphne Duplay. Duplay accepted a few minutes later.

"Suzanne Fuller."

"This is Daphne, Suzanne. What's going on? Did DoJ get in touch with you?"

"Yes. They made me a very nice offer. I talked to the Attorney General about it, then accepted the position. It's a dream job, Daphne, it really is. There's a problem, though."

"What's that?"

"I guess I've gotten spoiled racing around with D.K. I can't get to Ariel in less than a month from the time I leave here. I have about a week left getting ready to leave, but then it's a month – more like five to eight weeks – in transit."

"That long?"

"Passenger liners are slow, and there's no direct route. I was hoping to just pop over there and surprise D.K., but a month or two en route?"

"Ouch. OK, Suzanne. Let me look into it. I may be able to arrange something."

"Thanks, Daphne. Now that the deal's done, I just want to get going."

"By the way, Suzanne. Do you know D.K.'s boss's name?"

"Otto Pasha."

"OK. Thanks. Let me see what I can come up with."

Octavius Pasha didn't recognize the address of the incoming call request. He requested resolution from D Branch's database. Daphne Duplay.

Now that was interesting.

Pasha accepted the call request and the avatar of an attractive young woman appeared on his display.

"Otto Pasha."

"Hello, Mr. Pasha. I am Daphne Duplay. You may have heard of me."

"Indeed I have, Ms. Duplay. How can I help you today?"

"Have you seen that the DoJ had a new position approved by the senate's judiciary committee, Mr. Pasha? Principal Investigator for Official Corruption."

"Yes, I have, Ms. Duplay."

"It has not been announced yet, and will not be until she arrives, but they have hired Suzanne Fuller of Humphreys to fill this position."

Pasha's head spun. Too many coincidences here.

"As I recall, it was the chairman of the judiciary committee who bailed you out of jail five months ago, wasn't it, Ms. Duplay?"

"Yes, Mr. Pasha. If you are wondering whether I had some hand in engineering this solution to multiple problems, you would be correct. You see, sir, Deke Sharp is a very good friend of mine. I have other good friends as well, some in influential roles on Ariel. A word here, a word there, and sometimes things happen."

"I see, Ms. Duplay. And your reason for calling me today?"

"Normal passenger travel between Humphreys and Ariel is light, Mr. Pasha. There is thus no direct route. One must travel through Meredith or Elizabeth, on passenger liners, which are slow compared to some ships. Such as some ships deployed by D Branch, I understand. It will take Ms. Fuller some five to eight weeks to travel from Humphreys to Ariel.

"I was wondering if you had some way to expedite her travel, though possibly without the luxury accommodations of a passenger liner."

Pasha nodded. That would make sense if someone was coming through from Romeo or Juliet, for example. He would have to check.

"I understand, Ms. Duplay. I will look into it."

"Thank you, Mr. Pasha. Oh, and a word. Deke Sharp does not know that any of this is in the works. He probably knows of the new position, but not Ms. Fuller's hire. I am hoping to save it as a surprise for him."

"I understand, Ms. Duplay. We won't let the cat out of the bag."

Duplay's face lit up with a huge smile, and transformed her. Pasha could see now how she was so successful in her chosen profession. It was the sort of smile one wanted to see again.

"Thank you, Mr. Pasha. He's going to be so surprised."

Duplay nodded and cut the connection.

Pasha considered the empty display, suddenly lifeless.

He wondered how many things on Ariel 'happened' because of a word here or a word there from Duplay.

Nevertheless, in this case it was certainly welcome.

Pasha checked his field operatives' status and travel plans. *Medea* wasn't the only D Branch fast ship anymore.

D Branch had a way of communicating with ships traveling within the envelope, a method they had not shared with anyone else. Ships within the envelope could detect each other. Oh, it was fuzzy and indistinct, and position and velocity were impossible to nail down, but they could see each other.

In particular, they could detect ripple in envelope-space from each other's engines. Could, in fact, detect variations in those engines.

Thus if you modulated the engines of a ship in the envelope, D Branch ships could pick it up.

Oh, it was slow, and effective only for short messages, but short messages could be sent to a ship traveling within the envelope.

Matt Deckard was Ariel-bound from Juliet on the D Branch ship *Osiris*. Like Sharp's *Medea*, *Osiris* was a fast ship, frigate-sized but with an attack ship carrier's engines and a heavy cruiser's guns. *Osiris* was also registered as a Federation Navy Ship, the FNS *Osiris*, and had multiple aliases in Navy records.

Most of *Osiris'* aliases were the names of gods in the Egyptian pantheon, as *Medea's* were in the Greek pantheon.

Deckard got an incoming message alarm – unusual in the envelope, but not unheard of – and brought it up on the display. He watched it play out, a letter at a time.

OSIRIS DIVERT HUMPHREYS CALL HQ ON ARRIVAL

No question that it was a legitimate message. Only D Branch knew how to transmit and receive messages with ships traveling in the envelope. He sent a short message back.

OSIRIS ACK

Having acknowledged the message, Deckard considered the message he'd received. Humphreys was at least on the way to Ariel, not clear the other side of Federation space, which is likely why *Osiris* had been chosen for whatever the assignment was.

Deckard adjusted course for Humphreys, and had the computer calculate the deceleration curve required to drop out of the envelope within a day's spacing of the planet.

Suzanne Fuller got a short mail.

> **Pickup Humphreys Navy Shuttleport approx. three days. Time to Ariel Navy Shuttleport approx. twelve days. More info soon.**
> **– Otto**

Only one question ran through her head. How many people did Daphne Duplay know? Then again, Duplay had had to ask her the name of Sharp's boss. So she couldn't have known him already.

In any case, Fuller had to get a move on. Only three days left.

The movers were coming tomorrow to pack her personal things, mostly her clothes. She already had a great offer on the house. The houses on the little park were highly desirable and didn't come up for sale often, so there had been a bidding war for it. She settled for three times what she had paid for it ten years ago, selling it furnished.

She wasn't going to move furniture interstellar, and she had a good eye for interior design. The furniture helped pump the sale price, and then she didn't have to sell the furniture.

Osiris dropped out of the envelope and Deckard adjusted course and started her toward Humphreys. Then he called D Branch. Specifically, he called Otto Pasha.

"Pasha."

"Matt Deckard here, Otto."

"Ah. Excellent. Matt, I have a passenger for you to ferry to Ariel on the rest of your trip."

"A passenger, sir? He is D Branch, then?"

"No, she's not D Branch, but she is in the know. She has worked for us in the past."

"Very well, sir."

"You will be ferrying Suzanne Fuller. She is the new Principal Investigator for the Ariel Department of Justice. We're doing them a favor by cutting the commercial transit time."

"Understood, sir."

"Send me your arrival time at the Humphreys Navy Shuttleport, and I'll have her meet you there."

Two days after the first, another mail for Fuller arrived.

Ship is in-system. Pickup Humphreys Navy Shuttleport tomorrow at noon. Arrive Ariel Navy Shuttleport in twelve days.
– Otto

Friday. That was lucky. She would be able to hire people to transport the three heavy shipping trunks to the shuttleport and load them on the shuttle.

She assumed it would be a shuttle like Sharp's.

There should be room.

Deckard watched the shuttleport coming up as the shuttle descended. He had sent the slip number to the address Pasha gave him for his passenger once it was assigned.

A female passenger. That was interesting. Twelve days in close quarters. You never knew. Maybe he would get lucky.

Then again, a principal investigator in the Justice Department? That was an end-of-career position. She was probably in her mid-fifties.

Well, we will soon see.

There was a van parked alongside the pad as the shuttle came down. Anyone with it would stay inside until the engines spooled down. Two much dust flying about.

When the dust had settled, Deckard opened the door and extended the ramp. Two big, burly guys and a woman got out of the van. They were clearly there for cargo transfer.

She, on the other hand, couldn't possibly be his passenger. Early to mid thirties and absolutely stunning. Beautiful. Gorgeous. Oh, this could be a fantastic trip.

"Ms. Fuller?"

"Yes, that's me."

"I'm Matt Deckard."

"Pleased to meet you, Mr. Deckard."

The two guys were unloading what turned out to be three pretty serious cargo trunks.

"You'll have to show them where you want these stowed, Mr. Deckard. I think they'll fit."

"Yes, we can use the floor tie-downs. This way, fellas."

Once the trunks were aboard the shuttle and tied down to the pop-up floor handholds, Fuller dismissed the cargo loaders and their van.

She walked up into the shuttle and deployed one of the jump seats. Deckard watched, and she seemed most competent with the equipment.

She noticed his watchfulness.

"Not my first rodeo, Mr. Deckard."

Deckard got into the command chair and strapped in, then gave the shuttle take-off instructions to return to *Osiris* at where she was docked at Humphreys Station.

The engines spun up and the shuttle leaped up into the air.

Once the shuttle had latched onto *Osiris*, Deckard and Fuller moved into *Osiris'* main cabin.

"I've put in for departure clearance, Ms. Fuller. We're coming right up. How are you for weightlessness?"

"Already taken my pill, Mr. Deckard. I'm good."

"Excellent. There won't be much of it, but it's a low acceleration area until we're clear of the station."

"I understand, Mr. Deckard."

Once clear of the station, *Osiris* made for the envelope at frigate speed, concealing her true capabilities. There was now one gravity aboard ship.

Deckard turned the command chair around to face his passenger.

"So, Ms. Fuller. We have one day to the envelope, ten days in the envelope, and one day from there to Ariel."

"Excellent, Mr. Deckard. It was going to take five to eight weeks on commercial passenger liners."

Deckard nodded.

"Yes. No direct route, and they're a lot slower than *Osiris*."

"I understand, Mr. Deckard. I'm afraid I got spoiled by all the time I spent on *Medea*."

Medea? That was Deke Sharp's ship, the class leader. In fact, *Osiris* was called a Medea-class ship.

"We're going to be together twelve days, Ms. Fuller. Please call me Matt."

"And you should call me Suzie, Matt."

"So you're going to Ariel to become an Ariel DoJ principal investigator?"

"Yes, I was a senior investigator for the DoJ on Humphreys."

"Wait. You're the woman I saw in that press conference last month."

"Yes, that's right."

"Were you really the shooter in the Four Billionaires Case?"

"No, Matt. I did say 'neither confirm nor deny.'"

"Yes, but that always means yes, Suzie."

"Not in this case, Matt. D.K. did all the shooting."

"D.K.?"

"Deke Sharp. I call him D.K. I'm Deke Sharp's girlfriend. That's the big reason for moving to Ariel."

Deke Sharp's *girlfriend*?! Oh, shit. No nookie on this trip then. Screw *Deke Sharp*'s woman? Even if she was amenable, he might just as well shoot himself and save Sharp the trouble.

Oh, well, at least she wasn't hard on the eyes.

Fuller saw his reaction.

"You know D.K., Matt?"

"Everybody in D Branch knows Deke Sharp, Suzie, or at least knows of him. He's the most senior Senior Field Operative in D Branch. A legend. The man you can't kill. You can even blow him up, and he'll just come back at you. *Medea* is his ship. Permanently assigned. You know. Just in case he wants to go somewhere. I'm surprised he didn't go to Humphreys and pick you up himself."

"Well, we're intending this to be a little surprise for him."

"He doesn't know they've hired you into the Ariel DoJ?"

"No. There's been no public announcement yet, and everyone involved is keeping it a secret for now."

"Wow. That's cool. You would be one hell of a surprise for anybody, Suzie. I think that's great."

Fuller dimpled and smiled.

"Thank you, Matt. And what are you to D Branch?"

"Field Operative. Just six years out of college, but I have all of my training in. I just finished up an assignment on Juliet and had to space past Humphreys on my way home anyway. I got diverted to pick you up."

"And *Osiris* is your ship, Matt?"

"No. She was given to me for this assignment. Nobody in D Branch has their own ship except Deke Sharp. Nobody."

Fuller nodded.

"Well, on my last trip in *Medea*, we had seven people, four adults and three children. We used the shuttles for bedrooms. So how about I take the shuttle with my trunks in it for my bedroom, and you take the other?"

"That sounds good, Suzie. Then someone lounging here in the main cabin won't keep the other awake."

"Exactly. So we have twelve days together, Matt, and I have a question. Do you play cards?"

There was one thing Matt Deckard knew by the time they got to Ariel.

Never, ever play cards with Suzanne Fuller for money.

Deckard didn't, and he was glad of it.

When Fuller exited the shuttle on Ariel, there was a van and a rental car waiting. Two beefy fellows got out of the van, and Daphne Duplay got out of the rental car.

Deckard waved the cargo men into the shuttle, while Duplay ran up to Fuller.

"Suzanne!"

Duplay gave her a big hug, which Fuller, at first startled, returned.

"Come along. We're going straight to D.K. He should be home by now."

"What about the trunks, Daphne?"

"They have instructions to deliver them to the loading dock of D.K's building."

"All right."

The rental car took them into town and let them out under the porte cochere of the building.

"You going to dismiss the rental, Daphne?"

"No, I need it to get home. I just need to get you in the door."

Duplay walked up to the main door buzzer, pushing Fuller out of the camera view to one side. She buzzed the correct unit.

"Yes?"

"D.K. It's Daphne. Buzz me in."

The door lock buzzed and Duplay opened and held the door for Fuller.

"You know where you're going, Suzanne?"

Fuller nodded.

"Top floor, left, second unit on the right."

"Have fun."

Duplay pulled her close, kissed her on the cheek, and then was into the rental car and away.

Sharp was just relaxing with a drink after a day in the office when the door buzzer rang.

Daphne? What was she doing here?

He buzzed her in, then looked around the living room. Hmm. Put that pair of socks he had just taken off into the hamper. That was about it. He normally kept a pretty clean house.

There was a knock on the door, and Sharp walked over and opened it. It wasn't Duplay.

"Suzie?"

"That's Principal Investigator Fuller of the Ariel Department of Justice, Mr. Sharp."

"Principal—"

Sharp grabbed at the door frame as he almost fainted. Fuller grabbed his other arm and helped him stay up.

"Oh, that was a surprise, eh?"

Sharp's head cleared.

"Yes, you might say that. It's you they hired?"

"Yes, D.K. I'm here on Ariel for as long as you want me."

"Oh, Suzie...."

In Residence

Sharp had not set an alarm the previous night. When he woke, the sun was climbing to mid-morning.

Fuller was already awake, cuddled up to him. He couldn't believe his good fortune. What he had thought impossible, was now reality.

"Good morning, sleepyhead," Fuller said.

"You're really here."

"Yes, I'm really here. Until you throw me out, anyway."

"Don't hold your breath."

Fuller smiled and kissed him.

Sharp got out of bed and went into the bathroom, sitting in the shower stall. As every morning, he removed each prosthetic in turn, washed and dried off both them and the skin around the connections, salved the skin, then replaced it.

He then took a normal shower.

After his shower, Sharp took his morning medications. He then shaved his scalp and face rather than have them grow in patches.

He also applied makeup to his face and scalp to even out the patchiness from the skin grafts and artificial skin around his eyes, ears, nose, and mouth.

Sharp walked out into the bedroom and made a cup of espresso with the espresso machine in his bedroom. Fuller watched him from the bed.

"Can you make me one, too, D.K?"

"Sure. At some point I should show you how to run this machine in case I'm not around."

Sharp went out on the balcony, still nude, with his espresso and lay down on a chaise in the growing sunshine with a sigh. Fuller dashed through the shower, grabbed her espresso, and joined him, lying out nude in another chaise beside him.

The slight on-shore breeze, laden with the scents of the sea, kept the sun from being too hot.

"This is a really nice view, D.K. Away from the city and out to the ocean. And I love the smell of the sea. Can we swim out to that little island?"

"Oh, yes. I've done it often. The beach is nice, too. Lay out in the sand."

"I don't like tan lines, D.K."

"The beach here is a nude beach, Suzie."

"Oh, that's sweet."

"Yeah. Beach is nude, but custom is to wear a cover-up in the building."

"I can do that."

They lay in the sunshine. Sharp drifted in and out of sleep.

"You going in to the office today, D.K?" Fuller asked during one of his waking periods.

"No, I'm recovering."

"From what?"

"From your welcome home party last night."

"I don't need any recovery."

"Yeah, well, you spent a month getting here, so you weren't slaving away in the office every day."

"No, only twelve days getting here. Otto had someone stop at Humphreys and pick me up. In *Osiris*. It's just like *Medea*."

"Who was it?"

"Matt Deckard. He said he was coming back to Ariel from an assignment on Juliet when he got diverted to pick me up."

Sharp nodded. One of the young up-and-comers. He was young to be assigned one of the Medea-class ships. Otto must like what he sees there.

"What did you two do for twelve days?"

"None of *that*, if that's what you mean. I told him I was your girlfriend, and he was a complete gentleman. Never even hit on me. So mostly we played cards."

"He any good at cards?"

"He could stand to learn the odds a little better, but he has a good poker-face. No tell I could spot."

Sharp nodded. Concealing the tell was a good talent for an operative.

And he wasn't surprised that Deckard hadn't hit on Fuller once she had told him she was Sharp's girlfriend. Sharp had a reputation among the other field operatives, one he had been careful to cultivate.

The reputation of being an extremely dangerous man to cross.

Deckard probably wouldn't have touched Fuller if she had sat naked in his lap.

"So when do you start your new job?" Sharp asked.

"Monday. Then on Tuesday, I think, they're going to have the announcement that I'm here."

"They going to announce the corruption angle?"

"Yeah. They already announced it with the position. I told the AG I was afraid the bad guys would go to ground. Cut out the corruption and lay low. He said that would also solve the problem."

"He's right, you know."

"Yeah, I know. But I wanna catch 'em."

Sharp nodded. Fuller was silent for a while.

"D.K?"

"Yeah."

"Do you think it would be OK if I used the DV engine for a

while?"

"I don't see why not, Suzie. Don't forget, they arrested Pasha, too. He was not amused."

"Oh, yeah. That's right. OK, well, that will help a lot. They're going to like it a lot if I can hit on somebody in the first three, four months."

"They?"

"The AG and the chairman of the judiciary committee."

"Senator Jeffries?"

"Yeah. He's a good friend of Daphne Duplay. He's the one who bailed her out when she was arrested."

"Daphne has a lot of friends, Suzie."

"Yeah, but you know she set this whole thing up, don't you?"

"What whole thing?"

"Me being here. Them offering me this job. Daphne put the whole thing together. And when I couldn't find a way to get here in less than five weeks, I asked her about it, and the next thing you know, Otto diverts a ship to pick me up."

"Really."

"Oh, yes. She's terribly fond of you, D.K. She arranged for me to move to Ariel to make you happy."

"Well, she was certainly successful at that."

"Yeah. She was great. I like her a lot."

Sharp didn't ponder overlong about the curiosity of his wife – near enough – being friends with his erstwhile part-time mistress. All the people involved were adults, were in fact good people, and they had not overlapped. Not really.

"Suzie?"

"Yes, D.K?"

"I meant to ask you. What did you do with your house on the garden?"

"I sold it."

"That's too bad."

"No, it's OK. I made a killing on it, and I got out before they screwed it up somehow."

"They were going to screw it up?"

"No, but they could. There's always people who are never happy. Want to improve things. Most of them have very vague notions about what kind of thing would actually be an improvement. I got out at a real good time."

"Ah. I see. Good. I'm glad you're not sad about it."

"No, it's good. But I did have a thought."

"Yes?"

"I'm making great money. You make great money. I have a big chunk of cash from selling the house in New Denver. We could afford a second house. A getaway in the country somewhere. Some place quiet. Away from the city. For on the weekends. What do you think?"

"Sounds good to me, Suzie. If you do as good a job finding us a place as you did for yourself in New Denver, it would be a good investment."

"OK, D.K. I'll start looking around."

"Oh, and ask Daphne about it, Suzie. She knows a lot about what's going on."

"When she's not causing it, you mean?"

"Yeah. Then, too."

"D.K., why did Daphne never settle down with one of her man-friends and raise a family? Does she not want kids?"

"She's afraid to, Suzie. She told me about it once. Some congenital defect in her family. Really nasty. Reappears every other generation. She doesn't want to deal with that. Doesn't want to inflict that on a child."

"Oh. I see. How sad."

Sharp shrugged.

"She took a different path, Suzie. She's happy."

Fuller nodded.

"What about us, D.K? Those don't really work, do they? In that way, I mean."

She nodded to his prosthetic genitals.

"No, they don't. But there's an alternative."

"Adoption?"

"Well, that's an alternative, too, but there's more. Field operatives for D Branch spend a lot of time in space. Long-term exposure to low-level radiation isn't good for genetic material. So every field operative for D Branch has a hidden stash of sperm or eggs in a freezer in medical division. I have some young Deke Sharp genetic material stashed away in the freezer."

"That's great, D.K. I thought we would figure something out, but I didn't think of that."

"You want kids, Suzie?"

"Yeah, I do. Not right away. I have a few more years before it gets pressing, but yeah, D.K., I want kids. And you?"

"Oh, sure. I like children."

"And you're good with them. I thought Sarah was going to go completely to pieces when you left Humphreys."

Sharp nodded. The future looked good.

Have to retire from D Branch at that point, though.

No field missions when one had kids dependent on them. It wasn't fair to the children to have their father going out and getting shot at all the time.

Or blown up, for that matter.

They lolled away the morning, then went into the kitchen for a light lunch. Neither had yet gotten dressed.

"I suppose we ought to put some clothes on at some point," Sharp said.

"Easy for you to say, D.K. All my clothes are in shipping trunks down on the loading dock."

"We better call building staff and have them bring those trunks up before they leave for the day."

"Then I'd better get dressed again in what I wore yesterday."

They both got dressed, then called down to the dock. Soon, three large trunks were sitting in the middle of Sharp's bedroom.

"My word," Sharp said.

"Hey, a girl needs choices. You have a lot of room left in that closet."

"Maybe not enough room for all that."

"Another good reason to buy another house."

Fuller unloaded one of the trunks into the closet, then joined Sharp out on the balcony for a drink.

"Yeah. There's too much. Maybe a dresser would help. And I need to call Daphne and see about house-hunting."

"You should call her now. She's always busy evenings. I should go into the office at least for a little bit tomorrow, so that might be a good time to start."

"Hi, Daphne. Suzanne."

"Suzanne! Did you guys have fun last night? Was it a surprise?"

"Yes and yes. When I told him I was the new principal investigator for Ariel DoJ, he almost fainted."

"Deke Sharp? Almost fainted? Oh, my."

Fuller giggled.

"Oh, Daphne, you should have seen him. He went pale and

TOO SHARP TO HOLD

grabbed at the doorframe to keep from going down. I had to help him into the room."

Duplay shook her head.

"Well, I'm glad it all worked out, Suzanne."

"I am, too, Daphne. Thanks again. But I had a different favor to ask you today."

"Go ahead, Suzanne. Shoot."

"We're thinking of getting a country house for the weekends. Something private and cozy, and far away from the busy-busy of the city. Some place we can raise kids, when it comes to that."

"Wow. Sounds nice."

"Yes, Daphne, but I have to find it first. D.K. said to ask you."

Duplay nodded.

"Let me do some looking around, Suzanne. You have a timeframe in mind?"

"To buy? Soon. To look? Well, I start my new job on Monday, and I'll be pretty busy for a while after that. But I have tomorrow, and D.K. ought to go in to the office tomorrow. That may be too soon for you, though. And you may already be busy."

"I'm busy tomorrow evening, Suzanne, but not during the day. Let me poke around this afternoon."

"OK, Daphne. Thanks!"

Fuller thought that Duplay would use her time on Friday researching real estate agents and locations. She was flabbergasted to get an email late that afternoon from Duplay.

Meet me Union Station tomorrow 8AM.
– DD

"I guess Daphne's taking me house hunting tomorrow," Fuller said to Sharp over dinner.

Dinner was delivery from Piatti's, the little Italian place around the corner.

"Really? That's great."

"Yeah. I had hoped she would put me in touch with a real estate agent, or suggest locations to look at or something, but she's going along."

"That sounds like a lot of fun."

"Oh, yeah, Daphne's great. I'm looking forward to it."

The Country House

Fuller took a self-drive cab to the train station, even though it was only about a mile from Sharp's condo. Knowing how exhausting house hunting could be, she didn't want to use up a lot of energy getting there.

She walked into the main lobby and looked around for Duplay. Duplay saw her first.

"Hi, Suzanne."

"Hi Daphne. Thanks so much for the help."

They hugged, and then Duplay motioned her to follow.

"Come on. We have a train to catch."

Once seated in the train, Duplay explained the setup.

"This is a commuter train. The vast majority of commutes in the morning are inbound, and a lot of the inbound trains sit here until the evening's outbound commutes. But you have to take at least some of the trains back out to the 'burbs for runs during the day."

"Yeah. That's the same as on Humphreys. So where are we going?"

"End of the line. This is the west shore line, and runs west from New Destin on the flat plain between the hills and the ocean. Where we're looking is past that, but the real estate agent will pick us up at the last station. The railroad continues on past that point, but it's all freight from there on."

The brakes released and the train pulled out of the station. The sun was on their left and behind them, and there was an occasional glimpse of the ocean seen between the buildings. They went just a couple miles and stopped.

"This is a milk run on the way out now," Duplay said. "It makes all stops, so it'll take us an hour to the end of the line. Running with the commuting direction, you get express trains that make a couple stops and then race into the city. In the other direction, it's more like thirty minutes."

"I see. Not so bad, then. You said we're going past the end of the line, though?"

"Yes, Suzanne. But I know something most people don't. They're going to extend the commuter runs further down the coast. Not right away, but say in three to five years. Ultimately, it will be well under an hour's commute by train from where we're looking today."

"Oh. Nice."

"Yeah. The car trip is not fun, but the train is handy."

As the train was slowing for the final stop, Duplay gave Fuller some background on the real estate agent they were meeting.

"Stephanie married a former client of mine, and we became friends. They retired early, and she got bored, so she went into real estate. She's pretty good, at least for high-end properties."

The train stopped and they got off. A woman waiting on the platform walked up to them.

"Daphne. Good to see you."

"Hi, Stephanie."

They hugged, then Duplay waved to Fuller.

"My friend, Suzanne Fuller. Suzanne, Stephanie Borden."

They shook hands.

"It's good to meet you, Suzanne. And you're looking for a property out on the west coast here?"

"Call me Suzie, Stephanie. Only Daphne calls me Suzanne."

Borden chuckled.

"And call me Steph, Suzie. Same reason."

Fuller chuckled, then answered the outstanding question.

"Yes. We're both employed in the city, but we want a weekend escape. Something we can retire to eventually. Somewhere we can raise kids other than the city."

"I see. As Daphne said. I have picked out some properties to look at for this first run. Your reaction will help me bracket your desires for other trips if we need to."

"I understand, Steph. Lead on."

In a rental car, Duplay took the back seat so Fuller and Borden could talk.

"Daphne indicated you're open on price?"

"Yes. We both make stupid amounts of money, and I have the proceeds of a house sale on Humphreys. I made a killing."

"You're new on Ariel, then?"

"I am. My husband's been here quite a while, but he grew up on Humphreys. We grew up in the same neighborhood, and he and my brother went to school together."

"Ah. Newly married and you're pooling households now?"

"Right. So I sold my house on Humphreys and moved here. My husband has a nice condo downtown, but it's not a place to raise children."

"Well, the commute from here is long, but it's not too bad if you can work some of the time from home. And it's definitely a much better place to raise children."

It was twenty minutes' drive west to the first house on Borden's list. It was in a neighborhood on a quiet street. The houses here were big for the west coast.

"Hmm," Fuller said, looking around. "Not sure we're into a neighborhood like this, Steph. Not a lot of privacy."

Borden nodded.

"OK. Noted. Let's look inside, though, and see what you

think of the kitchen and such."

"All right."

They spent over two hours looking at various properties, with Borden noting Fuller's plusses and minuses of each. It was almost noon when they came to the last property on Borden's list for today.

Borden briefed them on the way.

"This last house is something I thought of as a bit of an outlier. I wasn't sure we'd get to it. But, based on what you've said this morning, it may be very close to what you're looking for. It's a big property, and a big house. On the expensive end of what we've seen today, but it checks most of your boxes, I think. We'll see."

The self-drive renter drove through a small city center, a cute downtown with coffee shops and boutiques clustered around a small park.

"This is the downtown for the village."

"Nice," Fuller said. "Homey."

The renter turned at the city center, heading south for the coast. The houses thinned out and the trees thickened into woods, then the road hit a tee and the car turned west. A quarter-mile on, it slowed, then turned south into a private drive. The gate drew back, then the car proceeded into the property.

"This is a big property," Duplay said from the back seat.

"Yes, it's forty acres, all wooded."

"Nice."

The car pulled up in front of a house that was set right into the trees. There was no clearing to speak of. There were trees, and there was house.

The house was one story, low slung and nestled down, as if it were almost a rise in the ground. Ivy crawled up the stone walls between large windows with views out into the woods. There was a porte cochere in front of a massive wooden door, inset with stained glass.

"Oh, it's so pretty," Fuller said.

"Almost primitive," Duplay said. "A throwback."

"It was built in that style, but it has all the modern amenities," Borden said

They got out of the car and Borden unlocked the front door, then waved them in.

They entered directly into the living room, a stone fireplace across the room in front of them, a beamed ceiling above.

It took Fuller's breath away.

"I feel like I've come home, to a place I've never been."

"It is homey, isn't it?" Borden asked.

"It's remarkable."

They walked through the central portion of the house. The master bedroom and bath, with two large closets and French doors out onto a patio. A guest room, also with en suite bath. The kitchen.

The kitchen was a chef's dream, with two built-in ovens, two microwaves, two warming ovens, and full-size separate freezer and refrigerator. An eight-burner professional gas stove was set into the island, the work triangles carefully thought out.

A large eating area set into a half-circle of windows was off to the rear of the house, but not walled off from the kitchen. The central windows were French doors out onto the patio.

"Oh, my. A cuisine center," Duplay said.

"I thought this kitchen might be a bit much," Borden said.

"Oh, no," Fuller said. "My husband is a notorious gourmet. He might hire someone – or a team of someones – in to cook, but there isn't anything one couldn't prepare here."

Borden nodded.

"Now, there is a basement under this central portion, while the two wings are built on slabs."

"Two wings?" Duplay asked.

"Yes. This is listed as a six-bedroom house, but you're talking children, and you also noted the need for working from home."

"Six bedrooms? On one story?" Fuller asked.

"Yes. It's a sprawling house. This way, Suzie."

Borden led them back to the living room. Off one back corner, a windowed corridor led to two bedrooms with a shared bath. The wing was diagonal off the main portion of the house, and each bedroom had windows on two sides looking out into the woods.

"They're lovely rooms," Fuller said.

"The woods are pretty," Duplay said.

"The other wing is similar," Borden said.

"I want to see," Fuller said.

Borden led them into the other wing. It was a mirror image of the first, off the other corner of the back wall of the living room. The other end of the fireplace wall.

"Again, very pretty," Duplay said.

"I thought one wing could be for the children, the other for your offices," Borden said.

"That makes sense," Fuller said. "It's a huge house, though."

"There's one more thing you should see, Suzie."

Borden led them back around, through the living room, to the back of the house. She opened the French doors from the eating area out onto the patio.

The patio had a barbecue setup to rival the kitchen. The bedroom wings of the house angling out to either side enclosed the patio and a garden beyond. The garden wasn't instead of trees, but planted into the trees.

"Oh, how pretty," Duplay said.

"It's beautiful," Fuller said.

"This way, ladies," Borden said.

She led them down a path through the gardens, past the end of the gardens and through the trees. After a hundred yards, the trees thinned out and stopped.

They stood on a headland sixty feet above the beach below. The sparkling ocean stretched to the south.

"Oh, my God," Fuller said.

She looked, and there was a stone stair set into the headland down to the beach.

"This is incredible."

Fuller sat heavily on one of two stone benches on the headland, just drinking it all in.

"This is a private beach, three miles long, owned in common by the dozen houses along this stretch," Borden said. "It's posted at both ends."

"It's amazing," Duplay said.

"How much is the asking price again?" Fuller asked.

Borden told her. It was a big number, but it wasn't *that* big. Her Humphreys house had been an oasis right in the middle of the city, almost adjacent to the downtown. Not an hour and a half's drive out into the country, half an hour past the last commuter train stop.

Location, location, location.

And her house had been completely paid off. She had the entire proceeds available.

Still, it was a big number. The proceeds of her Humphreys house, plus a mortgage. Given their salaries, they could swing the mortgage.

The other thing about it, though, was that it was a good investment. Borden had told them that private beaches weren't allowed anymore, but this setup was grandfathered in.

Also, Fuller knew that the commuter lines were going to be extended. That cute city center would be the new last stop. The availability of the commuter trains there would pump the price of this property a lot. If they ever got in trouble with the mortgage, they could sell the property. With that private beach, the property alone would draw big money, house or no house.

"Tell the seller's agent you think you have an offer coming."

They were on the mid-afternoon milk run back into the city.

"She saved the best for last," Duplay said.

"She sure did. From my point of view, at least. I know people who would prefer one of the earlier houses she showed us, but not me."

"Really?"

"Oh, sure, Daphne. It wasn't any more expensive than that pseudo-Tudor monstrosity. And someone will buy that one."

"With close neighbors and all. Yuck."

"And that pseudo-French Renaissance eyesore across the street."

"Yeah, Suzie. I think they better watch those houses don't go to war with each other."

Fuller chuckled. The history of France and England during that period surely suggested the possibility.

"So you think you're really going to do it, Suzanne?"

"I have to talk to D.K., but I think he'll like it. The beach is a really big deal. And the house is amazing. A true gourmet kitchen, and that very masculine living room. And imagine being a kid and growing up there."

"Kids might prefer a neighborhood, with other kids running around."

"They'll get plenty of that at school. Running around after

school, for that matter. They can take a cab home. But think of being a teenager and having parties on that beach."

Duplay nodded.

"So it looks like it worked out."

"Oh, it sure did, Daphne. Thank you so much."

"Glad to help, Suzanne. It was fun."

Once back at Union Station, Duplay was quick.

"Bye, Suzanne. I have to go get ready for tonight."

"Bye, Daphne. Thanks again."

Duplay waved a hand over her shoulder as she rushed off.

When Sharp got home, he found Fuller out on the balcony. This late in the day, the sun was behind the corner of the building, and she was dressed, just looking out over the ocean as shadows lengthened.

"How'd it go today? See anything interesting?"

"I found the house."

RICHARD F. WEYAND

Planning The Future

Claude Allard got home that evening, sat in the big chair before the gas fireplace, and sighed. Marie brought him a drink, said nothing, and left him to his thoughts for the moment.

He was getting too old for this.

He and Marie had a place in the mountains north of New Destin. A nice place in the woods. They usually went there on weekends. Used to be they went on Friday night, but that was too much for them now. They went out on Saturday morning, if they went at all.

Some weekends, they just stayed in the city, both of them too beat to consider the trip.

His seventieth birthday had come and gone. Oh, that didn't mean as much as it once did. Lifetimes were longer, people often lived into their early hundreds, or even into the hundred and teens.

But one did get weary. Longed for a quieter life than the hustle and bustle of the city.

Being the director of D Branch wasn't exactly a normal job, either. There was so much going on all the time, and not always without controversy. The latest hullabaloo had been around the execution of the four billionaires on Elizabeth.

The Navy had caught the most flack on that, as it was officially a Navy operation. Admiral Jurgens, the Chief of Naval Operations, had wanted assurances. But Allard had seen the evidence. They were guilty, no doubt about it. There were others that were iffy, but Pasha and his crew had drawn the line conservatively and there was nothing to apologize for.

That wasn't by any means the only thing D Branch had going on. Keeping track of it all was getting to the limit of what Allard could handle.

Marie came in and sat in the next chair, just to keep him company. She had always been supportive, but he knew she longed for a quieter life as well.

"Maybe it's time I retire, Marie. Get the ball rolling in that direction, anyway."

"That's up to you, Claude. Always has been. You know that."

"Yes, I know. And thank you for that. You've never pushed."

"I know better than to push on you, Claude. You're the pushback sort."

Allard chuckled. Yes, he was. If she pushed on him to retire, he'd be there till he was a hundred.

"I should probably give it a year – maybe more like two – to let everybody get in position."

"That's fine, dear. I can wait a couple of years. Whatever you think is best."

She took a sip of her drink and sighed.

"It would be nice to move to the mountains and stay there."

"You found the house? Really?"

"I think so, D.K. I'm really interested in what you think."

"Did you wear a camera, Suzie?"

"Of course."

Fuller had worn a hat while house hunting. One of her surveillance hats. It had captured video and sound of anything she had looked at.

She had clipped off the end of the trip – the spectacular house in the woods, beginning with the pretty city center – and sent it to Sharp now.

"There you go, D.K. From the city center out to the house."

"All right, Suzie. Let me give it a look."

Sharp went into the kitchen, made himself a drink, then joined Fuller out on the balcony. He logged into virtual terminal and watched the video.

When the video finished, he came back to the here and now with Fuller on the balcony.

"That's amazing. I was thinking, Oh, this is pretty good. You know. Like we talked about. Then you walked out onto the headland. It's the same view we've got right here."

"Yup. No elevator down to the beach, though. Stairs."

"When we get old, we can put in an elevator."

"Yeah, that's true, I guess. What did you think of the house?"

"Good. It's big enough, even for kids and such. The patio and gardens are pretty. The kitchen is amazing. But I think the thing I like best is the living room."

"You have to see it in person, D.K. It was like coming home to a place you've never been. I was ready to just stay there."

Sharp nodded.

"I can see that. It's kind of far, though, isn't it, Suzie? The trip into the office won't be fun."

"Daphne has an inside scoop there, D.K. They're going to extend the commuter trains. Couple years. That city center will be the new last stop."

"Oh, ho! Daphne always knows what's going on. Scratch that objection, then. The commute will be bad for a while, but that's OK if you know it's going away. Train rides are just more time to get work done. In the car, it's harder, even with self-drive cars."

"So what do we do now, D.K?"

"Well, we have work to do this weekend. Scan the listings. Anything up to and including that price. Sixty-, seventy-mile range of downtown. Try to find something better. If we strike out, then I think we have a winner."

"What about the price? It's not cheap."

"For what it is? It's cheap enough. Surely something we can do. At some point we sell this place, and it's a premium property downtown, completely paid off. And that doesn't include my portfolio."

"Your portfolio?"

"Oh, sure. Including hazard pay, I've made a lot of money, Suzie, and I just haven't had the time to spend much of it."

"Wow. I was thinking a big mortgage."

"Well, a mortgage, sure. Not sure how big it has to be. One does want some money set aside. Liquidity. Diversification. You know."

Fuller nodded.

"And I have savings, too. We need to put our finances on the table, Deke. See what all we've got. Make a plan."

"Agreed. But the timely work right now is comparison shopping. We should both see if we can top this house."

They worked on it all day Saturday, then again on Sunday. They would find possibles and send listings to each other. Go through them every hour or two.

They built into their considerations the availability of the commuter trains from the cute city center. Not there yet, Sharp was willing to bet on Duplay knowing what was going on.

Dozens of listings went back and forth over a day and a half. At noon Sunday, they gave up.

Lying out on the balcony nude in the sun, they talked it over.

"So no challengers, D.K?"

"Not really. Not to my mind. There's always something – or a couple somethings – that make them less desirable than that first house you found."

"Yeah. Schools, or size, or style, or commute. Something that doesn't fit."

"Yep. So I'm good."

"Time for finances, D.K?"

"Sure. This afternoon."

"OK. And in the meantime?"

"Lunch on the balcony?"

"Deal."

When they got to finances, Fuller was shocked by Sharp's portfolio. It was several times the size of hers.

Fuller had been pretty frugal, all things being considered. The house was her big extravagance, and it had paid off handily. She had also been a careful investor – her degree was in finance, after all – and had made good gains.

Sharp, though, was in another league. As a junior investigator for a government department, she had not made the big money until her promotion to senior investigator at almost thirty years old.

Sharp, by contrast, had been highly paid from the get-go. Field operatives for D Branch took insane risks, and the salaries and hazard pay had been designed to compensate for that. That early money had had more time to grow.

On top of that, Sharp had had a busy career. Much of his time had been spent on expense report. Buying the condo had been his big extravagance, but it had paid off handsomely as well, in that it had grown in value steadily while relieving him of rent payments.

Sharp's savings had also been carefully invested with the help of some of the financial people at D Branch. That and a little creative investing, because Sharp sometimes had inside knowledge of things that were going to happen. Buying puts in organizations where bad news was on the horizon was the big moneymaker.

"I can't believe this, D.K., but we could probably buy that house cash on the barrel."

"Yeah, but that's not the smart move, Suzie. We need some liquidity, some diversification. It's easy to get in trouble otherwise. Some big expense, or a string of bad luck, and blooey."

"A mortgage then?"

"Sure, but not on the house. On the condo. I pull equity out of this property. If we get in trouble, the bank can take the condo, but the house isn't entailed."

"Ooo, I like it. What's the condo worth?"

"D Branch had it appraised after all the repairs, to prove to building management that the property had been completely restored."

Sharp added a number to their spreadsheet, off to one side.

"That much?"

"Top floor, ocean view, and a walk to downtown? Oh, yes. And I can probably pull eighty percent of that out in equity."

"Wow. We can buy the house cash."

"Yes. You need to ask this agent what she thinks the offer should be. It'll probably go back and forth a bit, but find out what she thinks we should offer."

"Let me send her a quick mail and see what she says."

"On a Sunday?"

"Prime time for real estate agents."

There was a short wait, then Fuller had her answer.

"She says properties are closing about seven percent below ask. She suggests bidding ten or twelve percent below ask."

"Make it ten percent. We don't want to tick them off and have it fall through."

"And earnest money, of course."

"Of course."

There was a delay, with Fuller in virtual terminal mode, then she perked up.

"Done."

"OK. Now we see what they come back with."

An hour or so later, the counteroffer came back, splitting the difference.

"Should I split the difference with their counteroffer, D.K?"

"No. Sixty percent towards them. That gets us to seven percent below asking, which is probably what they expected."

"OK. Seven percent below asking. Got it."

Half an hour later, Fuller had an answer.

"D.K! They accepted."

Sharp nodded.

"That it was a cash offer, and not contingent on mortgage approval, appraisal, and all the other typical nonsense probably played a role. And they got seven percent below asking, which is sorta the going rate. What have they got for a closing date?"

"A month. A bit more actually."

Sharp nodded.

"I'll talk to the bank tomorrow about an equity mortgage on the condo. Shouldn't be a problem. Not for this property."

Monday morning, Claude Allard arrived in his office and looked around. Looked at his inbox in virtual terminal. Looked out the windows at the park-like grounds of the building.

Well, no sense putting it off.

He put in a meeting request to Octavius Pasha.

A meeting request – not a call request – from Claude first thing Monday morning?

Hoo, boy. That's the sort of meeting where big things happened.

Pasha just hoped it was good news.

He sent an acceptance for an immediate meeting.

"Yes, Claude."

"Otto. Come in, come in. Catch the door on your way."

Pasha closed the door behind himself and went in to sit in one of Allard's guest chairs.

"Otto, I'm getting too old for this shit. I just turned seventy, and I have a nice getaway up in the mountains. I'm retiring. I'll give you a year or two to get up to speed."

"Me, Claude?"

"Yes, you. Oh, there's analysis section and support section and all the rest, but everybody and their brother-in-law has an analysis section. The Navy. Treasury. All of them.

"What makes D Branch special, and always has, is field operations. We do shit nobody else can do, and we do it well. Again and again. Like this latest thing on Elizabeth. That was really well done. Clean and precise. No overreach.

"I've been watching you for years, and you're it. Unless you turn it down, I guess."

"Turn it down? No, I won't turn it down, Claude. I'm just trying to think of who to put in field operations."

"What about Deke Sharp?"

"Deke Sharp is the best field operative we have, Claude. Pull him out of the field and park him behind a desk?"

"If he's the best you've got, who better to bring up a new crop of field operatives? Who better to ride herd on the ones you have now? He set the standard, let everyone else try to live up to his standards. Is he respected by the other field people?"

"Yes, sir. He's a legend to them. Nobody better."

"Well, there you have it, then. Who else would they respect as much?"

Pasha nodded.

"No one, sir."

"So you have a year, maybe two, to learn my job and teach him yours. Then Marie and I are off to the mountains."

"Yes, sir."

Back in his office, Pasha gave some thought to how to spring this on Deke Sharp. Probably just like Allard did. Both feet, jump in.

"Hi, Otto."

"Hi, Deke. You got time for a walk?"

Sharp had just gotten off the phone with the bank. They would call him back later today. So right now was probably a good time to take a walk with Pasha.

"Sure, Otto. Meet you downstairs."

They met at the doors out to the walk around the lake and set off for their park bench. Sharp wondered what was up, but didn't ask any questions. Pasha made small talk.

"I saw DoJ announced Suzanne Fuller in a press release this morning. Nice choice."

"Yeah, Suzie'll clean things up over there. No doubt about it."

"I believe it. And you two are together now?"

"Oh, yes. I can't believe it, but she's as stuck on me as I on her."

"Why can you not believe it?"

"You know."

Sharp waved his hand up and down his body, indicating his injuries generally.

"She's better than that, Deke."

"Yeah, I know. I do now, anyway."

"You're a lucky man. Always have been."

"I think you're right, Otto. Actually, I need to talk to you about that."

"Hey, I called the meeting. I get to go first."

"All right."

They got to the park bench and sat down. Pasha turned toward Sharp.

"Claude's retiring, Deke. I'm taking D Branch. You're taking operations. We've got a year to get ready. Maybe two. Then Claude's outta here."

Sharp threw back his head and laughed.

"What's so funny, Deke."

"Sorry, Otto. Can't help it. I wasn't looking forward to telling you I'm retiring field ops in the next couple years. No more field work once Suzie starts on kids. It's not fair to the children. Or Suzie, for that matter."

"No shit."

"No. No shit."

"Well this whole thing works out perfect, then. I was afraid you'd be pissed off, Deke."

"I was afraid you'd be pissed off, Otto. All the stuff we did, over the years."

"Well, we can just keep doing it, Deke. Just one level higher."

"And me not getting shot at or blown up. Yeah."

"Sometimes, Deke, despite your worst fears, things just work out."

When Fuller got home that night, Sharp had news.

"How was your first day, Suzie?"

"Great. This is going to be fun. How about you, D.K?"

"The bank approved an equity loan at eighty percent of the appraised value."

"Really?"

"Oh, yes. D Branch used a top appraiser, to placate the building management, and the bank is fine with his appraisal."

"Wow. That's great."

"But that's not the best news."

"It's not?"

"No. I just got promoted to assistant head of field operations for D Branch. Sometime in the next two years, Claude Allard is retiring, Otto is moving up to director, and I'm taking field ops."

"You'll be out of field ops by the time we have children."

"Yep. It wouldn't be fair to you and the kids to be going out and getting shot at. I'll be a desk pilot."

"Oh, D.K."

Sharp got a big hug for that, then Fuller pulled back.

"Let's go out to celebrate."

"Sure, Suzie. Where?"

"Some place simple. How about Piatti's?"

"OK."

It might have seemed weird to dine out with Fuller at the same restaurant he had eaten at so many times with Daphne Duplay, but Sharp was so invested in the relationship with Fuller by now it never even crossed his mind.

Settling In

There was a lot of settling in over the next six months.

Octavius Pasha, Assistant Director of D Branch, got an office adjoining Claude Allard's office, where he spent afternoons. Deke Sharp, assistant head of field operations, moved to an office adjoining Pasha's, where he spent mornings.

Pasha was reading all of Allard's incoming mail as well as his own, while Deke Sharp was reading all of Pasha's mail. The half day spent in proximity to their superior allowed them enough time to discuss situations and responses, problems and solutions.

Pasha got access to all the records of the other section heads, and he and Allard talked about the other section heads, and their strengths and weaknesses, frequently. Sharp got access to all the records of the other field operatives, and he and Pasha talked about the other field operatives, and their strengths and weaknesses, frequently.

Sharp had been right about Matt Deckard. He was on Pasha's fast track as potentially being the next Deke Sharp.

Claude Allard had been right that Pasha had what it took to run D Branch, and relied on him more and more as time went on. Pasha sometimes returned calls for Allard as acting director, and those calls seemed to go well. People who had interacted with him later mentioned to Allard that he seemed competent and on top of things.

Pasha, for his part, was pleased with Sharp as well. His ability to perform analysis on his feet, from partial data – which was why Pasha had hired him, and which had served him well in the field – served him well in managing the field operatives as well. Field operatives who appeared before him learned to have done their work properly before bringing it to the boss. Sharp's camera eyes caught everything, and his ability to not blink the prosthetic facades of those cameras – at all – could be unnerving.

In reports, too, people learned to be thorough in their analysis and conclusions. Notations such as 'needs refinement,' 'needs clarification,' or – the worst – 'needs foundation' on returned reports were motivators to do the work properly first, and only then submit it.

These sorts of things enhanced Sharp's legendary status among the field operatives, rather than estrange him from them. To be the best, they strived to please him.

D Branch was shifting with the change in personnel, but it wasn't declining.

Seeing Deke Sharp promoted to assistant head of field operations, Octavius Pasha's heir apparent, Matt Deckard was happy he had been a proper gentleman when ferrying Suzanne Fuller from Humphreys to Ariel.

He was also happy about his assignments. He had gotten the impression that Pasha was grooming him for senior field operative status. Tough assignments that challenged him. Important assignments that required a delicate touch. Assignments requiring timely resolution, often using one of the Medea-class ships for transport.

Those assignments continued under Deke Sharp. If Matt Deckard had caught Pasha's interest, it was clear that he had caught Sharp's interest as well.

The Federation Department of Justice was tasked with determining the proper compensation for the victims of piracy.

Anything they determined would probably go to court before it was all over, delaying the payment of that compensation potentially for years.

There were two ways to calculate those payments. One was the wrongful death amount specified in law. That was normally reserved for cases of accidental death, however. The other way was unjust enrichment, the money that was made due to an illegal act. That was a much larger number. Perhaps ten times.

The families of the four executed conspirators pushed for the wrongful death amount, but FDoJ filed for unjust enrichment, plus penalties. That huge ask got the families to the negotiating table, and they settled on the wrongful death amount times three, for willful and malicious behavior, plus interest for the time since death.

The interest was a sticking point, too. The families pushed for minimum interest payments, while the FDoJ proposed interest at the rate of growth of the conspirators' investment portfolio. Again, they settled, using the average discount rate paid on annuities in the marketplace over the period.

For his part, Dominic Trask was as good as his word. He ponied up a million credits per victim to their survivors. He also got the other duped partners in his investment group to shell out a total of another two million. The list of survivors Trask got from the FDoJ.

Knowing how easy it was for someone not familiar with having any money to piss it all away within months and end up penniless, Trask set up annuities for the survivors, so that they would have a stream of payments into the future.

That annuity structure attracted the attention of investigators.

Suzanne Fuller, too, had settled in. One of her first actions on getting into the new position was to pull all Department of Justice communications into the D Branch data visualization engine.

When they announced Fuller as the new principal investigator for official corruption, she had been afraid the corrupt officials would change their behavior. Go to ground, so to speak, to keep from getting caught.

She used that to her advantage, asking the data visualization engine to highlight the ways in which communications within the department had changed after she had been announced. Following those changes upstream had been instructive, especially those communications streams which had disappeared after she came aboard.

Fuller uncovered one minor ring of officials selling lenient plea deals, plus one more-senior official accepting bribes from criminal defendants, botching prosecution evidence so they won on appeal. All were convicted on corruption charges.

Hank Branson had proved as good as his word, letting her have her head and go after whatever she found wherever she found it. Senator George Jeffries helped by sending her any communications the Senate Judiciary Committee received about corruption.

Both were pleased with the work she was doing. The Ariel Department of Justice was getting cleaned up, and everybody knew it.

Some people, for whom Fuller's research had turned up evidence not quite good enough for conviction, were convinced to retire rather than have her go after their bank accounts and other communications.

Fuller would have preferred convictions, but Branson was philosophical.

"You got them out of the department, Suzie. That's what's important. They are no longer a problem. And instead of spending all that time on seeking evidence for a conviction – which you might or might not get – you went after someone else. Maximize your impact overall. That's the key."

Fuller had reluctantly agreed initially, but, in hindsight, he had been right.

Fuller also investigated Trask's annuities structure for payments to the survivors of victims of piracy. There had been victims from Ariel, so it was in her purview.

She found that Trask had been meticulous in setting up the payments. First, it was not a ruse to delay the disbursement. The actual money promised had been transferred – in cash or in kind – to respected insurance companies selling annuity products.

Second, Fuller found that the discount rates and payments were at market levels, the sort of thing anyone could buy on the market, and were not set up to reduce payments for kickbacks.

Fuller published her report on the structure, and other planetary DoJs accepted her analysis.

Dominic Trask had done right by the victims, and Fuller had proved it.

The house closed on time. Sharp's condo was now mortgaged, but they owned the beautiful house in the woods along the west shore free and clear.

Weekends were spent at the house. They took the train out on Friday evenings, followed up by a rental car for the half-hour from the last stop of the suburban trains.

They were in the house four months when it came out that the transit company was planning on extending the west suburban commuter trains to West Coast Village in another two years. Property values in the area jumped, including theirs.

In a shock to many, and to many other men's dismay, Daphne Duplay retired. She married one of her clients, a man ten years her senior who had long been considered one of New Destin's most eligible bachelors.

Even more shocking to many was when, two months later, Duplay became pregnant with her first child. What they didn't know was, in some ways, more shocking still. While it was his child, Duplay had in vitro fertilization using one of Suzanne Fuller's eggs.

The two had become unlikely good friends. When Fuller pressed her on why she didn't want children, Duplay had told her the story.

"Why not just use one of my eggs, Daphne? This day and age, a genetic infirmity like that need not be a reason not to have children."

Duplay had agreed, then abruptly retired, marrying a man who had loved her but had wanted children.

The two couples were close, and Tim Hansen and Daphne Duplay often went out to the west coast house with Sharp and Fuller for the weekend. As frequent guests, they kept their things in the left bedroom of the otherwise unused east bedroom wing.

The west bedroom wing of the house was where Sharp and Fuller had their offices. Sometimes they would leave town a day or two early, or stay a day or two late, working from home.

Mostly, though, the house was for the weekends.

At least for the time being.

Sharp and Fuller were laying out nude on chaises on the

patio. The footprint of the house and the layout of the house and patio put a portion of the patio in the sun from mid-morning to mid-afternoon. This Saturday mid-morning, they were unwinding from the week in the office.

"Oh, this feels so good. Buying the house was the right thing to do, Suzie."

"I'm glad you think so, D.K., because otherwise we spent an awful lot of money on the wrong thing to do."

Sharp chuckled.

"No. No, this was definitely the right thing to do. How about a swim in the ocean this afternoon?"

"Sure, D.K. Have you thought about lunch yet?"

"No. You?"

"Maybe. Tim had something he wanted to try. On the grill, I think."

"Works for me."

Hansen and Duplay came out from the house, also nude, and settled into the other two chaises.

"Oh, this is great," Hansen said.

"Oh, yeah," Duplay said. "I'm cold all the time now."

She was coming up on three months along now, and her baby bump was becoming more apparent, especially when nude. Her breasts had grown as well, the nipples darkening somewhat.

"Yeah, that's much better," Duplay said.

"Tim, did you have something you wanted to try for lunch?" Fuller asked.

"Yeah. A friend of mine mentioned it. We brought some thin-shaved lunch meat out with us. Ham and roast beef. He said you grill it on the grill, just big clumps of it. Grill the buns, then serve the lunch meat on the buns with cheese. Really spices it up."

"That sounds great," Sharp said. "When you want to start, let me know."

"OK, Deke. Give it an hour or so. I'm really enjoying the sun today. It was gloomy in the city all week."

When the guys got up to go and fix lunch, the girls stayed behind in the sunshine.

"This is such a great place, Suzanne. I'm really glad you bought the house."

"You found it for me, Daphne. You and that agent of yours. And that after you created the job here on Ariel, and had them hire me, putting me together with D.K. That's two I owe you."

"And what do you call this, my dear Suzanne?" Duplay asked, waving at her belly. "Me, going to be a momma. Something I could never do otherwise, without the most personal gift of yourself possible."

"There's other eggs, Daphne."

"Yes. Of someone I don't know and could not love. No, thank you, Suzanne. I'm very happy as things worked out."

"I am, too, Daphne. I am, too."

Sharp and Hansen came out from the house, discussing the arrangements for who did what making lunch. Both of them had donned aprons, Fuller noticed.

"Ha! Aprons," she said.

"For barbecuing? I would hope, Suzanne. I don't want any damage to those dangly bits. I enjoy them too much."

Fuller laughed and lay back in the sun with her friend, as their husbands made lunch.

Life was good.

Fuller attended Duplay as the men fretted in the waiting room. Hansen didn't want to watch and had asked Sharp to keep him company.

Finally, the doctors called them in to the birthing room. Duplay looked radiant if exhausted, holding the baby to her breast. Hansen walked forward and kissed Duplay on the forehead. Duplay lifted the blanket off the baby's head.

"Our son, my love," Duplay said softly.

Hansen looked down at the newborn.

He was the most beautiful baby in the world.

Please review this book on Amazon.

Author's Afterword

"Too Sharp To Hold" was difficult to write, although not because of the book itself. My health issues slowly receded, but various medical procedures and recovery took a long time. In all, this book took eighty calendar days to write, with twenty-five non-writing days in that period. My writing days were also about half as productive as normal, at 1450 words per day or so. There were days I just couldn't see very far ahead.

That's almost unprecedentedly slow, but it wasn't the book's fault. I was also in unprecedentedly poor health after a heart attack and congestive heart failure earlier in the year. The holidays intervened as well, and I do like some time off of my seven-day-a-week writing schedule during the holidays.

As always, I wrote into the dark, making up everything as I went along. I only learned who the bad guys were as the D Branch team themselves did.

There were surprises along the way. Dominic Trask wasn't the big baddie after all; he was a victim of his investment partners. Deke Sharp came up with the idea of the paraglider setup as a way of escaping a penthouse condo in the city, and Dr. Weatherly added a balloon rig as she put it together. Deke Sharp and Suzie Fuller became an item on the mission, as one would expect, but that they became so bonded was a surprise.

"How could it be a surprise to you if you wrote it?" you ask? Simple. Once the author defines the characters in a book, they're off and running. They are who they are. Whether they fall deeply in love or get sick and tired of each other is out of the author's hands. The writers among you will get that.

In Sharp and Fuller's case, two competent and dangerous

people found someone they could understand and trust, and who could understand and trust them. Given who they were, that would be rare to the point of uniqueness. Fuller's beauty was almost beside the point for Sharp, and Sharp's injuries didn't matter to Fuller at all. She had found a man she could trust, who was as competent and dangerous as she was – at least – and who was good with kids on top of it all.

Love, honor, duty, and loyalty are, in my opinion, the four great pillars of civilization, and my consistent themes. Why do I think that? Take any of them away, and imagine the impact. Love – in the agape sense, love of one's fellow man – where are we without it? Where are we without honor? Or duty? Or loyalty? At the same time, name one thing you would add to that group that would have the same impact by its absence. In my mind, there's no contest.

Love, honor, duty, and loyalty are riding high here. Sharp's not kidding when he says if the Humphreys police tactical team had killed one of Camden and Thompsen's children he would have killed them all on general principles.

With Sharp's appearance, Trask and Anderson both see the chance to redeem themselves of being sucked into Thomas and Thurl's treachery, and they take it, each in their own way. Daphne Duplay sees the opportunity to help Deke Sharp with his problems and takes it, arguably to her own detriment.

And Deke Sharp, with children by Fuller on the horizon, contemplates retirement from D Branch to properly meet the duties of fatherhood.

Overall, this book was fun to write, if frustrating because of my health issues. As I write this, word counts have picked way up, writing days are more effective, and I look to be getting back in the saddle completely at last.

There is one more Deke Sharp book – at least – and I

anticipate it will go much better if my health holds.

I hope you enjoyed reading this book as much as I enjoyed writing it.

Richard F. Weyand
Bloomington, IN
January 8, 2025